Also by KELLI ANN MORGAN

THE RANCHER
REDBOURNE SERIES BOOK ONE
COLE'S STORY

THE BOUNTY HUNTER
REDBOURNE SERIES BOOK TWO
RAFE'S STORY

JONAH
DEARDON MINI-SERIES
BOOK ONE

Available from INSPIRE BOOKS

When Ethan emerged from the fireplace, it was hard to make out his features...

"Well, that was unpleasant," he said wryly as he pulled a handkerchief from his pocket to wipe his face.

Laughter bubbled to the surface, and she placed a hand over her mouth in an attempt to contain it—to no avail.

"You think that's funny do you?"

Grace thought for a moment before nodding wholeheartedly. He rubbed a finger-full of soot from his face, and before she could get out of his reach, he wiped it across her cheek.

She gasped in mock affront, and he tapped her on the end of her nose.

A low, hearty laugh erupted from Ethan's generally serious façade. The rich, deep tones of his amusement seemed to light the otherwise dark room. He brushed the rag over his face, the soot smearing in streaks against the darkened flesh tones of his face.

"Here," she said with a breathy chuckle, "let me do it." She set the lantern on the fireplace mantle and took the cloth from him. She wrapped it around her hand and with one finger reached up to his face, carefully wiping away the smudges.

Ethan's breathing became heavy and he lifted his hand and wrapped his fingers around her wrist, bidding her to stop. Grace knew if she looked up at him she would be lost. They were standing so close. She bit her lip.

Ethan groaned. He raised his hand to her face, delving his fingers into the hair just behind her ear and caressed her jawline with his thumb.

She looked up. Couldn't help herself. The lantern's light flickered in his eyes and his thumb found her lips. Her bosom swelled with anticipation as he slowly lowered his head toward her, his mouth slightly open. Grace curled her hands into the shirt tucked at his hips and closed her eyes, waiting for the moment his lips would meld with hers.

the Blacksmith

REDBOURNE SERIES BOOK THREE
ETHAN'S STORY

KELLI ANN MORGAN

inspire books

Inspire Books
A Division of Inspire Creative Services
937 West 1350 North, Clinton, Utah 84015, USA

THE BLACKSMITH

An Inspire Book published by arrangement with the author

First Inspire Books paperback edition December 2013

ISBN-13: 978-1-939049-07-0
ISBN-10: 1939049075

Printed in the United States of America

PRAISE FOR THE NOVELS OF AMAZON BESTSELLING AUTHOR

KELLI ANN MORGAN

"A delightful read with much intrigue, tension, laughter, and love. Dive into this adventure where you will find true heroes and heroines with great strength, courage and hearts of gold!"

—*Tennille Rasmussen*

"Excellent story. Well-drawn characters. The plot is full of shocking twists and turns you don't see coming. Ms. Morgan delivers a well-written read that is enjoyable to the end."

—*Rocky Palmer*

"The Blacksmith is Kelli Ann Morgan's most romantic book yet. It has the perfect mix of fun, romance, and Old West adventure…"

—*Grant Morgan*

"Strong characters and a compelling story make this an unforgettable trail ride…"

—*RaeAnne Thayne,*
USA TODAY bestselling author on THE RANCHER

"…stimulating and remarkably written…"
—*A. Eric* on THE BOUNTY HUNTER

"Ms. Morgan is a consummate story teller and she does it with style and emotion in such a way that you can't help but savor every last word."

—*Kerrigan* on JONAH

ACKNOWLEDGEMENTS

Dreams really do come true…which wouldn't have been the case for me without all the love and support of the people around me. Thank you to everyone who has been there in one way or another as I work hard to live my dreams.

To all of my incredible readers who continue to inspire me. None of this would be possible without you!

To my amazing alpha reader, Grant, and my wonderful beta readers, Rocky, Tennille, and Jennifer, whose insight and eye for detail have been priceless in the production of this book. Thank you for all of your wisdom, encouragement, and feedback. You ROCK!

To all those of my friends and family who took the time with me to bounce ideas and evolve this story. You know who you are. THANKS!

To my son who fills me every day with the kind of love and devotion the Redbourne family was built on. He loves my books and has grown to love my characters almost as much as I have. He has even started writing books of his own. I am so proud of you and your accomplishments, kiddo. Love you!

And, as always, to my wonderful, creative, talented, and supportive husband who continually spends innumerable hours talking through plotlines, proofreading manuscripts, cooking, and all the countless other tasks that are required to allow me the time needed to make our dreams realities. Thank you, baby, for loving me every step of the way. You are the love of my life! My hero!

As always,
To the two biggest heroes in my life,
Grant and Noah, for a believing in me, loving me,
and sharing me with my characters.

the Blacksmith

REDBOURNE SERIES BOOK THREE
ETHAN'S STORY

CHAPTER ONE

Kansas, Late November 1869

"What makes you think there is treasure in these hills?" Grace Nolan called to Jack, her fourteen-year-old brother, as they trudged through the tall brush on what she hoped was their land.

Jack shrugged and turned back to look at her.

"Look, Gracie! There it is," he called from the top of a small incline just a few feet ahead. "We're here!" Jack ran forward, briefly out of sight, showing no regard for the darkness.

Grace sprinted the last few steps to where Jack had stood moments before and squinted against the blackness of the night. The sky, full of stars and a slivered moon, offered little light, but sure enough, a high-pitched roof appeared above the tall grasses that had grown wild with years of neglect and lack of livestock.

But all that was about to change.

Home.

Grace cautiously made her way down the side of the hill

and stood in front of the large, rundown house, grey in the moonlight, and stared. Boards covered the broken windows and tall weeds and grasses filled the flowerbeds. Finally, she was far away from *him* with a place she could call her own.

"We'd better get inside before we freeze out here," Jack cautioned, rubbing his hands together. He ran toward the house and jumped up over the porch railing.

"Jack, be careful." Grace whispered into the moonlit darkness as she walked around the side of the house. She pulled her knapsack tighter around her shoulders.

The Nolan Farmhouse had been abandoned by her grandfather and his little family long before she'd been born, and she was grateful it still stood. Though barely. And it seemed to be empty.

Grace moved her way to the front of the house. She placed a foot gingerly on the first step and lifted herself enough to test the wood. It held. After repeating the process several more times, she found herself on the long wrap-around porch, standing in front of the heavily boarded door.

She shivered. Even with her thick woolen coat, the cold seemed to seep into her bones. She knew Jack was cold too. It wouldn't be long before winter set in and if the boards on the doors and windows were any indication, there would be a lot of work to do before then if they were going to survive the season.

"I found a way in over here." Jack peered around the corner on the west side of the house and motioned for her to follow.

Grace looked at the door, then back at her brother with a raised brow.

"Come on," he called, then disappeared the way he'd come.

Reluctantly, she picked up the hem of her skirt and followed. Jack stood next to a large window with a grin spread across his face. Two large planks had been removed and leaned against the house.

"After you," he said, sweeping the air and bowing.

"Not a chance," Grace replied with a smirk. "You go first."

"If you insist." He laughed and hurriedly climbed through the opening in the broken window.

Silence.

"Jack?" Grace called quietly.

Still silence.

"You coming?" Jack popped his head out from the window.

Grace jumped.

She closed her eyes briefly and shook her head. With a quick exhale, she tossed her bag inside the window and climbed in after him. Her skirt caught on something on the windowsill, throwing her off balance, and she fell against a cloth covered couch, effectively ripping the bottom of her hand-me-down dress.

Poof.

A cloud of dust puffed upward. Grace coughed loudly and waved her hands in attempt to clear the offending powdery grime from her breathing area. A straggly lock of hair fell onto her face and she attempted to blow it away—to no avail.

Above her, Jack's footfalls extended from one end of the house to the other. Grace pushed herself away from the couch and stood, attempting to brush the newly acquired dust from her dress, and scanned the room. She couldn't see anything in here.

A glimmer of light came from the next room. She moved toward it.

"It still works." Jack looked up from the newly lit lamp and he held it up above his head, illuminating what appeared to be the kitchen. His eyes were wide and hopeful, as if he'd just stumbled on a great wonder.

She smiled at her little brother. Their father had passed a little over eight years ago, when Jack had only been three and

Grace twelve. They'd just lost their mother a few months back, and all they had now was each other.

The light slowly dimmed until it finally extinguished.

"I think that's a sign." Grace said. "Let's get some sleep."

"Aw, Grace. Do we have ta?" Jack said, resigned.

"Yes." She paused. "And then we'll do some exploring in the morning," she said in a quietly excited rush.

Grace could feel his mood lighten immediately.

"There are two couches in this room." Jack ran back toward the room where they'd entered the house.

"I'm well acquainted, thank you very much." She had no idea how he was able to see so well in the dark—especially since her eyes still had not readjusted. She laughed and slowly followed him.

"Ouch," she squealed as her shin hit something hard.

The other couch.

Grace leaned down and rubbed the offending area, willing the pain to subside. It took a few minutes, but the initial shock of the hit turned to a dull ache. She felt the length of the couch and grabbed a hold of the cloth that covered the furniture and carefully pulled it back.

"Let's push these couches together," she said softly.

"Mmhmm," was the only reply.

"Jack?" Grace guessed that her brother had already settled himself onto the other couch and was near asleep. She wasn't surprised. Their trip out West had taken longer than expected and with the anticipation of finally arriving at the Kansas farmhouse, they were both exhausted.

"Jack," she called again.

"I thought you wanted us to get some sleep," Jack whined, but he got up and helped her push the couches together.

"It'll be much warmer this way." Grace lay down on the couch next to Jack, folded the dusty cloth's over to make a thicker blanket, and tucked it up around them.

Just a few more hours and daylight would mark the start

of their new lives as the Nolans of Kansas.

Home.

"I noticed a light flicker on for a few minutes in one of the windows at the old Nolan place tonight," Ethan Redbourne announced to his family as they sat around the dinner table eating supper.

"Must be some hooligans sneaking into that old house. Raine," Jameson Redbourne turned to his eldest son, "maybe you should take a couple of your brothers out there tomorrow and make sure there won't be any trouble."

"Yes, sir," Raine said, puffing his chest out a little farther, his new shiny deputy badge pinned to his vest.

Ethan smirked as he got up to clear his dishes. "I'll come along," he called from the kitchen, pumping some water into the sink to wash his hands. He still had a lot to do, but he figured the cool air would do him some good.

Raine nodded.

"Me too," Will said.

"And me," Tag chimed in.

All eyes turned to Ethan's youngest brother, Cole. He looked up from his food and scanned the faces of all those staring at him.

"What? I'll be there. Maverick's needing a little exercise anyway." Cole showed a lot of pride in his new horse and took every opportunity to ride the black Arabian stallion.

Ethan preferred geldings. Stallions were often unpredictable and dangerous. He guessed that was why Cole liked them.

If the light at the Nolan place had come from squatters or hooligans, Ethan figured that the sight of five of the seven Redbourne brothers would be enough to scare off any man. He smiled as he dried his hands on the cloth that hung from the cabinet next to the stove. He never got tired of being with his family.

With six brothers and a baby sister, it was hard to get lonely around Redbourne Ranch. Most of his siblings were home tonight. All but two. Levi would be coming out from Utah with his new bride for Thanksgiving and they were planning on staying at the ranch through Christmas, but Rafe was another matter entirely.

Rafe was the brother he had been closest to growing up. Ethan had always looked up to him and Rafe had always been there whenever he needed him—especially after his accident, but his brother hadn't been around much over the last year. Ever since his betrothed left him standing at the altar, with no explanation, he'd become more closed off to everyone around him and had not stayed home for more than a week at a time.

Ethan walked back into the dining room and sat in his chair, next to Hannah. "Hey, sis. I saw Gordon Blythe in town today and he asked after you."

"Ooooo," his brothers all cooed in unison and everyone at the table turned to look at her.

She blushed and slapped him playfully on the shoulder. Hannah looked down at her plate and folded her lips together.

"Well," she said after a moment and looked up all too eagerly, "what did he say? What did you say? Oh, I hope you didn't embarrass me. You didn't say anything to embarrass me, right?" Her words got faster the more she spoke.

Ethan's grin spread wide on his face.

"Ethan Redbourne, what did you say?" she pleaded anxiously.

"Nothing much." He shrugged his shoulders. "Just that you liked him so much that you kiss your pillow every night pretending it's him and that you practice writing your name as Mrs. Hannah Blythe." Ethan tried to keep a straight face.

Hannah gasped. "Mother!" she squealed, obviously horrified.

Ethan laughed, as did the rest of the family.

"Aw, don't get all riled up, sis. I just told him you are well, but he should come find out for himself."

Hannah's eyes fluttered shut for a moment and she took a deep breath. When she opened them again, she slugged Ethan in the shoulder.

He laughed again.

"So, when's he coming?" she asked.

Ethan looked at her. "What time is it?"

Hannah opened her mouth wide, then closed it again, squinting her eyes at Ethan.

He held up his hands. "I don't know, Hannah. Honest I don't."

His little sister turned back to stare at her food, but he didn't miss the hint of a smile that touched her lips. She was pleased. He was glad. Gordon Blythe was good folk and the kid was well aware that Hannah had seven older brothers. Ethan smiled to himself.

"Bizcochos fritos," Lottie, the family cook, said as she laid a plate full of delicious looking scones in the middle of the table.

"I think I'll take mine out in the shop," Ethan said as he stood up. "You know they are my favorite." He kissed the older Spanish woman on the cheek. "Muchas gracias, Lottie."

She blushed under his appraisal and wiped her hands in her apron.

He reached for one of the delectable treats, placed it on a cloth napkin, and scooped some of Lottie's honey butter onto the center. It immediately started to melt over the hot chunk of fried bread.

"Ethan, we hardly get to see you anymore. You're spending so much time out there," Leah Redbourne said, placing a hand on his forearm. "Won't you stay inside a while longer?"

"It'll be worth it, Mama. I promise." Ethan leaned down

and kissed his mother on the forehead. "Just wait and see."

She smiled up at him.

"I'll see you lot in the morning," Ethan said, looking at Raine.

He picked up his hat and shoved it onto his head before heading out the door. When the fresh, crisp air of autumn hit his face, he paused and took a deep breath. Ethan relaxed against the cool iron railing and carved pillar he'd added just a few months ago to the back porch steps and took a bite of the warm scone as sweet melted honey butter oozed onto his fingertips.

Ethan glanced out over Redbourne Ranch. He loved it here. All was quiet, except for the occasional nicker of the horses in the stable and the gentle lowing of cattle in the fields. It was a Friday night and most of the ranch hands had headed into town for a game of cards.

Something wet landed on his cheek and he looked up into the clouds. The moon peeked out, casting a beautiful blue glow in its path. Tiny white flakes of snow floated softly to the ground. The first fall of the year.

There was still so much to do. He pushed himself away from the porch and headed into the shop. He had to finish his project before these cool autumn nights turned fully into winter. The building was still warm from the work he'd done earlier in the day. A broken plow, two wagon wheels, and various metal tools that needed to be fixed, littered the floor and shelves, but he would leave those for tomorrow. Tonight was the time to work on *his* project.

It wasn't long before he had the coals in the forge glowing with a deep orange-red hue. He squeezed the accordion-like bellows, forcing out strong bursts of air. Small flames came to life for a few moments and the coals brightened as they grew hotter. He poked at the forge with a steel rod, stirred the embers, and left the metal to heat. He only had two more to complete before the project would be finished.

Ethan glanced out the window. His family was still gathered around the table, finishing their supper and sweet treats. He quickly unbuttoned his shirt and hung it on the hook at the far end of the room and exchanged it for the black leather apron hanging there. He caught his reflection in a hanging metal plate near the door. His focus immediately fell to the garbled flesh of his shoulder and upper chest . He rotated his shoulder, watching how the scars moved in the dim light of the room.

It had been a long time since he'd applied the salve to the area and the skin felt tight.

"You're not still bellyaching over a few little scars, now are ya?"

Ethan whipped around, instinctively reaching for his shirt. He knew that voice and relief washed over him.

"You're not still whining about being left at the altar, now are ya?"

Rafe emerged from the shadows, wearing a long duster and a gun belt. "Naw."

"Me either," Ethan replied with a grin.

Rafe laughed. He stepped forward and pulled Ethan into a firm embrace. "How've you been, little brother?"

Ethan clapped his brother on the back. "Can't complain," he said nonchalantly. "I have a warm bed to sleep in and a hot meal waiting for me every night. You should try it."

"Can't," was all he said in reply.

"How long you staying this time?"

"What are you doing out here?" Rafe asked, setting Ethan aside to lean over the forge. He squinted at the hot metal in the fire.

Ethan didn't miss how easily Rafe had changed the subject.

"How do you do it?" Rafe pulled off his coat. "It's hotter than hell in here." He stepped over to the coat rack in the corner of the room, stopping at the large concealed surprise Ethan had been working on for weeks. "What's this?" Rafe stepped behind Ethan and started to lift a corner of the blanket.

Ethan pushed his hand away. "Not yet."

Rafe raised an eyebrow, but didn't say anything.

Ethan reached up to the wall and grabbed his tongs. After shoving his hands into his thick leather gloves, he used the tongs to reach into the forge and retrieve the steel rod, aglow with heat. He carefully moved it to the anvil in front of Rafe and set it down. He picked up his iron mallet and began to stroke the hot metal, molding it into the shape he needed.

"It's not that hot out here. Once you get used to it," Ethan said, returning to a comfortable topic. "Besides, it's worth it to see something I've worked so hard to create come to life," Ethan told him between pounds. "These are also supposed to be a surprise. You should go into the house and let Mama and Dad know you're here. They don't say it, but they've been worried about you."

"I'd rather stay out here and help you. It seems like it's not much different than my pottery. Only your materials are hot instead of wet."

The two brothers looked at each other and laughed.

"And just how many people can sit with you at *your* wheel and work at the same time?"

"Oh, all right," Rafe resigned. He picked up his coat and walked out into the light dusting of snow that had draped over the ground. "But I'll be back," he said as he turned back to face Ethan. "You know how much I hate surprises."

"Not this one," Ethan called loudly with a grin, closing the door behind his brother. He pulled the formed metal from the anvil with the tongs and dipped it in the water bucket at his feet.

Not this one.

CHAPTER TWO

Sunlight percolated through the boards across the east-facing window. Grace, still prone on the couch, glanced about the room, now lit enough to show the cobwebs and thick layers of dust hovering over every wall and crevice. This place was going to need a lot of work.

She lay there, her breath visible in the air, and willed herself to stay a few minutes longer. But, she realized, the longer she stayed put, the harder it would be to get to work. Her body ached all over and she was unsure she'd be able to stand, but she tossed the dusty wool covering off of her, sat up, and briskly rubbed her arms against the deep winter's chill that had settled into the room. She glanced over at Jack, who still slept peacefully beneath the dirt encrusted couch and chaise coverings.

Winter was definitely on its way. Grace climbed up off the couch and tucked her side of the blankets up under her brother. The trip to Kansas had been a long one. When the stage had finally reached Stone Creek last night, the grocery had already closed, so rather than waste precious money on a hotel room and supper for the night, they'd decided to walk the rest of the way to the Nolan Farmhouse.

Grace was thankful she'd given in a few days ago and

purchased the loaf of bread and jar of berry preserves in one of the small towns they'd passed through. She quickly gathered her knapsack and made her way through aisles of abandoned cobwebs back to the kitchen. In the light of day it was even worse than she'd thought it to be last night.

Outside, she said to herself. *We'll be eating outside on this lovely morning.*

She reached into her knapsack and pulled out a thin shawl. She needed to purchase some yarn and other materials in town to make them some winter ready clothing. But for now, this would have to do. She readjusted the bag over her shoulder and tiptoed past Jack. She'd let him sleep a while longer. There was a lot of work ahead of them and he needed his rest.

"You're not trying to sneak out on me now, are ya?"

Grace turned to see Jack, one eye open, staring at her with a grin.

She smiled, shook her head, and climbed out the window. It didn't take Jack long to follow.

The ground was aglitter with a thin layer of frosted snow. Grace shook and rubbed her arms, grateful they had been able to sleep, despite the cool temperatures. She dusted off the top step and sat down, gazing out over the property and wondering how much of this land belonged to them. She made a mental note to visit the notary in town to see about getting a copy of the land records.

"It's beautiful," Jack said as he joined her on the porch.

Together, they sat and ate their humble breakfast. She noted how her little brother, who usually seemed to swallow his food whole, took his time to savor each bite. Grace regretted that they had not been able to save more money before their trek west, but they would make do. They always had.

"You sure this place is ours?" Jack asked after he'd pushed himself off the stairs and turned to look over the place.

Grace joined him, raising a hand to block the rising sun

from penetrating her closed lids. The warmth of it felt good on her face. "Yes. Grandfather paid his last mortgage payment more than a year before they'd left for New York. Isn't it wonderful?"

"Yeah, but why didn't he try to sell?"

"They did, but folks were in a bad way back then and nobody was buying. Don't you remember all the stories he used to tell?" Grace looked at Jack, who shrugged. "I guess not. You were just a baby when Grandfather passed on." She smiled. "You're so big now it's hard for me to believe you were ever that small." She pushed teasingly on his arm.

He smiled back.

"Hey look, it's a water pump. I wonder if it's still working." Jack pointed behind her. He didn't wait for her to respond before darting toward the metal spigot. He pumped it a few times, but nothing happened. He ran back to the house and picked up a short iron rod that had been leaning against the steps and clanked it a few times against the spout. He lifted the handle and started to pump again, hope alight in his eyes.

"Jack, it's been twenty-five years. I don't think tha—"

Splash. Spurt. Splash.

With each pump, more water shot out—dirty at first, but it worked all the same.

Grace sucked in an awed breath, then rushed over to her bag and pulled out two small tin cups. "Miracles," she said aloud. They'd certainly seen enough of them over the past few months.

The water was cool and tasted as good as any as it passed over her parched lips.

"Well, that's one thing to cross of the list," Grace said with a giggle. This was real. They were home.

"Not another list? Can't we just *do* something."

"There's plenty to do, Jack. Look around. But, we will get to it much more quickly and efficiently if we know what needs to be done."

The morning air was crisp and she rubbed her arms again. It didn't seem to bother Jack. He was ready to explore, but Grace knew that making a plan would serve them better in the long run.

"Let's go back inside. We can start our inventory there on what to keep, what should be tossed, and what needs fixing."

Jack groaned.

Grace ignored him.

"Once we've got our list, we'll need to head into town and get some supplies, and then we'll get started." She hoped they would have enough money to purchase a few necessities to get them ready for the winter ahead, including at least one horse—preferably two.

The house was in total disarray. To Grace's amazement, many of the furnishings were still intact, but most of it would need to be carted outside and burned. Some of the cloth covered items had holes and scratches where she guessed animals had gotten in and had made homes over the course of several Kansas winters. The thought made her shudder and she glanced over at the couch on which she'd slept. She shoved the idea from her mind.

Crack.

Grace jumped at the sounds of splitting wood.

"Sorry about that," Jack said as he pulled the last plank off the front door and opened it. "I thought we might want a way to get our supplies inside." He still held the last of the nailed wood in his hand.

Grace looked from the board to the black iron pot-belly in the kitchen.

"Jack, why don't you see if you can start a fire?" She pointed to the stove.

As she walked through the house with her pencil and paper in hand, she realized that most everything inside would have to be tossed. However, there were a few salvageable items—chairs, table, couches. She was bewildered that her family had left so many things behind when they'd headed east and suddenly wished she had her mother or her grandfather to tell her about this place and why they'd left so quickly.

In the hallway, a large draped tablecloth or covering of some sort hid a large and bulky object from view. Grace's heart skipped a beat.

Could it be?

Carefully, she lifted the edge of the material and pulled.

"Ah." She took a step back. It was the most beautiful grandfather clock she'd ever seen with an intricate gold design lining the outer casing. She wondered if it was one her great-grandfather had built. He'd become a master craftsman of fine clocks, among other things, after he'd abandoned his life as a bandit.

It read seven minutes past three.

Hmmm.

Grace stepped forward and reached to open the door that protected the chimes. It didn't budge, but she squealed when a small family of mice scattered at her feet. She would have plenty of time to ogle the newfound treasure when they returned from town. The kitchen had a plethora of pots and pans, dishes, and other utensils, but most were rusted or tarnished. Getting the house back in order was going to be a lot of work.

Jack whooped. "That old plank burned through pretty quick, so we'll need to collect some wood, but I fixed the blocked flue and it looks like we'll have heat tonight."

They moved out to the barn.

To Grace's delight, there was a small wagon-like cart that could be hitched to a single horse. The wheels looked rotted and the paint was chipped and worn, but it was a good find. An old rusted plow, various shovels and other tools, and a few dusty buffalo pelts were added to their list.

While it was too late in the season to worry about now, Grace wanted to be prepared enough that they would be able to plant a small crop come spring, and she scribbled down a note to remind herself to speak with the blacksmith in town to see about repairs to the plow, the cart, and some of the other equipment.

The walk into Stone Creek would take them a couple of hours. If they wanted to return with enough light to get anything accomplished today, they needed to get going.

"Grace, come quick."

Grace couldn't tell if it was urgency in Jack's voice or excitement. She lifted the hem of her skirt and dashed toward the back of the house. Jack stood at the base of the open cellar, peering inside. He pointed.

The dust had been disturbed on the old wooden stairs, and by the looks of it, recently. Grace scanned her surroundings. They hadn't seen any other signs of people being at the farm, but the hairs on her arms suddenly stood on end. She'd never really considered they would have to defend their property and quickly wrote 'shotgun' on her list.

"Close it up, Jack. We need to get going."

"But—"

"Come on, Jack," she said firmly, leaving no room for dispute.

When she turned around, a cluster of sticks and hint of color caught her attention. She tramped over some tall grasses and tugged at the foliage. A beautiful swirl of twigs and willow, crumpled berries, and burlap ribbon were formed into a unique wreath. Some of the shoots had been snapped and the ribbon was frayed and had been bleached with age. After a little cleaning up, it would be a nice addition to their new home. She lifted it up next to the window of the barn and hung it from a nail that protruded from the corner of framed glass.

I'll clean it up later, she thought, satisfied at the find. *I just need to add ribbon to my list.*

Grace and her brother cleared the clutter from in front of the cart in the barn and wheeled it out into the yard. She didn't know how long the wheels would hold, but at this point, they had no other means to get supplies back to the house. They would have to at least try.

With Jack on one side and Grace on the other, they started to pull the cart in the direction of town.

Boom. Boom. Boom. The loud pounding came in quick succession.

"There's smoke coming from the Nolan place," Raine yelled from the other side of Ethan's door. "Let's go."

Ethan darted out of his bed. He grabbed the shirt draped over the back of the chair next to his washstand, and threw his arms through the holes. He sat down, pulling both legs of his pants on at the same time and then yanked on his work boots.

When he reached the bottom of the stairs, his mother stood there with a hot buttered biscuit and two slices of bacon. He grabbed them, kissed her on the cheek, and skittered out the front door.

Raine and Rafe were already mounted and ready to ride. A handful of buckets were tied to each of their horses. He glanced around, but didn't see Cole or Will.

"Dad needs them to help with the new herd this morning," Rafe said, seeming to know Ethan's thoughts as always.

Ethan strode to the stable where the foreman already had his horse saddled. Two buckets had been strung from the saddle horn.

"Thanks, Marty."

The man simply tipped his hat in acknowledgement.

Ethan pulled himself up and rode out into the yard after his brothers, who'd already started out. Smoke could only mean one of two things. Either the house had caught fire, or someone was holing up in the old place. Neither option was preferable.

It was only a short fifteen minute ride over to the Nolan place and by the time they arrived, the smoke had already cleared and the old farmhouse seemed quiet.

"Blasted all, Grace. This isn't working," a voice carried from the opposite side of the house.

Ethan and his brothers rode around the house to where a young man and woman were positioned in front of a small one-horse cart, each had a hold of a pole on either side, and were attempting to pull it. It was quite a sight, and Ethan had to check himself from laughing out loud at their predicament. They were sure to get nothing for their troubles but a handful of slivers. Tenderfoots. What were they thinking?

"That's because you're doing it wrong." Ethan couldn't help the snort that accompanied his words.

He regretted them immediately when the young woman turned around startled, her green eyes alight with defiance. She was the most beautiful woman Ethan had seen in a very long time and he sat up straighter in the saddle. He darted his glance between her and the boy. Siblings. They had to be. The youth was much too young to be her husband. At least, he hoped.

"Excuse me," she said, setting her pole on the ground, "but if you have a better idea on how to get this cart to town, I'd love to hear it."

Raine and Rafe both had grins spread across their faces—their eyes open wide in disbelief. At his size, it wasn't very often that anyone talked to him like that. Especially a woman. His brothers both immediately dismounted and removed their hats with a nod of greeting.

"As a matter of fact, I do," Ethan replied, staying astride his mount.

The young woman stood there, her hands on her hips, and with a raised eyebrow dared him to try. Her lips were full and pink and Ethan wondered what they would look like if she smiled.

That's enough of that, he scolded himself silently.

"Well?" she asked expectantly.

Feisty. That kind of spunk would serve her well. Or get her into a heap of trouble.

Ethan cleared his throat and climbed down from his horse. He handed the reins to Rafe and walked closer to the woman. He opened his mouth to say something, but didn't voice the words. He glanced upward and noticed the open barn doors and, without a word, turned away from her to walk into the large run-down building. Ethan immediately saw the object he'd hoped he'd find there—a harness with leather straps. It was old, but not so far gone as to be useless. He gathered the contraption, threw it over his shoulders, and walked back to where the woman still stood silent by the cart. He dropped it on the ground in front of her and turned for Storm, his grey and charcoal gelding. Ethan could feel her eyes boring holes into the back of his head and he smirked.

Raine and Rafe had tied their horses to a weathered hitching post next to the large maple that dominated the yard.

"If you don't mind my asking, ma'am, who are you?" Raine asked, taking a step forward and moving his vest so that his deputy badge would show. "You do realize that taking property that doesn't belong to you is against the law," he said before she could answer.

Rafe took a turn around the immediate perimeter of the property. If anything was off, his brother would find it. Ethan reverted his attention back toward the woman as his brother disappeared around the side of the house. She looked up at Raine, as if noticing him for the first time, and dropped her hands to her side.

The kid pushed his way in front of her. "This is our property. It belongs to us," he spat out in her defense, standing with high shoulders and an arched back between her and Raine.

"It's okay, Jack," she said calmly with a reassuring curve to her mouth as she reached to place a hand on his forearm.

Her brother backed up beside her.

"I'm Grace Nolan, deputy." She reached out a hand to him.

Ethan led his horse over to the cart and removed his saddle. He carried it back to the hitching post and draped it over the beam. The harness was meant for a smaller horse, but if he used the outer holes, he would be able to secure it well enough to fit Storm. The wheels on the cart looked older than dirt, and he wasn't sure they would make it all the way to town, let alone return with a full load.

"This place belonged to my grandfather," Grace continued. "God rest his soul. It's just me and my brother, Jack, now. And we've come back to claim our farm."

She stepped closer to Raine, and Ethan laughed when his brother reached up and tugged on the collar of his shirt at the neck.

"Is there a problem?"

"Back from where? This place has been empty my whole life and you sure don't look older than me," Raine said.

"Our family left here before we were born," Grace raised her chin defiantly, but her tone remained cool, "but grandfather never sold the house or the land. Which I believe, deputy, means that you all are trespassing."

Ethan guffawed. No one talked to Raine like that either.

All eyes turned on him.

"Looks like the two of them slept inside last night." Rafe saved him as he appeared from around the far side of the house. "And three others have been sleeping down in the cellar."

"Three oth—" Grace's voice trailed as her eyes darted about the grounds. "We just arrived last night. It's only the two of us. There's nobody else."

Grace looked up at Ethan who had moved his gelding directly in front of the cart between the poles.

"There *is* nobody else, right?" she whispered. This was the first time there had been any break in the woman's courageous façade.

Ethan looked up at Rafe, who nodded.

"If Rafe says that someone has been sleeping in that cellar, then you can trust that someone has been sleeping in that cellar."

"I knew it," Jack said, turning to face his sister. "I told you something wasn't right."

"Don't worry," Ethan turned to Grace and looked her straight in the eyes—those beautiful eyes—"we'll take a look. You'll be safe."

What was he saying? He'd only just met the woman and he had no idea if she was telling the truth or spinning a tale, but something told him she was who she claimed. His mind told him to stay far away from this woman, but the rest of him wanted nothing more than to be near her.

"Thank you," Grace offered quietly.

Ethan acknowledged with a quick nod of his head. He lifted the straps he'd secured around Storm and fastened them to the poles of the cart and finished by hooking the metal clip into the ring.

"And that's how you get a cart to town. Excuse me for a moment, ma'am." He tipped his hat and walked over to where his brothers stood.

"I'll see her into Stone Creek. I don't trust that cart at all." He turned to Rafe. "You two, find out who has been staying in their cellar."

Raine smiled. "Just who is supposed to be the deputy around here?"

Ethan said nothing.

"You're sweet on her," his oldest brother said, tilting his head and squinting his eyes, scanning Ethan's face as if to confirm his suspicions.

Ethan raised an eyebrow. He had just met the woman. How could he be sweet on her? Although, she was beautiful and when she spoke to him, a hollow space formed in his gut. He shook his head.

"Ah, I get it. *You* want to take her to town." Ethan tried diverting the insinuation. "Maybe you're the one who's taken with Miss Nolan."

"Sure, I'll take her," Raine called his bluff. "I'm headed there anyw——"

A deafening screech split the air. It sounded like a small child had screamed out in agony.

Raine immediately jerked his hand to the gun at his hip, all playful expression leaving his face and they all rushed toward the barn where the sound had originated. Rafe stood just outside the open doors, while Ethan held out his arm to keep the young woman and her brother back at a safer distance.

Grace darted a glance at Ethan, somehow seeking his reassurance. He took a step toward the raggedy barn door and was greeted by a high-pitched yipping, growl-like sound.

Coyotes.

Grace rushed to his side.

Boom.

She jumped and instinctively Ethan threw his arm around her shoulders.

With one squealing whimper, all went silent.

Rafe, still aiming his gun, disappeared inside the barn with Raine on his heels.

"Wait here, Miss Nolan." Ethan squeezed, then let go of her and headed into the barn after his brothers. He grabbed an old shovel that hung from the nails just inside the door.

A lone coyote lay dead on the ground, blood accumulating beneath his head.

"Did you kill it?" Jack rushed into the barn and stopped cold when he saw the inert animal at Rafe's feet.

"It's dead all right." Rafe nudged the creature with the toe of his boot. "But where'd he come from?"

"Incredible," Jack said with an appreciative tone.

"Shhhh." Ethan placed a finger over his lips. He'd heard something, but it didn't sound like another coyote.

The unmistakable mewing of kittens now seemed to fill the barn. Ethan stepped around the coyote and spotted two little fluffy kittens—one grey and the other cream—huddled together in a dirty old blanket peering out from open doors of a broken cabinet, tilted to one side.

How did I miss them? He'd just been in the barn a few minutes before and had not heard or noticed the little family that had taken residence here. Ethan fell down to one knee to get a closer look and his insides twisted tragically inside him.

A warning hiss alerted him to the mother cat, staring at him from the corner. She picked up the motionless body of a small kitten by the scruff of its neck and carried it to the others. Ethan noticed deep gouges in her neck and side and realized she had been trying to protect her young from the coyote. He reached out to her. She needed help. But she swiped at his hand, drawing blood.

"Ach." He sucked in a gulp of air and shook his hand as it immediately started to sting.

"What is it?" Raine asked, peering over the top of the cabinet. He looked down. "So, that's what he was after."

The mother cat began licking the tiny, lifeless kitty. Blood stained the otherwise orange color of its fur and deep teeth indents marked the area where the coyote had gotten a hold of it.

Ethan dropped his head. It was his fault. He should have shut the door. Why hadn't he just shut the door?

Something had to be done. The mother wouldn't survive those wounds without help, but he couldn't do it alone without gaining her wrath.

"Rafe, a little help, please."

In moments, Rafe stood behind him and crouched down. "It's pretty bad, Ethan. She's lost a lot of blood and that gouge looks pretty deep."

"No!" Ethan said more firmly than he'd intended. "Fix it. Please."

"It's not like a wagon wheel or tools that you can mend with fire and a hammer, little brother, she's a living thing."

"Exactly. She was protecting those she loves and I think that's worth something, don't you?"

Rafe clapped him on the shoulder. "Good point, Ethan. We'll need to get her home. Mama will have her salve and clean rags," he looked around at the dust and cobwebs at every turn, "unlike here." He glanced down at Ethan's hand. "And it looks like you could use some cleaning up too."

Ethan looked around for something clean he could use to wrap them in. The blanket the kittens occupied was old, ratty, and filthy. Rafe had spoken on many an occasion throughout his years in medical school about the importance of keeping wounds clean and dressing them.

He looked at the door, knowing full well that Grace Nolan stood just on the other side. But what other choice did he have?

She'd find out sooner or later anyway, he tried to justify to himself. *Might as well be sooner and save us all some trouble.*

Ethan quickly undid the buttons on his shirt. He took a deep breath, looking around the old building for something he could use as a cover. There was nothing that would suffice. He tugged on the shirt, but before he could get it over his shoulders, Rafe stayed his hand.

"Wait," Rafe said. "You're prepared to go out there?" he asked with a raised brow. "Like that?" Rafe nodded to the open section of his shirt.

His older brother, doctor turned bounty hunter, had always been patient and sensitive to Ethan's fear of showing his scars to anyone—especially the idea of exposing them to any woman.

"Here," Rafe said as he removed his shirt. "Use mine." He held out the garment for Ethan, then pulled his black leather vest back over his shoulders.

Ethan breathed a sigh of relief as he reached out for Rafe's shirt.

"Thanks."

"Now, if you two will stop playing dress up, you can get the mother, and I'll grab the kittens," Raine said as he stepped around the large set of broken cabinets.

"She needs to know they are safe," Ethan told them. "After I collect her in my arms, just place the kittens next to her inside the shirt. Hopefully, she won't see much of a need to fight after that."

"When did you get to be so smart?" Rafe asked with a wink, mussing Ethan's hair.

Ethan shook his hair back into place as he bent down and scooped up the mama cat with the shirt. She scratched and clawed at his arms, shredding part of the shirt. One claw snagged on the button hole and while she was attempting to remove it, Raine set the kittens in the shirt next to her and her entire demeanor visibly relaxed. With another quick tug, her claw came loose and she nuzzled against her babies.

Ethan wrapped his arm protectively around his little bundle and tucked the edges of the shirt up around them. He took a deep breath and walked out of the barn, surprised to see Grace standing there, a shotgun in her hands and pointed at the door. She must have pulled it from Raine's saddle holster.

She lowered the gun with a sigh. "I'm not even sure I know how to use this thing. But I wanted to be prepared for anything that might come out of there."

Ethan took a step toward her, courage finding its way inside him. "And are you?" he asked with a raised brow. "Prepared, I mean, for anything that might come out of there?"

She swallowed, not taking her eyes from his. "Well, I wasn't prepared for you, Mr..."

Ethan realized they hadn't even introduced themselves yet.

"Redbourne," Ethan supplied. "Ethan Redbourne."

CHAPTER THREE

Grace bit her lip and gripped the shotgun in her hand. Ethan Redbourne had emerged from the barn in an open shirt that exposed his flesh down the center of his chest. Her mouth went dry and suddenly she yearned for a glass of water. A wiggling bundle, swaddled in something akin to a man's red shirt, was carefully enfolded in Ethan's arms.

"Grace, there was a whole little family of kittens in there." Jack burst from the barn and dashed toward her. Breathless, he stood and regaled her with a recount of everything that had transpired in the barn. "But the coyote killed one and hurt the mother. But that one over there," he pointed to one of Ethan's brothers, "killed it and now they're going to try to nurse the mama back to health. Look, he has them right there."

"Jack, it's not polite to point," Grace said with a smile. "Wait, did you say there is a dead coyote in my barn?" There had been so many things she hadn't considered when they'd made the decision to come to Kansas, and having dangerous wild animals in her house or her barn had certainly not been a part of the plan.

A tiny little face emerged from the bundle Ethan held. Its wide grey eyes, near the same color as its ears and sections of its face, stared up at her.

"Kittens, huh?" she asked, reaching out to scratch the small fluffy kitten on the top of the head and behind the ears.

She giggled and glanced back up at Ethan.

"I imagine they can't be any older than two, maybe three weeks at most. We need to get them back to Redbourne Ranch. We're your closest neighbors, just over that hill, around the copse of pine trees, and down about a mile or so."

Ethan's brothers appeared from the barn. One carried the dead coyote and the other a ratted old blanket all wrapped up. They set down their loads in front of the cellar doors and moved to join her, Jack, and Ethan.

Grace raised her hand to her chest and she looked over at Ethan, whose facial expression said it all. "How many?" she asked.

"Just one," Ethan told her, a sad expression daunting his otherwise handsome features. "Miss Nolan," he said, "these are my brothers, Raine," he pointed to the deputy, "and Rafe."

"Ma'am," they both said in unison as they each tapped on the front brims of their hats.

"Thank you," she said sincerely. "I don't know what we would have done if you hadn't been here."

"We'll need to be burning those carcasses before they attract any other unwanted guests," Rafe said.

"The wood in the pile looks like it is completely rotted through. We'll have to see if we can't find a fallen tree over in the pine grove." Raine pointed in the direction Ethan had told her was their ranch. "Jack, you want to come along?"

"Really?" Her brother turned to look at her, his eyes pleading for some adventure. "Can I?"

Grace looked from one brother to the next. "You'll keep him safe?" she asked with only the slightest hesitation.

Raine tipped the edge of his hat. "Will do."

Neither she nor Jack were accustomed to their new home, but the Redbournes seemed to be good men, and it would be nice to have firewood for the cold nights.

"Mind your manners," she said with an approving nod at Jack.

Raine took her brother over to where the horses had been tied to the old hitching post, and he handed the reins to Jack.

Suddenly, she wasn't sure it had been such a good idea. They had never really been around horses and now she was going to let him just ride off with a perfect stranger. What had she been thinking? She held her breath as Raine showed her little brother how to mount the horse. At first, he looked a little unsteady, but quickly the expression on his face changed from one of apprehension to excitement.

Jack waved as he and Raine rode past the rest of them on their way out.

Grace hoped they wouldn't be gone long because time was passing and she still needed to get to town for supplies. She didn't want to put that off any longer than was necessary. There was so much work to be done. The chill in the air reminded her just how quickly winter was coming.

The kittens in Ethan's arms had started squirming and it looked as if he were having a difficult time keeping them inside the shirt. She reached out and took the little white and grey one she'd petted earlier from him into her own arms. It found her fingers and rooted around briefly before it started to suckle.

Grace giggled, then became serious when she saw the mother cat, lying so still.

"Will she make it?" Grace asked, concerned for the babies.

"Not unless we can get these wounds cleaned and bound quickly. She's lost a lot of blood." Rafe walked up to Ethan. "May I?" he asked as he reached for the mama.

"Excuse me for a moment," Grace said and quickly moved for the house, the kitten tucked in her arm. He crawled up her neck and snuggled his face in just below her jaw.

She found her large knapsack-like traveling bag and opened it, the soft fresh scent of lavender filling her nostrils. It only took a moment before she located the bar soap she'd purchased a few weeks ago in a small town along their route to Kansas. With it clasped tightly in her hand, she returned to Ethan and his brother, then held it out.

"Will this help?" she asked hopefully.

"Ethan," Rafe asked, "do you still have those handkerchiefs Mama wanted us to deliver to Mrs. Flinders?"

"Yes. They're in my saddle bag" Ethan said, already making his way back toward the hitching post beam.

"Yes, Miss Nolan, I think your soap will do quite nicely."

Grace handed him the soap. She grabbed the bucket next to the stairs, set it down in front of the pump, and began to fill it with water. She didn't dare set the kitten down for fear that something else might happen to it, but he was obviously getting anxious and tried to wriggle from her grasp.

"Allow me," Ethan said, appearing out of nowhere. He finished filling the bucket, picked it up and carried it to the cart.

Grace noted his strong arms, straining against his shirt, contracting with the slight weight of the bucket. She took a moment to admire his broad shoulders and slender waist. When her eyes traveled farther down to his firm buttocks, she blushed and quickly turned away. She'd never looked at a man in such a way, but she couldn't deny he was beautiful.

When they reached the cart, Rafe turned around, the expression on his face unreadable.

"I'm sorry, Ethan."

"I'm sorry too. Thanks for trying." Ethan set the bucket on the ground and walked over to the porch. When he returned, he had the other little kitten. "They won't survive without their mother," he said matter-of-factly.

Rafe took the cat over to the place where the other carcasses lay.

"We can't just let them die," Grace said, hoping that was not what he had been implying.

"I have a friend in town that may be able to find homes for them," Ethan volunteered.

"Why not just leave them here?" She motioned to the house.

"Do you know how to take care of a kitten that hasn't been weaned from its mother?" Rafe asked seriously from behind them.

"No, but I learn quickly," Grace said as the little grey calico climbed up onto her shoulder. "Do you?" She pulled him back down into her arms.

"Learn quickly? I'd like to think so." Rafe's face cracked into a smile.

"You're teasing me," Grace said playfully.

"When are the rest of your things arriving?" Ethan inquired, pulling a sugar cube from his pocket and feeding it to his patiently waiting horse.

Things?

Ethan's little cream colored friend had climbed beneath his vest, his face barely poking out from the leather and seemed perfectly content to be there.

"We each brought whatever we could carry. I'm afraid it's not much. But that's exactly why I need to get to town." When her kitty climbed up the front of her and nudged her face with his, she decided she had chosen the much more spirited of the two.

Ethan must have sensed her distress. He walked over to her with his hand extended. The kitty immediately crawled into his palm.

"Let's get you to town. These little guys will be okay until we get back. Hopefully, we won't be gone more than a few hours." He strode up the stairs and set them in an old crate. He pulled on the boards covering one of the windows and when they came free, he set them across the top of the open box.

We?

The sound of approaching horses pulled her attention from the direction her thoughts were heading. Raine appeared first, followed closely by Jack. She breathed a prayer of thanks. Each had a bundle of wood rolled and tied to the back of their horses. When they got closer, Grace could see that Jack was still a little nervous, but he sat up straighter in his seat when he saw her. He was proud of himself. She was glad.

It wasn't long before a big fire roared to life in the make-shift pit they'd constructed in the dirt at the far edge of the yard. Jack and Grace collected some of the things around the old farmhouse they had determined would need to be thrown out and added them to the fire.

The heat felt nice against her skin. She glanced up and caught Ethan staring at her from across the fire. A different type of heat rushed into her cheeks. She almost hated to admit it, but she was pleased.

Ethan strode around the blaze.

"Are you ready?"

"Grace," Jack said with a look of pleading in his eyes, "can I stay here with Rafe and Raine?"

She looked at the small cart and realized it only had seats for two. If Ethan took her into town alone, there was sure to be talk, and that is not how she wanted to start off her new life here. She wouldn't mind getting to know him a little better, but she'd already seen the damage a few gossips could do and refused to let that happen to her...again.

It was settled. Jack could ride in the back of the cart.

"I think you should come with us, Jack."

He dropped his head, looking slightly dejected.

"Okay," she said reluctantly, hoping he would change his mind, "you can stay if you trust me enough to pick out your horse."

His head shot up, a smile touching the corners of his mouth.

"Oh, no you don't. I'm coming."

Grace forced herself not to smirk.

"Well played," Ethan whispered against her ear before

walking over to his brothers.

Tingles cascaded down her neck and shoulders to her toes. Yes, it was best if Jack came with them.

"I hope you don't mind, ma'am, but I think Rafe and I will stick around and put out the fire. We'd also like your permission to look through the cellar to see if we can't find out who has been staying down there." Raine looked at her expectantly.

Grace nodded. She'd nearly forgotten that Rafe believed three people had been sleeping in her cellar. "That would be lovely. Thank you all for your kindness and your help. It's been quite neighborly of you. If you'd excuse me."

She shuffled past them and into the house to retrieve the small handbag with her money tucked inside. She counted out just over half of it and stuffed that into her bag, then glanced about the room looking for a place she could hide the rest. She spotted the beautiful grandfather clock that she had admired earlier.

Perfect.

Grace took a step forward and tripped over a curling rug in the hallway. She slammed into the stone wall in the entry and fell to the ground along with a few loose pebbles and dusty rubble. She reached up for a protruding stone to gain enough leverage to pull herself up off the ground. It shifted in the wall when she pulled, but it did not fall out.

Once in a standing position, she hunched over and wiggled the loose rock. With a little extra encouragement, she was able to slide it out of place. She peered inside the now empty hole. It was even more inconspicuous than the clock, although, she realized she would have to hollow out a small area to be able to fit the money.

With a quick glance out the window, she saw the Redbournes and her brother still standing close to the fire engaged in conversation. There wasn't much time. She picked up the rusted metal poker next to the fireplace and hastily carved out a piece of the mortar. Satisfied when the wad of bills and a few coins fit into her makeshift cubby, she replaced the stone and ran her hand over the wall and then stood back just a little. It looked perfectly in place.

Deep breath, she told herself as she brushed at the wrinkles in her dress and walked outside to meet up with them.

"Is everything all right?" Ethan asked as she walked up next to him.

"Yes. I just needed to collect my bag." Grace held up the purse with the funds she would need for today's purchases.

Ethan nodded his head. "Shall we?" He held out a hand.

Breathe. Just breathe.

She placed her hand gently in his and he helped her up onto the seat of the cart. Jack jumped into the back. After Ethan tossed his saddle in next to her brother, he climbed up onto the seat next to her.

Grace dared a glance at Ethan. He smiled and snapped the reins. They jolted forward, the wheels protesting the exercise.

This was going to be a long ride.

CHAPTER FOUR

Crack!

The cart jerked to the right. Ethan reached out and wrapped his hand around Grace's waist in time to stop her from falling to the ground. He pulled her close to him on the seat, but her nearness made him heady. He jumped down off the cart to inspect the broken wheel and give himself a little distance.

What was it about this girl that was making him act like a fool schoolboy?

"Looks like we walk from here," he said bluntly. "Miss Nolan, you can ride Storm."

She looked with apprehension at the horse.

"You do know how to ride a horse?"

"Not exactly, but like I said before, I'm a quick learner." She swallowed hard.

"It's fun, Gracie," Jack said as he hopped down from the back of the cart.

Ethan raised a brow. He unhooked Storm from the cart and grabbed the saddle from the back. It only took him a few minutes to secure the tack and then he motioned for Grace to join him next to the horse. His appreciation for her grew as she grabbed a hold of the hem of her dress and marched right up to him, fear-be-damned.

He helped her up into the seat, but hadn't thought about adjusting the length of the straps. "Your feet won't reach the stirrups here," he motioned to the leather foot holders, "so I'll need to adjust them or you'll have a hard time keeping yourself upright." Ethan quickly made the modifications. "We'll take it slow. You'll do just fine."

"What about the cart?"

"It's not going anywhere." Ethan mustered a smile. He had worried that these old wheels wouldn't make it all the way to town and chastised himself for not making the quick trip home to get some of his tools or a wagon. Luckily, they were only a couple of miles outside of town and it wouldn't take long for him and Jack to make the trip on foot. He reached for Storm's reins and clicked his tongue. Once there, he could stop by the smithy and get what he needed to make repairs enough to get the cart into town.

They reached Stone Creek just inside an hour. Mr. Pierce, the town's blacksmith and Ethan's mentor, sat behind the main floor window in the restaurant having lunch. One of Dinah's meat sandwiches with egg on rye bread sounded wonderful about now, but Ethan figured it would be inappropriate to leave Miss Nolan to her own devices while he enjoyed the delectable treat.

As they crossed the main boardwalk toward the mercantile, Raine pulled into town in one of the Redbourne wagons.

"I thought you might need this," he said, pulling up alongside Ethan. "Ma'am." He tipped his hat at Grace.

"Where were you an hour ago when the cart snapped a wheel?" Ethan asked sardonically.

Raine ignored him. "Miss Nolan, I just thought you might want to know that we believe there are prospectors squatting in the farmhouse," Raine said, leaning over from the buckboard seat, his elbow resting on his knee. "We found maps and mining tools, along with a few canteens and other supplies. Rafe believes they are on foot and headed toward the wooded hills that separate our properties."

"What do we need to do, Mr. Redbourne?"

Raine jumped down off the wagon. "Rafe locked a heavy chain around the handles of the cellar doors for now. We will need to talk to these people. Hopefully, there won't be any trouble and they'll move along with little encouragement."

"Thank you, deputy."

"We'll be back around tonight to check in on you, but Ethan here will take real good care of you in the meantime." Raine winked at him and headed for the sheriff's office. Ethan felt like punching his brother in the face.

Jack scanned the town. Ethan speculated he was looking for the livery. His dad had just delivered a dozen or so Quarter Horses and Morgans to Mr. Phillips and Ethan was glad that the Nolans would have some good stock to choose from.

"Do you know what you need to get??"

Grace pulled out a small piece of paper from her handbag and held it up in front of him.

"Let's get started." Ethan gathered Storm's reins and walked with Grace and Jack over to the mercantile. He tied his gelding to the hitching post just to the side of the building.

"Mrs. Day?" He called as the bell on the door chimed when they opened the door.

The shopkeeper was on a ladder in front of them, placing jars of Lottie's jam on the shelves. She turned around and looked down at them through her small wired spectacles.

"Why Ethan Redbourne, what brings you to town?" She climbed down the ladder to face them and picked up a pencil.

"This is Miss Grace Nolan and her brother, Jack."

"Nolan? As in Horace Nolan? Out at the old Nolan place?"

"You knew my grandfather?" Grace asked eagerly.

"Knew him? Why he was like my own father. Are you Gemma's daughter?"

Grace nodded.

"Oh, child, let me look at ya." Mrs. Day walked around the counter and placed her hands on Grace's shoulders. "You are a mighty fine looking young woman." She turned to Jack. "And what a strapping young man you've turned out to be." She looked back at Grace then behind them to the door. "And just where is Gemma? There is so much we need to catch up on."

"Mama passed away a few months ago. I take it you were close."

Mrs. Day tilted her head, some of the light now missing from her eyes. "I'm so sorry to hear that. She was a good friend." The woman placed a hand on Grace's shoulder, then squeezed. "So, what brings you to Stone Creek? I reckon it's been twenty years or so."

"Twenty-five," Grace supplied.

Ethan watched Jack move to the window and peer outside.

"Miss Nolan, if you don't mind, I am going to take Jack down to the livery so he can look over the horses Mr. Phillips has for sale."

No response.

"Why, did you know that it was your great-granddaddy who built that beautiful clock that sits in the loft above the church? It doesn't exactly chime on the hour like most clocks. But I think that's what gives it some of its charm." Mrs. Day walked back around the counter and leaned over. "Now, let's have a look at that list."

Ethan didn't feel much like sitting around town all day, waiting on a woman. He cleared his throat and took a step toward them.

Grace placed her paper on the table, and Mrs. Day busily glanced it over, nodding and marking things with her pencil. They started discussing which items would be best for now, which needed to be ordered in, and those that could wait until spring.

"Miss Nolan?" he tried again. He'd barely had out the

words before her brother stomped his foot on the wood floor.

"Grace!" Jack called loudly.

She turned with narrowed eyes and a raised brow.

Jack smiled. "Ethan is taking me to buy a horse. We'll be at the livery."

She glanced over at Ethan and pulled the corner of her bottom lip under her teeth. He could not drag his gaze from her perfect mouth,

"I'll join you as soon as we're finished here," she said and turned back to Mrs. Day.

"That's how you get her attention," Jack said, satisfied with himself.

Ethan laughed. He doubted highly that Miss Nolan would appreciate him yelling for her in public. They walked down the street to the livery where Mr. Phillips was brushing down a beautiful Appaloosa mare with a sorrel-like coloring he'd never quite seen before. Her mane was a light red color and she had a unique white marking on her forehead.

"She's a beaut, ain't she?" Mr. Phillips asked without looking up. He'd always seemed to know when he had visitors.

"She sure is, but she didn't come from our last herd."

"Nope." The liveryman set down the brush and reached into a bucket hanging from a nail just outside the horse's stall and grabbed an apple. "Hurley Devlin is back in town to spend Thanksgiving with his folks. She belongs to him."

Hurley Devlin? A pit opened up in Ethan's stomach. If ever a name fit a man, Hurley was the devil himself.

He reached up instinctively and rubbed his shoulder.

"What can I do for you, Ethan?" he asked as he held the apple out for the Appaloosa.

Ethan shook his head, thoughts from his past still haunting him. "Mr. Phillips, this is Jack Nolan," he said, placing a hand on Jack's shoulder. "He and his sister are new in town and in need of a couple of horses. Jack here would like to look at the new stock."

"Come on in." Mr. Phillips walked to the back of the livery ahead of them and opened the doors leading out into the corral. There were only three horses roaming the enclosed space.

"Where are the rest of them? Didn't my father deliver more than a dozen head?" Ethan inquired, puzzled by the few horses for sale.

"Fifteen to be exact, but when Hurley arrived early this morning and saw them, he bought up a straight twelve, and they've already been driven out to the ranch."

What in heaven's name did Hurley Devlin want with a dozen new horses?

Ethan saw Jack's hopes deflate—his smile fell and his shoulders slumped a little.

"Come now, Mr. Nolan, these are finely bred geldings and will be good, strong work horses," Mr. Phillips encouraged.

Jack walked out into the corral and one by one approached each of the horses. He rubbed their noses and they all seemed to like him well enough, but when Jack returned to where Ethan was standing, instead of the glimmer of excitement he'd expected to see there, he saw resignation.

"I guess I'll take that one over there." He pointed to the chestnut colored Morgan who continued to gnaw on the long grass that had grown over the fence.

"What's wrong, Jack," Ethan asked quietly.

"Aw, I don't know," he said, kicking at the dirt. "I guess I was just kind of hoping for a black one."

Ethan understood. When he'd first seen Storm, there'd been a connection and after he'd ridden him, there was no turning back. Storm was the perfect fit for him. Each of his brothers had experienced the same thing with their horses.

"Thank you, Mr. Phillips." Ethan reached out to shake his hand. "I think we're going to see if there are any out at the ranch that catch his fancy."

"Thanks, Ethan. And tell your pa that I'll be needing some

more real soon."

"Yes, sir."

"Well," Ethan started once they were back out on the street, "what else was on that list of your sister's?"

"I didn't pay much attention. Sorry." Jack waved and Ethan turned to see Grace waving at them from the boardwalk in front of the mercantile.

Ethan waved too.

Mrs. Day's three young boys were already filling the wagon with supplies and food stuffs.

Then, as if someone had just knocked Ethan in the gut with a mallet, Hurley Devlin appeared behind Grace carrying a large box that he loaded into the Redbourne wagon, then turned and placed one booted foot up onto the boardwalk in front of her.

Something he said made Grace laugh and she lifted a hand to her mouth to hide the grin that touched her features. Ethan had to do something. Hurley was not a man to be trusted. But his good looks and easy demeanor had fooled even the brightest of them before—including him.

"Devlin," Ethan said in a low, even tone.

The man spun around and with a satisfied smirk on his face reached out a hand. "Good to see you, Ethan. We have a lot to discuss, old friend. Grace was just telling me that you have been a great help in making her feel welcome to our little town."

Grace? He'd known the woman for all of five minutes and he was already using her first name? Ethan ignored the extended hand.

"What are you doing here, Hurley?"

"It's the holidays, Redbourne. It is customary to spend them with family. Besides, I've been working on a little business venture that may just bring me back this way on a more...permanent basis."

"I'm sure you have a lot to do, Devlin. I can help the lady

from here." Ethan hoped the tone in his voice would be enough to deter the man from lingering any longer.

Hurley pulled a unique looking brass watch from his pocket. "When the man's right, he's right." He returned the timekeeper to his vest and turned to Grace, taking her hand in his. "You are most enchanting, Grace. Can I call on you after I get settled?"

Ethan was surprised steam didn't blow out his ears. He had to focus on keeping his breathing even. After all, he'd only met Grace today and didn't have any claim on her. If she wanted to see Hurley, the choice was hers, but he would make sure she understood exactly what kind of a man he was.

"Of course, Mr. Devlin."

"Hurley. Please."

Ethan nearly choked on the deceivingly sticky sweetness of his voice.

"Of course, Hurley. Thank you for these."

Ethan hadn't seen the small bouquet of wheat strands held together with a ribbon in her arms.

Hurley bent down and kissed her hand, then turned with a grin. "See you soon, Redbourne." He tipped his hat and headed for the livery. Before he'd gotten even a few steps he turned back to Ethan. "Oh, I heard that Victoria just married someone from Pastoral Hill. It's too bad, really. You truly liked her." He paused for a moment, then met Ethan's eyes straight on. "How *is* that shoulder of yours?"

Ethan started toward him, but Raine came out of nowhere and stepped between them, effectively blocking his way.

"Not here," his deputy brother whispered. "Not now."

Hurley laughed. "We'll talk soon, Ethan." He pivoted on his heel and walked again toward the livery.

"Count on it," Ethan ground out under his breath.

Why did he still let Hurley get under his skin? He'd thought he'd let his bitterness go a long time ago, but seeing him again with that smirk on his face, brought back old hurts.

He needed to work in his shop. Pounding metal always seemed to calm him down and help him to see things clearly. He unwittingly rubbed his chest just below the shoulder.

"Who was that?" Jack asked, his voice laced with disdain—which somehow pleased Ethan.

"Nobody. He's nobody."

Grace set down that blasted wheat bundle Hurley had given her and walked back into the mercantile. When she emerged, she was struggling with a large crate. Ethan took a step toward her, but Jack beat him to it and ran to help her.

"Is it true, Raine?" Ethan turned around to look at his brother. "Did Victoria get married to that little bald weasel from Pastoral Hill?"

"Ethan," Raine started.

"Don't." He raised his hand. "I just want to know how Hurley Devlin, of all people, who doesn't even live here anymore, knew and I had to learn it from him."

Raine opened his mouth to say something, but Ethan realized he didn't want to hear it.

"Forget it."

"Ethan," Raine called as he started to walk away, "I'm headed home to get Will and Cole. They'll come help us unload the wagon."

"I'm sure Miss Nolan would appreciate the help."

"And Mama wants to meet the new unmarried woman who has moved into the place next door."

Ethan groaned. Just what he needed. Ever since Victoria had left him, it seemed his mother wanted nothing more than to find him the perfect match. So far, Ethan had been lucky. Women were scarce in Stone Creek and the surrounding towns, so finding eligible women to court didn't come easy. Not that she hadn't tried.

"Now, you just ask Ethan," Mrs. Day was saying to Grace as the two women exited the mercantile. "He knows the place."

Ethan stepped up onto the boardwalk. "Do you have what

you need?"

Grace looked up at him and smiled. "Mrs. Day has been very helpful. And she's going to order the things we couldn't find. Horses?" she asked, looking around.

"Ethan and his family are all ranchers, Grace," Jack piped up. "We're going to get the horses from them."

"Well, that's not exactly true. We do the breeding, breaking, and brokering of horses at Redbourne Ranch, but not all of us are ranchers."

"He said I could have a black one if I wanted."

Ethan laughed to himself. Color was only one of the factors people considered when making such a purchase. Temperament and strength were generally more important. Jack would learn, as would his sister, soon enough. Living in the west was going to be very different than living in the city.

"What else is on that list of yours?" Ethan asked, leaning over her shoulder. She turned to look at him, her face mere inches from his. He glanced down at her lips and regretted it immediately.

Get it together, Redbourne.

He cleared his throat and took a step backward. She handed him the piece of paper and he jumped down off the boardwalk to inspect the load in the wagon.

"Well, good luck, my dear," Mrs. Day told her. "Please don't be a stranger. And if you need anything else, you just send word through your brother or one of those Redbourne boys." She winked at Ethan.

"Thank you for all of your help, Mrs. Day. I'll be back when I figure out what else we'll need."

Mrs. Day hugged Grace and then turned into her store to help the other patrons in the mercantile.

Something cold and wet fell onto Ethan's cheek and he raised a hand to brush it away. Another drop touched his nose and he looked up.

Snow.

He loved watching the snow fall from inside his shop, but driving in it with a wagonload of food and supplies was another story. He hoped it would just be a few flurries for now. Ethan glanced up and saw Mr. Pierce unlocking the smithy. The cart would have to wait. Tomorrow, he would drag one of his brothers to help him load it into their wagon and he could take it back to his shop at the ranch, pull off the wheels, and try to fix what ailed it.

The list, Ethan realized, was still clutched in his hand. He opened it. Most of the items had been scratched off. Others had been circled and a few hadn't been touched. Some of the remaining items included a wagon, a team of horses, a cow, and various other farm animals. Written on the side of the paper was scribbled, '*goat at Day farm.*' Ethan guessed that Mrs. Day had sold Grace one of hers.

"Is it snowing?" Grace asked, making her way toward the front of the wagon where Ethan stood. "I love the snow."

"Remember that," Ethan said with a smirk as he helped her up onto the wagon seat. "Have you ever driven a wagon before?" he asked seriously.

"How hard can it be?" she replied with a slight shrug of her shoulders.

"Jack, have you ever driven a wagon?"

"My friends in New York had a sleigh that I drove once. It didn't end well."

Ethan shook his head. How were these two tenderfoots ever going to make it here? He untied Storm from the mercantile's hitching post and handed the reins to Jack. "There will be time to teach you both later, but for now, we need to get you both home."

Grace nodded. *Thank you*, she mouthed at him.

Watching her lips move did nothing to help him forget his attraction to her.

The bells on the tall, white church building sounded and Ethan looked up. It read seven minutes past one o'clock. He shook his head. Eccentric old clock.

They made it back to the farmhouse much more quickly than they'd come. Raine, Rafe—who'd donned another shirt—Will, and Cole all waited, still mounted, in front of the Nolan place.

"Just how many brothers do you have?" Grace asked, awe apparent in her voice.

"Six. And a sister," Ethan added for good measure.

"Eight children? Your mother must be something."

"Oh, she is something all right," Ethan said, still thinking about Leah Redbourne coming to 'meet' the new neighbors.

Stop! Ethan screamed inside his head. He realized that over the course of the last several hours he had started to feel comfortable with his beautiful new neighbor and her young brother. He liked her and it had to stop. They would all be better off if he simply did what he'd come here to do and then left well enough alone.

When they finally pulled up the drive, his brothers dismounted and waited for Ethan to stop the wagon. He pulled up as close as he could to the house. Luckily, the few flakes that had dropped earlier had been the only ones to fall.

With everyone pitching in, they had the crates, boxes, and sacks all unloaded within a quarter of an hour. And it couldn't have been soon enough. Ethan looked up to see a wagon emerging from the copse of pine trees separating their property from the Nolan's. His parents were here.

Suddenly, he had the urge to get on his horse and head home. He could use work as an excuse. After all, he still had plenty of projects to work on as well, including his own. He'd already finished the biggest of his projects, but he was still working on the smaller surprises.

Grace stood out on the porch staring into the house with her hands on her hips.

"I never realized just how much faster the work goes when a girl has a slew of strong young men helping."

Ethan snorted. How many times had he heard his mother say that many hands made light work? Ranch work was anything but easy, and yet they seemed to be able to accomplish a lot in short periods of time.

"This place has been empty a while. Time has taken its toll. You certainly have a lot of work ahead of you."

"I know," she told him, "but it's beautiful. And it's ours."

Ethan understood the draw of having a place of your own. While he loved living on the ranch, his shop was all his. A quiet place of his own.

Leah and Jameson Redbourne pulled into the yard. Ethan watched as his father reached up and helped his mother down. He admired them. They were still in love, even after nearly thirty years. He could see it every time they looked at each other.

Leah smiled up at her husband. His father reached behind her and picked up something wrapped in cloth. Ethan guessed it was a loaf of Lottie's bread and a jar of her jam.

His brothers dotted the porch, leaning against windows, the porch railing, and sitting on the stairs. They all stood as Leah approached.

"Well, you must be Grace Nolan. I'm Leah Redbourne. I see you've already met some of my boys."

Grace stepped forward and met his mother at the top of the stairs. "It's very nice to meet you, Mrs. Redbourne. Thank you for allowing your sons to help me this afternoon."

"We are just so excited to finally have some new neighbors. Welcome to Stone Creek." Leah handed the cloth bundle to Grace and reached out an arm to hug her.

"Looks like you're needing a few repairs around the old place," Jameson said as he glanced around the property. "My boys and I will do what we can to help."

Ethan smiled when Grace's cheeks filled with color. She placed a hand just below her throat and it took her a moment to speak.

"You've all been so kind. I don't know what to say."

"There's no need to say anything at all," Jameson said as he glanced over the porch at each of his boys.

Grace looked up and met Ethan's eyes. "Thank you," she said.

"Are your parents here, my dear? I would just love to meet your mother." Leah glanced past Grace into the house.

Ethan didn't miss the flicker of pain that crossed Grace's face at the mention of her mother, and a twinge of sympathy pricked at his gut.

"My father has been gone a long time, but mother passed away just a few months back. So now, it's just me and Jack," Grace said matter-of-factly.

"We're so sorry for your loss, ma'am." Jameson said with a brief nod of his head.

"I have an idea," Leah said with a smile.

Oh, no. Ethan didn't like it when his mother got 'ideas' in her head.

"Why don't you and young Jack come to Redbourne Ranch for Thanksgiving dinner?" Leah said with a satisfied grin on her face. "Trust me. You won't want to miss Lottie's sweet potato casserole."

Ethan nearly choked. Why did his mother hate him? He thought of all of the unfinished projects sitting in his shop—along with his own—and the last thing he needed was a distraction. His mother would complain about him being out in the shop and give him some nonsense about being polite and entertaining their guest.

"Oh, we couldn't intrude. Holidays are for family," Grace said graciously.

"Nonsense. Holidays include friends—new and old alike," Leah countered.

"You might as well say, yes," Cole told her. "She won't let up until you do."

Everyone laughed.

Thanksgiving Day was an entire event at the ranch—not only the food, but the three-legged races, the turkey catch, and the annual archery tournament—which Ethan was determined to win this year—were all a part of the big day. Leah Redbourne loved the holidays.

"Well, then, yes. It would be our pleasure to join you for Thanksgiving," Grace said with a resounding affirmation.

Ethan groaned. A tiny voice in the back of his mind told him that maybe Grace would be different than other women. Maybe he could let himself like her.

"Who am I kidding?" he asked himself aloud. He'd thought Victoria had loved him, but after he'd gotten hurt, she'd no longer been able to bear looking at him. And now she was married to that balding weasel of a man over in Pastoral Hill. No, he was meant to be alone. And the sooner he accepted that, the better.

"I'm sorry, what was that, son?" Jameson took a step toward him and placed a hand on his shoulder.

Ethan shook his head, but didn't answer his father.

One day. Thanksgiving was just one day. He could guard himself that long.

"Miss Nolan?"

Grace turned to him expectantly, her eyes warm and excited.

One day, he reminded himself.

"I'd like to take Jack over to Redbourne Ranch to select his horse. He didn't fancy any of the three Mr. Phillips had left at the livery."

"Three?" his father looked at him with knitted brows. "Must be a lot of folks needing horses in town. We just delivered fifteen head."

Ethan snorted. "Devlin bought a dozen this morning."

"What does Richard Devlin want with a dozen new stock horses?" Jameson asked.

"Not Richard, Dad. Hurley."

His mother's sharp intake of breath started a wave of his brothers all getting to their feet, looking ready for a fight.

"Mr. Devlin, the gentleman from Mrs. Day's store?" Grace asked.

"Hurley Devlin is no gentleman, Grace, be warned. You best stay clear of that scamp."

Before Grace could retort, Ethan stepped between her and his mother.

"Horses?"

"Mr. Redbourne, it is so nice of you to offer your horses, but I think choosing one in town will be fine. We have a lot of work to do, as you said before, and we need to get started before winter sets in." She glanced up into the sky as if expecting the snow to start falling again at any moment.

"Awww. Come on, sis. There will be plenty of time to work on the house. And you said yourself that we need some good horses. The Redbournes have the best horses in the territory—at least that's what Mr. Phillips at the livery said." Jack looked at her with exaggeratedly big eyes and it appeared as if he'd used the trick before.

Ethan could see her teetering. He wondered if it was a good idea to befriend the boy, who seemed to be quite the adventurer. In many respects Jack reminded him of his little sister—always up for a new quest.

Grace looked back and forth between them. "Jack, we don't want to impose any more than what we already have."

"Oh, it's no imposition, ma'am," Jameson said. "What the boy said is true. We do have the best stock around. That comes from good breeding and training. Mr. Phillips buys all his horses from us. We have another couple dozen head at home. You are welcome to come and select from the lot."

"I'm at a loss for words."

"That doesn't happen very often," Jack said with a wide smile.

Grace swatted mockingly at her brother's shoulder.

"Well, horses were at the top of our list. Are you sure you don't mind?"

"Ethan," his father turned to him, "why don't you bring Jack and Miss Nolan back to the ranch and help them select two horses that will fit their needs."

Ethan had been prepared with a speech on how much work he still had to do, but it wasn't very often that Ethan was asked to help out with the horses, and he jumped at the chance. He could be near her for a few more hours without risking his heart—if it meant proving to his father that he was as good a rancher as he was a blacksmith. That he could run the ranch, if given the chance.

"Yes, sir."

"Then it's settled," Jameson said with a firm nod.

Ethan descended the stairs and climbed up onto the wagon seat. "Let's go."

CHAPTER FIVE

The last thing Grace needed in her life was a man. She had escaped New York to start a new life, free from unhealthy romantic entanglements—in a place she could call her own. Discovering that her grandfather's old farmhouse still stood had been such a blessing, but she had not expected it to come with an entire family of handsome neighbors. Especially, Ethan.

Give me strength.

Grace glanced across the seat to where Ethan sat, reins firm in his grip, and she admired the strong set to his jaw. He had obviously been reluctant to have her join them at the ranch, but when his father had mentioned horses, something in his demeanor had changed.

"Thank you," she forced the words to break the silence. "It has been a long day. I imagine it has been for you too."

He nodded, but did not look at her.

She bit her lip.

Jack seemed to be getting used to riding as he looked more relaxed in the saddle than he had earlier today. Storm was a beautiful horse. His coloring reminded her of his name with white cloud-like swirls mingled with dark menacing colors. However, he seemed to sense Jack's apprehension and somehow was able to put her brother at ease.

It wasn't long before a small city came into view.

"I thought we were going to Redbourne Ranch," she stated, irritated at the quiver in her voice.

"This *is* Redbourne Ranch," Ethan replied, pulling the wagon to a stop at the peak in the road, overlooking a vast gulley littered with outbuildings, an enormous barn, and a large homestead in the center of it all.

"This…" Grace said with awe, looking over the immense property, "is where you live?"

Ethan smirked and for the first time since they'd left her house, he looked at her. "Isn't it remarkable?" he asked, scanning the pastures. He took a deep breath and closed his eyes.

"You really love this place, don't you?"

"Yes." He slapped the reins again and they descended into the yard.

A few minutes later, the wagon came to a stop. He jumped to the ground and walked around the buckboard to help her down.

Ethan's brothers had already taken Jack into the stable and were teaching him how to take care of a horse at the end of the day.

"He needs to be brushed and fed," Grace heard Cole coaching him when she stepped into the stable.

Ethan's young brother didn't look much older than Jack and she hoped they would become friends.

"The kittens are in the kitchen, if you'd like to go see them," Ethan whispered against the back of her ear.

His breath was hot against her skin. Gooseflesh cascaded down her arms and she chastised herself for her reaction to his nearness. He placed a hand on the plank of the first stall in front of her.

How had he taken care of the wagon and its horses so quickly?

"Lottie can show you what you need to do if you'd like to take one of them home."

Grace turned around. Big mistake. His face was so close to hers, she couldn't meet his eyes, so she closed her own and exhaled slowly.

"What about the horses?" she asked, afraid to open her eyes.

"Come on, boys."

Grace felt the heat from Ethan's proximity pull away from her and she opened her eyes. Jameson appeared in the doorway. Ethan stood up straight, and for the first time, Grace realized just how tall he was.

"We need to show these Nolan's some horses before nightfall."

"I'm sorry," Ethan said as he backed away from her and stalked out of the stable past his father.

Sorry? As much as Grace wanted to be sorry that she'd allowed him to be so bold, she wasn't.

Splash. The sound came from outside

"What in the—" Jameson ran out the door, followed closely by a running Cole and Jack.

Grace trailed behind, curious at the sudden commotion.

Damn, that's cold. And you're a damn fool, Redbourne.

Ethan didn't know how he'd allowed himself to stand so close to Grace.

Seamus, the family's giant black and white sheep dog barked at the edge of the water.

"I know, boy," he said, shooting out of the ice-cold pond.

Ethan had only wanted to let Grace know that the kittens were safe, but the faint lavender scent in her hair had intoxicated him and he found himself wanting to be closer to her. To be the one to put a smile on her face. To kiss her. She was beautiful, there was no doubt, but Ethan had seen her strength and goodness today, and heaven help him, he was intrigued.

Rein them in, Ethan. Allowing his thoughts to dwell on the sweet vixen was not going to do him any good. The chill from the water had started to seep into his bones, and he could feel his knees and hands beginning to stiffen.

"What in the hell are you doing, son?" Jameson demanded of his son. He took Ethan by the shoulders and briskly rubbed his upper arms up and down.

So much for impressions.

"Guess I got too close to the edge and Seamus bounded by me, a little too excited. Fell right in."

Seamus barked.

Jameson and Ethan laughed in unison.

"Are you all right?" his mother rushed to the edge of the pond with a bath sheet and a blanket. She threw the bath sheet over his shoulders first and then the blanket. "Come in and warm yourself by the fire."

Ethan allowed her to guide him toward the house, but then he caught Grace's gaze and held it. He could not make himself look away. Her eyes didn't falter either. How he'd allowed himself to be so forward with a woman he'd only just met was beyond him, but he was determined to keep his distance. If he could just make it through the next couple of days without allowing her into his life, he would be clear.

"Mama," he said, handing her the newly wet linens, "I'm going to change and after Miss Nolan and Jack have chosen their horses, we'll sit by the fire a while, okay? I'll be just fine. It's nothing. I'm fine." He repeated the last, mostly to convince himself. It had been a stupid thing to do, but it had seemed like a good idea at the time. He *had* to stop thinking about Grace Nolan.

Leah opened her mouth to protest, but as if sensing it would do her no good, closed it again. Ethan smiled.

"Señor Ethan," Lottie rushed after him from the kitchen door with a mug of steaming liquid. "You drink this." She placed it carefully into his hands and pushed the door open even farther to encourage him to go into the house.

"Thank you, querida, but I'm fine." Even as he said the words, Ethan could feel the cold seeping through him.

He lifted the cup and nodded at the two women, then at all the rest of the expectant onlookers. It was the look of concern on Grace's face that caught him off guard. He needed just a few minutes away from her and he would be fine. He pushed open the door and headed for his bedroom.

Once he was dressed in some warm, dry clothes, he scrubbed a towel over his wet head, then threw on a thick lined coat and met with the others out in the far pasture where some of the highest quality quarter horses and Morgans had been wrangled. Jack stood between a black quarter horse and a brown and white paint. It looked as if he was struggling with which horse to choose.

Women's laughter turned Ethan's attention toward a tan gelding with a cream-colored mane. The horse seemed to have taken a liking to Grace. It suited her.

"Your mother is worried about them staying at the old Nolan place alone in its current condition," Jameson said from behind him.

Ethan shivered. He hoped it was from the cold.

"You're not suggesting—"

"With Levi coming home with his new bride, I'm afraid we just don't have the room to keep them here."

Ethan breathed out a loud sigh of relief.

"So, we thought it might be good if you and Rafe stay at her place…"

"What?"

"At least until we can repair the windows and patch up some of the larger holes. And it might be a good idea to teach them how to protect themselves."

"But, Dad…" Now he just sounded like a whining child, but he certainly couldn't tell his father the real reason why he didn't want to be her protector, why he couldn't be near her.

"She's from the city, Ethan. She isn't prepared for life out here. And the Nolan house has been left in disrepair for far too long."

"I realize that, but I have responsibilities. I have work to do and I certainly don't have the time to play house with the new neighbor and her brother. Let Raine go. He's going to be the sheriff. What better person is there to protect her?" Ethan cleared his throat. "Them," he corrected.

"Ethan." Jack emerged from the pasture leading the Paint. "Ethan, isn't he beautiful? I'm going to call him Hound."

"He's a real sturdy horse, Jack. Nice choice." Ethan wanted to distract his father from their conversation. "And it looks like your sister has found one too."

Grace looked up at his words as if she sensed that he'd spoken her name. She smiled and the hollow hole in Ethan's gut swelled. Lord help him, but he smiled back. What was he thinking?

"Thanks for bringing us here, Ethan. Hound is much better than the others we saw in town." Jack brushed his new horse's nose with his hand. "When can I take him home?"

"I tell you what," Jameson said, "you can start riding him right away, but I think he needs to stay here at night—at least until we get your place fixed up a bit."

"You'll do that?"

"Now, it'll be your responsibility to feed, brush, and clean him. But, yes, he can have a stall here at the ranch."

"Where is Ethan? I need to see Ethan!" A loud booming voice carried through the yard and out to the pasture where they stood.

Ethan turned to see Mr. Banks marching toward them, his face flooding with shades of red and purple.

"Mr. Banks? What's wrong?"

"My mother-in-law, that's what's wrong."

"I'm sorry?"

"Myrtle's mother has come to visit for the holidays."

Jameson laughed and clapped their old friend on the back.

Mr. Banks took a breath and turned to Ethan.

"One of the springs on the carriage snapped and if I don't get it fixed by the time we head in to town for her appointment to have a new specialty hat designed for her at the milliners on Friday morning, I will never hear the end of it." The look on the man's face was almost comical, but Ethan was grateful for the excuse it would provide to head to his shop for a while.

"A simple wagon just isn't good enough for her, you understand?" He put a hand on Ethan's forearm. "I hate to bother you just before Thanksgiving, but…"

"Don't you worry, Ezra. My son will get one made up for you. He's the best blacksmith I've ever seen."

Ethan looked at his father, pride beaming from his face. How would he ever be able to tell him that he didn't want to be Stone Creek's new blacksmith? That all he really wanted to do was ranch?

"Of course, Mr. Banks. Why don't you tell me just what you need and I'll get to work on it and bring it by your place sometime tomorrow."

Mr. Banks handed him half of an old rusted spring and Ethan nodded. He started to walk away, but turned back over his shoulder. "And Dad, about the Nolans…I can't.

Still chilled when he closed the door to his shop behind him, he quickly got to work lighting a fire in the forge. It didn't take long for the small room to heat up. Ethan rubbed his hands together and reached for his gloves.

"You like her," Rafe said as he walked into the shop and closed the door behind him.

"Like who?" Ethan knew exactly to whom Rafe was referring, but he wasn't about to admit it.

"How long are you going to do this to yourself?"

"I don't know what you're talking about, Rafe." Ethan set the steel rod into the forge. "What exactly am I doing?"

Rafe leaned against the work table and folded his arms across his chest. "Not all women are going to be like Victoria."

"Are you really going to have this conversation with me?" Ethan picked up his mallet and with his tongs, pulled the hot metal from the fire. "You, of all people. After everything that happened with Tessa?" He set the top of the metal on his work area and started to pound and turn the rod, molding it against the hardened steel anvil.

"What?" Rafe said in a low, indifferent tone. "I'm doing pretty well for myself."

"You quit medical school."

Rafe shrugged.

"Changed your whole life and ran away from home and your family all because of a woman." Ethan kept reheating the metal and working it around until it had formed into a perfect circular coil. He dipped it in the over-sized pot of water and set it down to look at Rafe.

"What can I say? You're right," Rafe said. "I won't be ready to settle down for a while. But, come on, little brother. You're not me. Besides, I think she likes you too."

"That's not going to happen, and you know it. She'll get one look at my scars and I'll never see her again. Might as well save us all the trouble."

"Oh, get over yourself. You'll never know until you try." Rafe pushed himself away from the work table to peer out the window. "Have you told him yet?"

Ethan picked up the coil and set it back into the forge to heat the ends. "How can I? He is so proud of his son, the blacksmith, and he expects me to take over for Mr. Pierce."

"You do have a real talent with metal, Ethan. But that doesn't mean you have to be a blacksmith."

"Don't get me wrong. I am grateful for everything Mr.

Pierce has taught me, but—"

Knock. Knock.

The door opened and Jack popped his head inside.

"Whoa," he said with awe as he stepped inside the workshop. He looked over all the tools hanging on the wall. "Is this where you work? I mean, I know you said you were a blacksmith and all, but I never expected this. Will you show me?"

Rafe snorted a laugh. "We'll talk later." He turned and walked out to join the others.

"So," Jack said without looking up, "what do you know about making tools to look for buried treasure?"

Ethan wasn't sure whether or not the kid was serious.

"Who has buried treasure?" He asked with a raised brow and a half-smile.

"We do. I mean," he glanced up and met Ethan's eyes with intense focus, "my grandfather hid our family fortune before they moved to New York and I'm going to find it."

The kid *was* serious.

"And what does your sister think about this treasure?" He removed the coiled spring from the forge and pounded the end on the rounded surface to curl it sufficiently to hook into place on Mr. Banks' carriage.

"Aw, don't mind her. She thinks that grandfather was just telling a bunch of tall tales, but I overheard a small group of men in the mercantile," Jack's eyes were alight with excitement, "talking about how close they were getting and it would just be a few more days and they'd find it. The treasure. Our treasure."

"Okay, slow down. What men? And how do you know they were talking about treasure?" Ethan's interest was piqued.

"I told you, I overheard them talking about it while we were loading the wagon in town."

"What else did they say?"

"Just that they were supposed to meet sometime tonight at a place called, the Old Town Mill. Do you know the place?

Can we go?"

"What did these men look like, Jack?" Treasure or not, a group of men looking for something in a town like Stone Creek could only mean trouble. He needed to find Raine and let him know to be on the lookout.

Maybe they'd all have to make a little trip to the old mill.

Grace bit back her disappointment after watching Ethan retreat into his workshop. The Redbournes had been so kind to her and Jack. And they had given them two horses at such a good price. She didn't know how she would ever be able to repay their kindness.

At least tonight they would have heat. Jack had cleared out the pipe stove and, with the help of some of the Redbourne brothers, they had a stack of dry, un-rotted wood to burn.

She glanced around, looking for Jack.

Where has he gotten off to?

"That old place sure needs some fixing up. Why don't you and Jack stay here tonight?" Leah asked. "Tomorrow we can organize my boys and a few men from town to start making some of the larger repairs."

"You've done so much already."

"I can't in good conscience let you and your brother stay there, all alone, in its condition."

What was she trying to say? For once in her life, Grace had a place to call her own. She wanted to be there. Needed to be there. And she was willing to work hard to make the place livable.

"Mrs. Redbourne—"

"Leah, please."

Grace cleared her throat. "Leah, thank you, but I'd like to stay at my home tonight. We'll be fine. We have plenty of food and supplies, as well as wood for a fire, thanks to your sons. I would appreciate the help in working on some of the repairs. I'm afraid the only people we've met have been your family, Mrs. Day and her family, and Mr. Devlin, of course."

The smile on Leah's face faltered a little. "I understand, Grace. You want the new place to feel like home. I'll have Ethan take you home right after supper." She nodded and turned for the front door, then paused at the top step and spun around again to look at Grace. "I know it is none of my business, dear, so I'll just say this once and be done with it. Everything with Hurley Devlin comes with a hefty price."

"Why does Ethan hate him so much?" Grace wasn't sure it was her place to ask, but she wanted to know why there seemed to be so much bad blood between them.

Leah didn't speak for a moment, as if trying to collect her thoughts. "Hurley is a selfish man who only cares about his own agenda. Ethan," she paused, "well, Hurley took something from Ethan a long time ago and I'm afraid my son has not been able to forgive himself, or Mr. Devlin. We've all struggled with it, truth be told."

Grace knew something about what it was like to hold onto things for too long. She also had people in her life she needed to forgive.

"Thank you for sharing that with me." She linked her arm in Leah's. "We really should be going."

"Well, then." Leah patted her hand. "I will have my boys escort you home. With all the talk of unknown persons sleeping in your cellar, I would feel better if you would allow a couple of my boys to stay at the house with you tonight." Leah Redbourne reached out and rubbed Grace's shoulder.

The thought of Ethan Redbourne sleeping under the same roof as she, opened a hollowed space in her belly that seemed to immediately fill with flutters. She opened her mouth to respond just as Ethan walked out of his shop with an arm craned around Jack's shoulder and the other ruffling her brother's hair.

Grace's breath caught in her chest when Ethan looked up and met her gaze. Heat flooded her cheeks when he smiled. She got the impression he didn't do that very often.

"It's settled then," Leah said with a satisfied smirk. "If you'll excuse me a moment." She rushed off in the direction of her husband.

"Gracie!" Jack exclaimed. "Ethan said he'd make me some mining tools to help find grandfather's treasure."

"What?" The warm sensations that had tempted her belly moments ago, turned cold. She turned to Ethan. "You can't be seriously thinking of entertaining the notion that there is treasure in these hills." She shook her head. "Our grandfather was a great story teller. That is all."

"Come on, Gracie," he mimicked Jack.

Heat rose again in her cheeks at his use of such a familiar name.

"What could it hurt to do a little treasure hunting for the holidays?" Ethan raised an eyebrow, daring her to refuse.

"Jack," she tried to reason, "who knows how long we have before the snow falls? We have to get the house ready for the winter or we'll be frozen solid before spring."

Ethan guffawed loudly. "If you think for a moment that my mother will allow you to freeze, you are wrong. You'll have the whole Redbourne clan and half the town at your place on the day after Thanksgiving if she has anything to say about it."

Grace didn't know how to respond. In New York, folks took care of their own, but rarely did they offer to help a stranger. Living in Kansas was going to be very different than living in the city. Grace smiled.

"You asked for it," she told Ethan. "Once Jack has been given room to explore an idea in that hard head of his, it is near impossible to deter him. Be forewarned, Mr. Redbourne."

"Noted," he said with a smirk.

"Grace," Jack pointed. Grace turned around to see Ethan's mother standing on the porch looking directly at them.

"I think Mrs. Redbourne is looking for you."

Grace squinted at Ethan, then quickly turned for the house. The last thing she wanted to do was to go gallivanting in search of some legend her grandfather had concocted to entertain his grandchildren. Especially with Ethan Redbourne. And now, she had to allow him to sleep in her house. Maybe she could convince Leah to send one of her other sons.

Grace wondered where they would sleep. Having all of them sleeping on the couches in the great room would be highly inappropriate, but they'd scarcely had a chance to look over the house, let alone know where to put guests.

"I've just spoken to Jameson, dear, and Ethan and Rafe have agreed to accompany you home."

Grace's heart pounded hard inside her chest. She didn't want to be attracted to another man. Not so soon. Maybe not ever. And she feared that spending all this time with a man like Ethan would undo all the resolve she'd built up over the last few weeks. She couldn't fall again. Not yet. Her heart was still too fragile from the last time. Still, she couldn't deny he was a beautiful man, and it *would* be reassuring to have someone there to protect her and Jack, if those prospectors decided to return.

"They will bring you back tomorrow for the festivities." Leah rushed down the last few steps between them and pulled Grace into a firm hug. "I'm so glad you've moved in to that old place. It deserves some love and attention. I just know you'll be happy here. We are." She released Grace and stood back. "Welcome."

Grace couldn't help but like the woman. The whole Redbourne family in fact. They were so different than everyone at Coldhern Estates. Different than Lee.

CHAPTER SIX

Ethan took a deep breath.

"Thank you." Grace cleared her throat.

He nodded, not at all sure what he could say. He'd tried saying 'no', but even as he'd said the words, he'd known he would do it.

It wasn't like he was spending the night with Grace. He and Rafe, two trustworthy and respectful neighbors of the Nolans, were simply staying at the house. They would keep watch and make sure that a young woman and her brother were safe from any potentially shady intruders.

"Are we heading out to the old mill?" Jack asked, his eyes alight with anticipation.

Ethan swung a large pile of blankets over the back of the buckboard.

"We weren't invited," he said. But upon seeing the look of disappointment on the kid's face, he nudged him. "I guess we'll just have to find our own clues. People have been looking for that old treasure for twenty years. I think one more day will be fine."

"Thanks, Ethan," Jack said as he climbed up into the back of the wagon.

"I can't believe you are getting him all riled up. There is

no treasure," Grace told him.

"We'll see about that." Ethan had heard the stories of treasure being hid in the hills surrounding Stone Creek. He'd never really believed them, but he didn't want to give Miss Nolan the satisfaction of knowing that.

Ethan held out a hand to help Grace up onto the seat of the buckboard. When she didn't immediately take it, he closed his fingers over his palm and dropped it to his side.

"Your mother sure is protective, isn't she?"

"Can't be too careful. If there are people squatting at your place...well, it'll be better if we can just get them out before there's trouble."

Other than the few gamblers he'd seen in town, there weren't a lot of new people in Stone Creek. Jack said he'd seen some suspicious men at the mercantile. Maybe they'd been there with Hurley, but that didn't explain who may be sleeping in her cellar. If those men had indeed been with Devlin, they certainly wouldn't be holed up in some abandoned farmhouse.

So, who had been sleeping there? And why hadn't they just slept in the house? It seemed odd, but if anyone could figure it out, it was Rafe. That was, unless his brother chose to pursue another bounty.

"Do you think there will be?" Grace stepped forward and placed a hand on his forearm. "Trouble I mean."

Ethan looked down at her hand—keenly aware of her touch.

She pulled back her hand. "Excuse me."

He wasn't sure how to answer her question. If she kept touching him, they'd both be in a heap of trouble all right.

"You ready?" His voice had a gruff edge that he hadn't intended.

"Just give me a moment. I think I've forgotten something," she said as she gathered her skirt and whisked away from him.

Damn. It's going to be a long night.

Distance.

You have to keep your distance, Grace chided herself. After all her determination to stay away from him, she'd found herself yearning to connect with him, to touch him. And before she'd been able to stop herself, she'd found her hand resting on his forearm. When had she become so bold?

Wishy-washy. That is exactly what you are, Grace Nolan.

The wagon hit a small bump in the road that jolted her off her seat. She immediately jerked her hands down to clutch the bench and stop herself from sliding toward the stoic driver.

"Careful," was all he said. He was quiet, seeming quite content to simply listen to the cooing of night sounds the rest of the way to the house.

Jack had ridden in the back of the buckboard, his legs dangling off the rear. As they neared the front porch, he jumped off and ran up the front porch steps.

"It's just the same as when we left," he called out.

Rafe rode the perimeter of the house again before dismounting. Grace did not miss the exchange between Ethan and his brother as they opened the door to the barn.

"What is it?" Grace asked, not wanting to be ambushed if something was amiss.

Ethan cleared his throat, but it was Rafe who spoke.

"The chain lock I strung through the cellar doors has been cut clean through." He eyed her as if assessing her reaction. "There's no one down there now, but they've cleared out most of their things."

Grace stared at him, trying to process what he'd just told her. It took her a moment and something inside of her changed. She was tired of being afraid. Tired of worrying about what *could* happen. She needed to be strong. Somehow having the Redbournes here gave her some added courage. For now, that was enough.

"So, what are we going to do about it?" she asked, her chin held high.

"There's not much more we'll be able to do tonight. Let's just get you and Jack settled in for the night and we'll take a look around tomorrow." Ethan didn't look at her, but pulled the blankets from the back of the wagon, brushed past her, and marched up the stairs and into the house.

It was dark. She took a step inside the door, but stopped short when she hit a hardened wall of cloth covered flesh and fell backward, tripping over the small lip of the doorframe. Ethan's strong arms encircled her and pulled her tight into him, effectively stopping her fall to the ground.

"You should watch where you're going," he said, his voice huskier than usual. "Are you all right?" He released her.

"I'm so sorry. I...I..."

What was it about this man that made her ramble like a bumbling idiot?

"This might help." Rafe struck a match against its box and lit the wick of an old lantern.

Grace hoped that even with the light it would still be too dark to see the flushed color that she knew must be staining her cheeks. She didn't dare look up at Ethan.

"Thank you," she said, taking the light from him and pushing past Ethan in the doorway. She didn't stop until she'd gotten all the way up the long curved staircase and into the room she would claim as her own. She shut the door behind her and leaned up against it, her chest heaving with ragged breaths.

Lord, she pleaded quietly, *have mercy*.

Ethan opened his eyes just in time to see the early rays of

the morning sun peeking over the hillside as it rose from the east. It had been a long time since he'd slept until dawn. He sat up and glanced about him. Through the window, Ethan could see that Rafe was already awake and sitting out on the porch.

The morning air held a chill. Winter was not far off.

Ethan forced himself into an upright position, grabbed his hat from the back of the couch, and moved to join his brother outside.

"Still can't sleep?" he asked.

"I got plenty," Rafe said gruffly. "You seemed to have slept just fine. The sun got up before you. I don't know the last time that happened."

"I missed my bed." Ethan stretched, trying to rid himself of the tight strains cramping his shoulders and back. "And a few times during the night I could have sworn I heard something ticking. It wasn't that big old grandfather clock in the entry either. I checked."

Rafe laughed. "You should try a bedroll and the nice hard ground. It'll grow on ya. Maybe it'll stop you from hearing things too."

They sat for a while in comfortable silence.

"Let's hitch that wagon. We can be ready once Miss Nolan awakes," Rafe said, patting Ethan on his knee.

"Morning," Jack called as he leapt from the stairs and ran out to the stable without looking behind him.

Ethan glanced at Rafe and back to where Jack disappeared inside the old, run-down building. When he emerged, he carried an old bucket and a thin yellowed rag that looked as if it might disintegrate at any moment.

"Mr. Redbourne?"

Ethan and Rafe both turned to see Grace standing in the doorway and stood up.

"Good morning, ma'am," Rafe said with a tip of his hat.

"Ma'am," Ethan echoed.

She smiled at them and took a step forward.

"Would one of you be so kind as to drive me over to the Day farm? I bought a goat from Mrs. Day and thought it might be nice to have some fresh milk."

"She won't be expecting you today," Ethan said matter-of-factly. "It's Thanksgiving."

"If you're ready to go, ma'am, we can head back over to the ranch. Lottie'll have scrambled eggs, potatoes, and some fresh biscuits with strawberry preserves." Ethan's stomach groaned in protest. Normally, he'd eaten long before this time of day.

"I'll get to work," Rafe said as he pushed away from the railing and out toward the barn.

"Where's Jack?"

"Over here, sis," Jack called from the old rusting water pump. "Gotta get that stable cleaned up if I want to bring Hound home."

"That stable is going to need a lot more than water and a rotted sponge," Ethan said under his breath.

Grace ignored him. "The Redbournes have been kind enough to invite us over to their ranch for Thanksgiving," she called back to him. "It can wait until we can hire more help. Maybe another day or two."

Hire help? Grace obviously didn't know Leah Redbourne. Ethan groaned. He had too much work to do to worry about fixing up the woman's rickety old house, but when his mother was on a mission, there was no stopping her.

"Let's get going or we're going to miss the turkey run." Rafe was already mounted and the wagon was hitched and ready to go.

"What's a turkey run?" Grace asked, eyes wide and curious. *City girl.*

"Tradition."

Grace's eyes furrowed together.

"Every year we raise a couple of turkeys. On Thanksgiving morning, Pa turns two loose in the corral and all of us, Hannah included, get into the corral and it's like a race to see who can catch the first turkey."

Her brows knitted even tighter together.

"Whomever catches the turkey is named the king, or queen, of the feast."

"Why would you want to catch a turkey?" she asked innocently.

Ethan looked at her. Was she kidding?

"For...the feast."

It took a moment, but understanding soon crossed her face. "Wait. You mean you..." she swallowed, "...kill the turkey?"

Ethan nearly choked at the look of horror that popped open her eyes and her mouth.

"Where did you think Thanksgiving dinner came from?" he asked the moment he was certain he could ask the question without laughing.

She looked at him, closed her mouth, and then narrowed her eyes.

"From the kitchen," she said with a laugh. "I guess it makes sense," she said, an air of logic lining her tone. "There aren't a lot of people who raise turkeys in New York, and I guess I'd never really thought about it before."

"Let's go," Rafe called again.

"He's right." Ethan took the steps two at a time.

"Give me just one moment," Grace said, holding up one finger, a smile on her face. "I have something I'd like to give your mother." She quickly disappeared around the side of the barn.

Moments later, her high pitched scream had Rafe off his horse and around the corner ahead of him, and Ethan running toward the sound. When he reached her, her hands were cupped over her mouth and a tear leaked down her cheek. Rafe was hunched close to the ground. Ethan guessed another animal had scared the woman. Life in Kansas was a far cry from life in the city and the sooner she learned that, the better.

Rafe turned to look at him, a strange, knowing look in his eyes. He shook his head and stood up, his hand caressing the butt of his revolver.

"What?" Ethan asked as he looked around his brother at the ground.

"He's dead."

Dead?

She'd seen death. Her mother had just died, but this was different. She didn't know this man. Who was he? And how did he die? The thought startled her. Someone had died on her land. She couldn't help but wonder if it had merely been an accident or if something sinister had taken place today. Kansas was not at all like New York.

Ethan moved closer to her and wrapped his arm around her, guiding her back to the wagon. She turned her face and buried it into his shoulder, not wanting him to see her cry. She swallowed hard to keep her sobs from sounding. Once they reached the wagon, he pulled away and lifted her chin with a crooked finger and bent his face down to look at her.

"We'll get you and Jack back to the ranch. You'll be safe."

Grace hiccupped loudly, evoking a small smile to touch her lips. She nodded. When they'd left New York, she'd never imagined that she may be putting their lives in danger. What if something happened to Jack? She'd never forgive herself for running away from...from Lee.

"What's wrong, Gracie?" Jack asked, running toward her. "What happened to her, Ethan?"

"We'll talk about it once we get back to the ranch, Jack. Just get in the wagon. We need to go."

Jack hesitated.

"Now!" Ethan's voice was firm, but not unkind.

Grace turned to her little brother. "I'm all right, buckwheat. Just do as Mr. Redbourne asks."

Jack climbed up on the back of the wagon, grumbling.

"We can't leave him here, Ethan." Rafe walked up alongside them.

Grace eyed the two brothers. Surely, Rafe wasn't suggesting that they take a dead body with them back to Redbourne Ranch. They moved to the stairs, just out of earshot, but Ethan didn't seem to like what they were discussing one bit. His whole body became rigid and his motions were jerky at best. After a few moments, they returned to the wagon.

"Change of plans, kid," Ethan said to Jack. "You're going to be riding Rafe's horse, Lexa. Isn't she a beaut?"

Jack jumped down off the wagon as if he had just struck gold, grinning from ear to ear.

"Miss Nolan," Ethan started, "Rafe is going to ride with us. Back there. With him." He pointed to the corpse lying in the bed of the wagon.

She didn't know what he wanted her to say, so she just looked ahead and nodded.

Maybe leaving New York wasn't such a good plan, after all.

The short ride to Redbourne Ranch was made in silence. Jack still looked a little awkward astride a horse, but he was learning. And quickly. A soft smile touched her face as she felt the corners of her mouth upturn, however slightly. She hadn't seen her brother this happy in...well, ever.

When they approached the ranch, squawking noises carried through the air and she turned toward the sound. Sure enough, one of the larger corrals contained two flustered turkeys and it looked as if all of Ethan's siblings were standing on the fence, eagerly awaiting their annual turkey run.

Ethan jumped down off the wagon and strode directly over to his father. Jameson whistled and to Grace's amazement, every one of his children turned to look at him. In moments, the whole clan was gathered around the wagon and helped Rafe pull the body from the back and they carried him into a small building that looked like living quarters.

Grace climbed down off the wagon and Leah hurried toward her. "Are you all right?"

"I will be." Grace took a deep breath and lifted her chin. *I will be.*

CHAPTER SEVEN

"Who is he?" Jameson asked.

Raine stepped forward. "He was with a group of fellas I talked to yesterday in front of the Broken Pony. They said they'd come into town looking for a good game of cards. Last I saw him, he was sitting down at Bernie's poker table." He reached forward and felt the dead man's pockets.

Ethan guessed he was looking for clues as to the man's identity. "Coincidence they showed up the same day as Hurley?" Ethan asked.

Raine raised his empty hands. Nothing.

"Not a chance," Rafe said with a snort. "Ruffians like that, Hurley Devlin brought them in for sure. Maybe we need to have a little visit with our old friend."

"What do you think Hurley's up to?" their father asked.

"I don't know," Raine answered, "but we're going to find out."

"Jack," Ethan pointed at the kid, "overheard a couple of them talking in the mercantile. He believes they are looking for a treasure his grandfather left behind."

"Horace Nolan was a believer." Jameson looked over his shoulder to where Jack stood perched on the corral gate. He shook his head. "He searched for that old treasure until the day he up and left with his family for New York."

"You mean, there really is a treasure somewhere in these hills?" Ethan asked incredulously.

"That's how the story goes. Horace's pa wasn't a very nice man." Jameson shifted his stance and leaned against the stall door. "One of the legends says that he and a couple of his buddies up and robbed a big transport on the Santa Fe." Jameson pushed himself off the planks and hunched forward, his voice gradually becoming softer and more scratchy. "They claimed that Nolan hid the loot himself. I've heard it told that he used some of the silver and gold from his score to buy his claim on the land and that somewhere on Nolan property is an emerald treasure beyond imagination."

"Are the stories true?" Cole asked, eyes wide with anticipation.

Their father stood up straight and chuckled heartily. Ethan and his brothers laughed—except Cole. He narrowed his eyes at everyone as he glanced around and after a moment, started to laugh too.

"If there was a treasure hidden somewhere around here, I'm sure someone would have found it by now. It's been fifty years. Maybe more."

"What on earth is going on in here? Have you no reverence for the dead?" Leah Redbourne marched into the barn and motioned to the body lying on the cleared work table near the door.

The smile left Jameson's face.

"I've sent Marty out to retrieve Mr. Collins," Leah said with a little shake of her head, handing her husband one of her white bed linens.

The town undertaker was a widower who lived in a small room at the back of his shop in Stone Creek. It would probably be a good hour or so before Marty returned and Mr. Collins was sure to be right behind him with his black, soulless carriage. But, they couldn't very well just leave a dead man lying on top of the work table.

"I need to ride into town and speak with Sheriff Fogarty," Raine said quietly. "Ethan and Miss Nolan should probably come along. He'll have some questions."

Ethan nodded. "I'll get Miss Nolan's horse saddled and ready."

"There's no need for Mr. Collins to come all the way out here. We'll just take the body into town. I'm sure we'll meet up with him and Marty on the way." He turned to Ethan. "From what I understand, Miss Nolan is not very familiar with horses and it may be better just to let her ride anyway.

Ethan walked out into the yard to retrieve the wagon. He spotted Grace sitting on the front porch steps. Other than the downturn of her mouth and slight droop to her eyelids, she looked as if she were handling the situation quite well. Lottie sat next to her, rubbing her arms and Hannah was sitting next to her, a step lower.

Grace stood up when she saw him and Jack pushed himself away from the porch column. Ethan forced his mouth into a reassuring smile as he escorted the wagon around back and led the horses into the large barn through the back doors. Luckily, the new building was large enough to accommodate several wagons and horses. The other livestock had all been moved to the smaller barn at the back of the house.

Rafe picked up the body and laid it carefully in the back while two of his other brothers, Will and Cole, each filled buckets of water for the horses to drink. Ethan reached down to the sack sitting next to the open doorway and pulled out two rosy apples. He tossed one to each of his brothers, who, in turn, fed them to the horses.

"There's nothing more we can do for now," Jameson said. "Be safe, son. This wasn't an accident and whoever did it is still out there."

Leah stepped toward them and reached out her hand. Raine took it and leaned down to kiss her on her forehead. She closed her eyes.

Raine clapped his father on the shoulder and turned to Ethan. "Let's get on the road."

Ethan glanced at his mother, who was now tucked up under his father's arm.

"Don't worry, mama," he said. "It's early yet. We'll be back in plenty of time for the turkey catch."

Since they'd received the telegram informing them that Levi and his new bride would not be able to make it in time for Thanksgiving, their mother had experienced a touch of melancholy. He didn't imagine that finding a dead body in the neighbors grass had done anything to help.

Ethan was grateful that they had left the Nolan's place just after dawn. He wasn't about to let anything else get in the way of spending the holiday with his family—especially when they were all depending on him. He didn't know how many times he'd been reminded over the years how long it took to prepare and cook a turkey. This year would be a little different. He smirked at the thought.

Ethan guided the wagon back into the yard and strode to where Grace, Jack, and Hannah all stood. It appeared as if Lottie had returned to the house.

"We need to take him into town," Ethan said quietly, meeting Grace's eyes. "Raine thinks we should talk to the sheriff."

Grace swallowed. "I'm not sure I'll be any help," she said with a shrug.

Ethan held out a hand to her.

She looked down at it, as if weighing the option for its merits. After a few moments, she slipped her hand into his, which wasn't as soft as he'd expected it to be, and nodded. It was small, but work-roughened, and Ethan realized there was a lot more he had to learn about his new neighbors. Apparently, living in New York was not the high life he had always thought it to be. No. Grace Nolan's hands were not those of a pampered chit, but those of someone who had worked very hard.

Crack!

The loud boom pierced the otherwise quiet of the morning.

Grace ducked instinctively, then popped her head up to look around. "What was that?" she asked hastily.

Ethan's stance became rigid and he grasped the reins tighter and snapped them hard. The horses immediately lurched forward, nearly causing Grace to tumble from her seat. He looked straight ahead, as if focused solely on the town.

"Get down," he demanded as he whipped his head over his shoulder to look behind them.

Get down? The area in front of the wagon seat was too narrow. Where was she supposed to get down to?

"Ethan, I—"

He let go of the reins long enough to shove her off the seat. Her hip caught hard on the wooden ridge where her feet were resting moments ago and she bit back the cry that threatened.

"It's too narrow," she screamed up at him instead.

Raine pulled up alongside them, his gun drawn. "I can't see them," he called out to Ethan.

"Put your head down," Ethan shot her a look of warning, "and cover it with your arms."

Grace quickly did as she was told. People had told her that living in Kansas wouldn't be the same as New York, but she'd welcomed that idea. Now, she was beginning to understand what they had meant. New York was full of hustle and bustle. And there was a definite separation of classes. She'd wanted to make a new life for herself. And her brother. A life where they wouldn't be defined by their station. But she hadn't anticipated the dangers that would accompany that choice.

"Whoa," Ethan called.

The wagon came to a halt and Grace looked up, but didn't dare move. They were in town. The streets were empty. The only activity she could see came from the saloon across the street. She guessed that most folks were spending the holiday with their families or friends.

"Whomever it was, is long gone. Either somebody doesn't want us to find out what happened to this man, or they mistook us for Thanksgiving dinner." Raine holstered his gun and dismounted. "I'll check the Broken Pony for the sheriff."

"We'll go look for Mr. Collins," Ethan said. He turned to Grace and reached down a hand to help her up.

Her pride pushed her to disregard the gesture, but, she realized, she wasn't going to be able to move without his help. She placed her hand in his and he pulled her up, a little too hard, and she fell against him.

As she pulled back, as far away from him as she could muster, she glanced up. Their faces were still so close. She couldn't back away for fear of falling, so she just stood there, avoiding his eyes. Her hip throbbed and she clenched her jaw in order to hide the pain from her face.

"Are you…all right?" he asked, his voice low and husky.

"No." She couldn't say more.

Ethan jumped down off the wagon and held his arms up for her.

This time, her pride won. She ignored his hand and grabbed a hold of the handle on the side of the wagon and stepped down. A jolt of pain shot through her side and she slipped off the step into Ethan's arms.

"You can set me down anytime now. I'm fine."

Ethan eyed her with a look of unconvinced speculation, but he set her down all the same.

Grace smoothed her dress and pulled her shawl more closely about her shoulders.

It wasn't long before Raine reappeared with the sheriff in tow.

"Ethan," the sheriff said as they approached.

"Sheriff." Ethan nodded his head.

"And you must be Miss Nolan," he said with warmth. "I'm Sheriff Fogarty. Raine tells me you have moved back into the Nolan place. I heard about your mother's passing. I'm so sorry for your loss. She was a good woman." His warm smile was hidden by an overly large orange moustache that seemed too big for his skinny face, but it reached his eyes.

"Thank you," Grace replied.

"Now, let's see what you've got back here." The men all walked to the back of the wagon.

Grace noted a small bench in front of the town bank. She pulled up her skirt and walked the short distance with minimal difficulty. It seemed the more she moved, the less her hip hurt, but she just wanted to sit while the men discussed the morning's events.

The clickety-clack of another pair of horses caught Grace's attention and she turned to see a large, black, enclosed carriage-like wagon approaching from the direction they'd come. It halted directly in front of her. The side of the vehicle was painted with a cream-colored stripe and centered oval. J.B. COLLINS, Undertaker, was written in black.

The men helped Mr. Collins put the body in the back of his carriage. He drove a few hundred yards to the end of the dusty street and stopped.

"Miss Nolan."

She pulled her attention away from the undertaker and looked up to see Ethan, Raine, and the sheriff all staring at her. The sun peeked through an overgrown tree next to the mercantile and a burst of light hampered her view. She raised a hand to block the rays.

"If you don't mind, ma'am, I'd like to make a visit out to your place tomorrow. Being a holiday and all, it might be best if you just head back to the ranch with these boys and try to have a pleasant holiday." He tipped his hat. "Don't fret none. You'll be safe if you keep these Redbournes close." He winked.

Grace was relieved that she wouldn't have to talk about finding the man next to her rickety old barn. What would she tell him anyway? She'd lived in the Nolan farmhouse for exactly two days. She didn't know anything about the people here. She wasn't familiar with her land or even the buildings that surrounded her house.

"Thank you, Sheriff. It was very nice to meet you," she said, pushing herself into a standing position.

"The pleasure was all mine, ma'am." He turned to Raine and Ethan. "Gentlemen." He tipped his hat again and headed back toward the Broken Pony. "Oh, Miss Nolan," he called out, turning back to look at her, "a telegram came in for you yesterday, but everyone thought it was a jest since nobody's lived in that house for a couple of decades. But I reckon now, it was for you. I'll see that it's delivered."

A telegram? But nobody knew they were coming here. Unless...

She shook her head.

It couldn't be.

She groaned.

Fresh start, she reminded herself. *A clean, fresh start.*

Crack!

Jameson shot the small pistol into the air.

Chaos flooded the corral as Ethan and his siblings pushed and shoved, scrambling to be the first to capture the beloved bird. What had started out many years ago as a mishap had now become one of the Redbourne family's favorite Thanksgiving traditions. Jack and Grace had also joined in the fun.

Clucks, cackles, gobbles, and an abundance of other calls sounded as each person vied for the attention of their prey.

"Oh, no you don't," Hannah squealed just as Ethan was about to dive onto the largest of the two turkeys. She jumped up onto his back and tried to pull him to the ground.

"It's not going to be that easy, sis," he said as he swung her around, effectively flipping her into his arms. She flailed about, laughing and kicking. He set her down on the other side of the corral fence, but she wouldn't let go of his vest, so he slid his arms through the holes and left her holding the garment in her hands and he jumped right back into the middle of the action.

One turkey appeared to be cornered by Rafe, Cole, and Tag. They were moving in together as if in the midst of some truce, even while the others sought the other turkey. Ethan lay down on the ground directly behind the first group in hopes of catching an escaping turkey when they missed.

When Tag finally made his move and jumped toward the turkey, it ran along the fence-line, just out of his grasp, and Ethan was ready. Cole and Rafe both turned to follow it, but they tripped over Ethan's backside and landed on the ground. Before the turkey could escape fully, Ethan reached out a hand and caught its leg in a firm grip.

Laughter filled his ears and he glanced up to see Grace sitting on the ground, her face splashed with mud and a few whimsical feathers flying around her head and face. Ethan pushed himself up onto his knees and attempted to stand. His turkey pecked at his hand and he almost let go, but he made it to his feet without dropping it and handed the bird, by its legs, to his father. In two strides he stood above Grace and held out a hand to her.

She glanced up at him, straining her neck backward, and blew a feather from her lips.

Ethan hunched down and offered her his hand— something that was becoming quite familiar—and helped her up off the ground. "Nicely done," he said with a smirk.

"Thank you," she said, her voice dripping with sarcasm.

Ethan chuckled.

Grace stood up and walked toward the corral gate, and Ethan noticed that she was still limping, however slightly, and a twinge of guilt slugged him in the gut. He hadn't meant to hurt her, only protect her from their unseen attacker. He should have been more careful. He often forgot how strong he was and resolved to be more gentle in the future. She disappeared into the house with his mother, who he knew would help her clean up.

Rafe stepped forward with the second turkey tucked between his arm and body and disappeared with their father to prepare the birds for cooking. Once the birds were plucked and cleaned, Lottie and his mother would garnish and get the turkeys cooking. In the meantime, everyone would pitch in cutting vegetables and mixing dough for the rolls. The archery, shooting, and arm wrestling competitions would soon follow.

Ethan walked into the kitchen and over to the sink, where Lottie kept the lye soap. The whole house had been converted to washing hands before cooking, eating, or treating any wounds right after Rafe started medical school. It was something about avoiding sickness or spreading bugs or some such.

He sat down at the table and pulled a couple of potatoes toward him. Hannah already had a bowl near half full of snapped peas and Tag had just started shelling walnuts. Ethan picked up the knife that had been set on the table, but his attention was turned to the door when his mother walked in followed by their Thanksgiving guest.

Ethan pushed himself away from the table and stood up. Grace was dressed in a simple light purple dress and her soft brown hair was pulled back away from her face.

"Close your mouth, little brother," Raine whispered, patting Ethan on the shoulder before taking off his hat and sitting down at the table. He picked up the newly sharpened knife and began quartering the freshly washed golden potatoes.

Ethan cleared his throat and held out a chair for Grace.

"Thank you, kind sir." Her eyes locked with his and she smiled before sitting down at the table.

What am I doing? He had to get away from her before there was no turning back. Before he allowed himself to fall for her.

"Mama," he held up a finger, "I'll be right back." He could make the excuse that he needed to collect the ovens for cooking the dinner. No one could disagree with that.

"Why, Ethan Redbourne," Grace turned to him with narrowed eyes and a smirk, "if I didn't know any better, I would say that you were trying to get away from me."

Where was the Miss Nolan they met a few days ago? This Miss Nolan was definitely not the same woman. What was he supposed to say to that?

"I just have to get something from out in the smithy." He paused at the door. "You're welcome to come along, if that's what you think."

What?

"Your mother tells me you are a blacksmith. What does a blacksmith do, exactly?"

Meeeeeew. Ethan ignored Grace's question completely as the quiet sound caught Ethan's attention. He turned and looked in the corner of the kitchen to where two small kittens lay huddled together atop a blanket in a small basket.

Meeeow. He heard again.

Lottie stood in the entryway. He could feel her eyes on him and turned toward her with an apologetic smile. The smithy could wait. When he'd brought the kittens into the house, he'd promised the Spanish woman that she wouldn't have to lift a finger to take care of them. They would be his responsibility. Besides, if Grace was going to take these kitties home, she needed to learn how to take care of them.

He strode over to the counter and retrieved a bowl from

the cabinet, pulled a couple of rags from the drawer, and set them on the counter, keenly aware of Grace watching him. A pail of fresh milk sat next to the stove and Ethan quickly scooped a ladle-full of the warm liquid into the dish.

Careful not to spill the milk on Lottie's freshly cleaned floors, he made his way to the corner where the kittens were getting restless with hunger. He sat on the floor, dipped the edge of one of the rags into the bowl, and scooped the smallest of the two kittens into his arms.

"Leave it to Ethan to bring home a stray," Tag said with a grin.

"You should be the one to talk," Ethan said with a raised brow, putting the tip of the cloth against the babe's mouth. Immediately, it began to suckle.

"Fair enough," Tag laughed.

Tag and Levi, twins, had often brought home creatures of all sorts.

"Come to think of it, you might want to keep those kittens away from Genesis," Tag teased. "He might be getting old, but he still gets hungry."

"That collared lizard is so old," Ethan retorted, "I doubt he could do much harm, even if he wanted to."

Everyone laughed. Except Grace.

"You have a lizard? That lives…inside the house?" she asked in disbelief.

Tag nodded.

After a moment, her eyes widened with delight. "May I see it? Please?" She turned and looked at Ethan. "It won't really hurt the kittens, will it?" A slight crease formed on her brow.

Ethan shook his head.

"Nah," Tag piped up. "Genesis is real gentle."

Leah placed a large basket of newly washed apples in the center of the table. "It looks like that other kitten is needing some attention."

In a matter of seconds, Grace sat on the floor next to him.

"May I?"

Ethan showed her what to do with the rag as she scooped up the fluffy cream-colored kitten. She giggled as it greedily began to eat. He enjoyed seeing the wonder alight in her eyes.

"What should we call them?" she asked.

"How about Bob?"

"Bob?"

"Bob for that little fella," Ethan said. "And Cratchit for this one?"

"You want to name them after Dickens characters?" Grace asked.

Ethan was pleased that she had read Dickens. It had become one of his favorite tales. After everything that had happened with Victoria, he'd felt there were a lot of lessons to learn there about happiness.

"And why not?"

Grace shrugged her shoulders. "I guess Bob and Cratchit it is then."

When her kitty finished eating, she set the rag aside and lifted him up to look him in the face. She brushed his nose with her own. "Hello, Bob." She hugged the kitten into her. "You are the sweetest little thing," she said with a grin before allowing it to come to rest in the crook of her arm. When she looked down and brushed over its body with her hand, a stray lock of hair fell down onto Grace's cheek.

Ethan couldn't help but watch her. She was beautiful.

The outside door to the kitchen opened and Rafe stepped inside. He set his turkey on the counter. Just before the door closed all the way, Jameson appeared with his bird in tow, Cole, Jack, and Will right behind him.

"That was fast," Ethan said. He set his kitten back in the basket and stood up.

"Will, Jack, and Cole all came out and helped us pluck. I'm guessing they just wanted to make sure we will eat sometime today," Rafe said.

Turkeys often took quite a bit of time to cook. This year, Ethan had crafted two enormously over-sized Dutch ovens to accommodate the roasting of a whole turkey. With two, they could cook both turkeys at the same time without having to cut them up first. One of them would be cooked indoors in the hearth and the other in the fire pit just outside the smithy.

"It's just beautiful, Señor Rafe," Lottie said as she carried the large bird over to the sink.

"It's going to be a real feast tonight." Cole rubbed his hands together and licked his lips.

"Gracie," Jack said excitedly, "they let me help and everything."

"That was real nice of them."

"He's a natural," Jameson said with a firm nod.

Grace smiled. Ethan liked it when she smiled.

"Ethan, honey," Leah said, turning to him, "it's time to show everyone your surprise."

Ethan stared at her for a moment, wondering how she knew about his surprise.

Then it clicked. The Dutch ovens.

She was referring to the Dutch ovens. He breathed a sigh of relief. In the beginning, he hadn't told anyone else about the ovens—just in case they hadn't turned out the way he'd hoped. But when they were finished, he thought it might be a nice surprise.

The Redbournes loved their Dutch ovens. The annual Christmas cook-off had become a tradition and a few years back, Ethan had made enough for each person in his family to have one of their own.

He looked down at Grace, still sitting contently on the floor with little Bob. "I'll be right back," he said to no one in particular.

Ethan returned a few moments later, one pot in each gloved hand. Luckily, they had already been seasoned and were ready for cooking. The kittens were both sleeping soundly in their basket, all cuddled up together, and Grace was sitting at the table helping Hannah snap peas.

"Whoa! How heavy are those things?" Raine asked, standing and meeting his brother at the door.

Ethan handed one to him. It dropped to the floor with a thud. Color flooded the oldest Redbourne sibling's cheeks and he bent down to attempt to lift it again.

"Heavy," Ethan said with a smirk. He glanced over at Grace, who smiled at him.

With two hands, Raine lifted the oven from the floor and with each apparently arduous step his face grew redder.

"Aw, come on, Raine. It can't be that heavy. Are you going to let our little brother show you up?" The grin on Rafe's face spread wide across his face.

"You're right, Mr. Bounty Hunter. Maybe you should show us all how it's done." He gingerly set the iron vessel back on the ground. The knowing look on Raine's face put a smile on Ethan's.

Working with metal all day most every day had its advantages. Strength was one of them.

Raine backed away and leaned against the fireplace, folded his arms, and crossed his ankles.

Rafe strutted over to the large pot and lifted. His brow furrowed and his grin was quickly replaced with something akin to a grimace. He used both hands, but after only a few steps, Ethan took pity.

"We'll be here all day waiting for you two," Ethan said as he reached out for the handle. Today was a day for family and the last thing he wanted to do was injure their pride. "You both just needed gloves is all. Then it wouldn't have hurt your hands so much or been so hard to carry." Ethan lugged the weighty oven over to the counter where Lottie was stuffing the fresh-cut rosemary and thyme with a handful of salted and creamed butter below the skin on the turkey's breast.

Once the bird sat in the over-sized pot, Ethan and Rafe

collected the carrots, potatoes, and onions that had already been cut and placed them around the turkey. Lottie threw salt and pepper on top and Rafe slid the lid onto the oven.

"Señor Ethan, would you mind?" Lottie asked, pointing to the hearth.

Rafe laughed.

Ethan donned one of his gloves, but couldn't find the other. He reached down to lift the pot and Rafe also grabbed hold, wearing the other glove, to help. Together they carried the extra heavy cooker to the fire where Tag had a nice blaze. It would be a bit before they would have enough embers for the lid.

"Gracias," the cook said before turning to the other turkey.

"We already have the fire going out near Ethan's shop," Will said. "Marty is out watching it and stirring. It'll be ready shortly."

"Well," Jameson said loudly, "who's ready to shoot?"

Whoops and hollers sounded and everyone scrambled from the table. Ethan was excited to try out the new design on his arrows and hoped they would fare well in the competition. He headed for the door, but realized Grace still sat at the table. He was sure she felt out of her element. New Yorkers probably didn't have archery competitions, and with it just being her and Jack…well, it was time they learned how to celebrate Thanksgiving right. Despite himself, he wanted to be the one to teach her.

Ethan didn't wait for an invitation, but reached out, took a hold of her hand, and pulled her out the door. She didn't object and followed him with a giggle. When they walked into the smithy, Ethan was reminded of just how many projects he still had to complete. Branding irons, a wheat grinder, and a half-full box of nails for Mrs. Day's mercantile sat on the shelves, still unfinished. And then there were his own projects. While they needed to be completed before the first freeze, Ethan tried to push them from his mind.

They'll keep—one more day, he attempted to convince himself.

Grace's hand felt good in his and he hesitated, not wanting to let it go, but alas, the call of the competition got the better of him. He slid his hand from hers to retrieve his new archery equipment. The sensation of her touch lingered and he flexed his hand out and back in to shake the feeling.

"I'm told you spend a lot of time out here," Grace said, eying the shop with curiosity. She casually strolled through the small room, glancing over the walls and counters at the many artistic pieces he had created, but hadn't wanted to display.

She stopped at his small collection of books adorning a far corner shelf. He loved to read almost as much as he loved working with the horses on the ranch. Works of Dickens, Shakespeare, Washington Irving, and the Bible were among them. Suddenly, Ethan felt very exposed. Very few people had ever seen the inside of his shop—with the exception of his family.

What was he doing?

"There's a lot to be done," Ethan answered. He lifted the soft leather quiver from a nail in the far corner of the room and retrieved the final arrow of the new collection from the cooling bench next to the water bucket.

"I thought blacksmith's generally made and fixed practical things. I didn't realize you were an artist as well." When Grace reached for the corner of the blanket that shielded his latest creation from view, Ethan stepped in front of her, effectively blocking the action.

"Not yet," he bellowed. It came out more gruffly than he'd intended.

"Oh, I'm sorry," she said, retracting her fingertips quickly and placing them against her chest. "I didn't realize…"

Idiot, Ethan chastised himself.

"It's just…not finished yet," he tried a softer tone this time.

"What is it?"

"Ethan!" the muffled sound of his name reached them from the yard. "Are you coming, or what?"

"That's a question for another time," he said, not taking his eyes off hers.

Grace folded her bottom lip to bite the side, unwavering in her gaze.

They had to go.

"Ethan!" someone called more loudly this time.

"We should go," he said quietly.

Grace nodded.

Ethan reached for his bow, resting on a hook behind her—his face mere inches from hers.

"Excuse me," he said and cleared his throat as he stood up straight. He held the bow up for her to see and she smiled.

"We should go," she repeated.

CHAPTER EIGHT

No fire was ablaze inside Ethan's smithy, but heat decorated Grace's face and neck. Whether or not color actually stained her skin she was unsure. The moment Ethan opened the door, the cool, crisp air outside swirled inside and played with the wisps of her hair that wouldn't stay tucked into the large silver combs Leah Redbourne had used to pull her locks back away from her face.

Ethan stood in the open door way and lifted an eyebrow. He jerked his head toward the outdoors, motioning for her to leave. Grace had hoped that he would take her hand again, but with a bow in one hand and his quiver in the other, it was unlikely.

He slid the quiver up onto his shoulder and as she passed him, he carefully placed his hand at the small of her back and guided her out to where most of his family now stood, facing a row of three hay bales, each aptly marked with a red and blue painted bulls-eye.

"We'll take the best shot in three," Jameson called loudly. "Raine, Rafe, and Will. You three will start us off."

Each of the brothers he called took their places in front of their respective targets.

Grace was fascinated at the precision and time it took for

each of them to make their shots. Ethan, Cole, and Hannah lined up next. She watched carefully as Ethan took a deep breath and closed his eyes. When he opened them again, he exhaled and released his arrow.

Thud.

Dead center.

A mixture of protest and excitement filled the yard and everyone rushed to clap Ethan on the back. His face lit up with a smile—the kind she'd had yet to see on his guarded features. When he turned to look at her, heat once again flooded her cheeks. He winked at her, and a sharp intake of breath nearly strangled her.

She couldn't let anyone see how he affected her. Especially him.

The sound of approaching riders distracted attention from the game to the three figures racing up the road toward the homestead.

"Now, who'd be calling today?" Jameson asked, all hint of merriment lost from his face.

Grace was fascinated how each of the siblings had slung their bows over their shoulders and had holstered their arrows in one seemingly fluid motion. Even Hannah.

As the riders got closer, Grace recognized the familiar face of Hurley Devlin and two of the men who'd been with him in town and to whom she hadn't been introduced.

"Mr. Redbourne," Hurley said, tipping his hat at the head of the Redbourne family.

"Hurley," Jameson returned the courtesy.

"Please excuse the intrusion, but I've got a man missing. No one at my place has seen him since last night and I was hoping one of you might have."

"What are you playing at, Devlin?" Ethan stepped up next to his father. "You know as well as we do that your man is dead."

Hurley narrowed his eyes at Ethan. "Dead? What are you

talking about, Redbourne?"

"Now, Hurley," Raine said, moving his hand to the pistol that rested at his side. The motion pulled his jacket aside to reveal the deputy badge pinned to his vest. "A man was found dead out on the old Nolan property this morning. He wasn't from around here, and since you've been associating with a lot of strangers to Stone Creek recently, we guessed he might be one of yours. I imagine you wouldn't know anything about that?"

Grace shuddered. Stumbling over the corpse, seeing the empty, glasslike look in the man's bulging eyes and bluing tinge to his skin, had not been the highlight of her day.

"Dead? How?" Hurley demanded, sitting up taller in his saddle.

"Suffocation maybe."

"Maybe? What kind of answer is that?" Hurley huffed and swung his leg around his horse and dismounted. "Where is he now? This dead man you found in the middle of nowhere?"

All the Redbournes moved together and in an instant, each was armed. Some had drawn their guns, but Ethan and Rafe both had arrows drawn in their bows—all pointing directly at Hurley.

"Whoa, now. I'm not looking for trouble. Just answers."

"The sheriff has been notified and the body is with Mr. Collins," Jameson said. "You can find answers there."

"All right. All right. Just answer me one thing. Who found him?"

Silence.

Ethan's stance tensed. His head turned slightly toward her, but his eyes never left Hurley. Grace stepped up behind Ethan and placed a hand on his shoulder.

"I did," she said as she stepped out from behind the wall of Redbournes.

The expression on Hurley's face changed in a flash from disdain to one of concern.

"Why, Grace. I had no idea you were visiting here." His voice was coated with honey. "Are you all right?" He stepped toward her, but Ethan blocked his way, relaxing his draw and returning his arrow to his quiver.

"*Miss Nolan* is safe here with us."

"I can speak for myself, thank you very much," Grace said, ducking under the tip of Ethan's bow to stand in front of him again. "I am fine, Mr. Devlin. Thank you so much for your concern." She smiled.

"Hurley. Please."

Was that sadness she saw behind the man's eyes? To hear the Redbournes speak of him, he didn't have a soul, but she'd seen that worry before.

"I am sorry if you've lost a friend, Mr. Dev…"

He cocked a brow.

"Hurley," she corrected.

"I'm still planning on calling after you," he said, only a hint of a smile touching his dark and chiseled features.

"Not if I can help it," Ethan said under his breath.

Grace imagined he hadn't intended for her to hear it. She mused at the physical differences between Hurley Devlin and Ethan Redbourne. They couldn't have been more opposite. Hurley's dark hair extended the length of his collar, and his eyes were black as steel. Ethan was fairer—his blond locks cut short on the sides and stood up straight on top. It looked much the same as it had when he'd woken up this morning. Heat flooded her cheeks at the thought. And then there were his eyes—the color of warm honey. She could get lost in those eyes.

Stop it right now, Grace Nolan.

From what she could tell, their dissimilarities extended to their dispositions—except when they were with each other, and that just meant ornery.

"Now, you've seen she's fine, *Hurley*. It's time to leave," Ethan said. His jaw flexed.

Hurley took another step forward, but Raine stepped
between them. "Hurley, if indeed the man was your friend,
shouldn't you be heading into town to see the sheriff?"

Raine had holstered his weapon, but his hand did not
leave the handle. "I can't imagine what a friend of yours was
doing out at the Nolan place though. Any ideas?"

"Not a one, deputy, but I'm sure you'll keep me informed,"
Hurley said with narrowed eyes still focused on Ethan. After a
moment, he broke their stare and swung up into the saddle of
his horse. "Ma'am." He tipped his hat and motioned for the
two riders he'd arrived with to follow.

Grace glanced up at Ethan, his eyes narrowed and jaw
clenched.

What did he mean, 'Not if I can help it'?

Clank!

The hundred-year-old platter that had belonged to Leah
Redbourne's great-grandmother teetered on the edge of the
counter and Tag reached out just in time to catch it. The gravy
bowl, still full, was not so lucky. It tipped and before anyone
could stop its rapid decent, it crashed to the ground and
shattered, sending thick brown splashes and ceramic pieces
flying in every direction.

"We're okay," Tag called out quickly.

"Aw, Tag," Ethan said with chagrin. "Now we'll all have
to go change."

"I don't know that you'll ever change, ya ornery old cuss,"
Tag responded, earning him a snort from a couple of the
others.

Ornery? He guessed it was true. He had been a
little…reclusive over the last little while, but he hoped that his
new projects would change that—at least with his family.

"How are my dishes?" their mother asked from the other

room, the attempt at nonchalance poorly masked in her higher than normal pitched voice.

"Great-grandma's tray is safe with nary a scratch," Tag called back. He carefully walked over to the hutch where all of mama's special dishes were kept.

Each brother had taken his position in clearing, stacking, and washing the dishes. They'd done it so many times it had become almost an art. However, once in a while, there was a mishap.

Ethan pulled a towel from the bottom drawer next to the sink and dipped it in the sudsy water his brothers had carted in from outside and had set to boil. It was still hot and he gingerly wrung out his rag before joining Tag, who'd already dropped to the floor to wipe up the spill.

"There," Hannah said from the other side of the room where she and Lottie had just finished putting together a basket, filled with leftover turkey—though there wasn't much—rolls, and other foods, for Grace and Jack to take home with them.

Ethan smiled. After making sure that they had gathered all the shards of the ceramic bowl, he picked up the soiled braided rug and tossed it near the back door to be taken out to the water shed to be laundered.

When he walked back in the house, everyone had migrated to the living room.

"What do you know about my grandfather's treasure?"

"Jack!" The annoyance in Grace's voice was unmistakable.

Ethan leaned against the archway between kitchen and family room and folded his arms across his chest. Ethan had never thought much about the old legends. He'd always figured that's just what they were—legends.

"What?" the youth responded with brows slammed into a harsh angle. "He might know something that will tell us where it is." Jack looked back at Jameson as if hoping to confirm his suspicions.

"Sorry, son." Jameson shook his head.

Jack's smile faltered.

"I'm afraid I don't know much more than what I told you before. Those old stories have been around for a half century or so."

Jack scooted closer to Jameson's oversized cushion chair, his face suddenly bright at the mention of a story. "Tell us more. Please? Was my great-granddad really a bandit?"

Cole, who'd been lying with his new Stetson over his face and his feet resting on the short table in front of the couch, moved his hat and sat up. He set his feet on the floor and leaned forward with his elbows on his knees. "I thought you said that if there really was a treasure someone would have already found it by now."

Jameson shrugged his shoulders

"They're just stories, son. Don't know that there's any real truth to them."

"But how come you've never told us about these legends before?"

Jameson laughed. "It's been a long time since I've heard most of them myself."

Jack nodded anxiously and Ethan shook his head. The boy was only a good six years or so younger than him, but right now he looked like a little child, hanging on his father's every word.

Ethan glanced around at his family. Rafe and Will sat alongside Cole on the couch. Raine lay across the floor in front of the hearth with his arms behind his head and his feet extended nearly to the rocking chair where his mother sat braiding Hannah's hair in front of her.

The front door opened and closed and Tag stepped into the room, shook the chill from his shoulders, and threw another log onto the fire.

"Well," Jameson said, scratching his stubbly chin with the backs of his fingers, "let's see."

Ethan's scan of the room ended on Grace, whose stance had become rigid and all hint of merriment had left her face. She shifted in her chair. Her fingers reached up to her neck, and she hastily began twirling a cluster of her honey-colored locks. He wondered what had put her on edge so quickly.

"As I told you before, there used to be a group of young men around these parts that did some pretty crazy things when they got bored. They were always looking for trouble of one sort or another." Jameson looked at Jack. "Ulysses Nolan, your great-grandfather, was one of them."

Grace rubbed her neck and shakily lifted her hands to her mouth to bite at her thumbnail.

What in the world?

"Rumor has it that when they first carved the route for the Santa Fe Trail, the military and many wealthy landowners, entrepreneurs, and fortune hunters would use the trail to transport precious goods and cargo between Mexico and many of the eastern states to be shipped overseas toward Britain and other parts of Europe."

Ethan smirked. He remembered well his grandfather sitting them all down around the fire and recounting tall tales of adventures on the high seas, across the west, and to foreign lands. His father looked just like him right now, God rest his soul.

"One stormy afternoon just before Christmas," Jameson started in that voice that dared you to turn away, "your great-granddaddy and his pals had planned to rob one of the transport trains heading to the eastern states. But to their detriment, the men who travelled the route that day were not simple merchants, but outcasts from an ancient Incan civilization."

Rafe and Will now sat at the edge of the couch, and Raine had pulled himself into a sitting position with his arms wrapped around his knees.

"What's an Incan?" Jack asked in wonder.

"Incas were kind of like the Indians. They lived a long time ago down in a southern country now called Peru. The Spaniards conquered them and they all died out. We just learned about them at University." Will had just returned from England where he had graduated from the university in Oxford, and Ethan could already tell his brother was going to be impossible to live with.

"If they all died out, then the legends can't be true," Tag said as if he were now the smartest man in the room.

"Ah," their father said with a lifted finger, "but these men were from a secret group of Inca's who had survived the Spanish invasion and hid themselves far from their conquered brethren."

Ethan had heard the stories of legend from Mr. Pierce as they'd worked together in the smithy in town, but he had to admit, knowing that the legend involved a relative of Miss Nolan's intrigued him somewhat.

"These outcasts were Incan mercenaries who had been hired by a vengeful and wicked priest to escort him to the east. He had stolen the life spring of his village—a collection of ornately crafted chests of gold and silver full of thousands of beautifully cut and raw emeralds, green as the grass in the spring. He had believed they would be his source of extreme power and elevate him to godhood among men." Jameson scooted forward in his seat and braced one leg against the floor, while the other curled under him enough that he almost knelt on the wooden ground.

Ethan had to admit that his father did a better job at telling the story than Mr. Pierce. He sat down on the floor in front of Grace's feet, his forearms resting on his upturned knees.

"But when one of your grandfather's cohorts pulled his gun and demanded they empty the chests into his saddle bags, the malevolent priest threw his jewel encrusted golden spear through the man's heart."

Gasps erupted throughout the room.

"...a battle began, and there were severe losses on both sides until the last two standing were your great-grandfather and the priest."

Grace jumped to her feet. "If you'll excuse me for a moment." She half-smiled, but turned on her heel and nearly ran from the room and out the door.

Leah locked eyes with Ethan and tilted her head in two soft, but sudden, motions toward the entryway. Of course, she wanted him to go after Miss Nolan. He didn't know what to say to the woman, but reluctantly he pushed himself away from the wall and slipped behind the couch and toward the door as his mother had silently instructed. He grabbed his coat from the rack and quietly opened the door.

Grace stood at the bottom of the stairs, leaning on the iron railing for support as she stared up into the cloud laden sky.

"Are you all right?" he asked, inching down the steps toward her. She had to be cold without so much as a shawl to protect her from the wintery evening breeze.

She jumped at the sound of his voice, and turned to face him. "You startled me," she said, turning away from him again and rubbing her arms briskly.

Ethan placed his coat around her shoulders and sat down on one of the higher steps and leaned forward, glancing over the yard. "It's a beautiful evening."

"Yes, it is lovely," she said without looking back. "Thank you. For the jacket."

A few moments of silence passed between them.

"Mr. Redbourne?"

Ethan wanted to correct her, to tell her to call him by his Christian name, but he couldn't do it. He didn't want to look like he was following anything Hurley Devlin did. He didn't say anything and she turned around, finding a place on the stair next to him.

"I know it seems a little ungracious, you've all been real nice and all, but..." She bit her lip.

I wish she'd stop doing that.

He clenched his jaw and redirected his thoughts.

"Will you take me and Jack home?"

He wasn't sure what he'd expected her to say, but somehow the request didn't surprise him. She was new to Stone Creek. New to the west, and she'd barely had time to find the place, let alone get her bearings.

Ethan chuckled quietly. "Is that what you're so worried about? That we're going to keep you here forever?"

She smiled with pursed lips. "Of course not. I just..."

"I'll have the wagon ready in half an hour," he said when she didn't finish her sentence. He stood up and offered her his hand.

What are you doing, Redbourne?

Grace stared at his hand a moment before sliding hers into his grasp. He lifted her up. Her fingers were cold and Ethan could think of nothing more at that moment than warming them with his breath. He settled for reaching toward her and delving into the pocket of his coat to retrieve his gloves. They might be big, but they would be better than nothing.

He lifted her hand to slip on the glove, but she placed her other hand over his.

"You take them," she said quietly. "You'll need them to get the horses ready. I'll just go inside and get Jack."

Ethan didn't want to move. Didn't want to withdraw from her touch. This was ridiculous. He'd sworn a long time ago he would never give another woman the opportunity to hurt him the way Victoria had, and he'd lost all hope of ever being able to trust again. To love again. Yet, here was this woman who defied his wishes and knocked on that door—daring him to take a chance.

How did he let himself get to this point?

"Hmhmmm," Rafe stood at the doorway. "Ethan, can I

talk to you for a minute?"

Grace stole her hands from his with a nod and slipped past his brother into the house.

"Miss Nolan is ready to go home," he said sensibly. "I'll go get the wagon ready." And he skittered down the last couple of steps and in the direction of the barn.

"Ethan," Rafe called him back.

He turned and Rafe joined him in the yard.

"I'm leaving."

"We'll all go together. Just give me a few minutes to get the horses hitched and the hay and blankets loaded." Ethan turned back toward the barn.

"Ethan!" Rafe said a little more harshly.

"What?" he retorted, matching Rafe's tone.

"I'm going after a bounty."

Ethan felt like he'd just been slugged in the gut.

"This guy's real bad, little brother. He's killing innocent people. Pawnee."

Rafe would never be able to resist—especially where his beloved Pawnee were concerned. He'd spent nearly a year living among their people and had returned a changed man. How could Ethan deny him justice?

"Women. Children."

"Okay, Rafe. I get it. When are you coming back?"

"I don't know."

"Christmas?"

"I'll try."

Ethan caught a glimpse of Grace through the front window of the house. "What about Miss Nolan? And Jack?"

"I'll stay there with you tonight and head out just after first light." Rafe patted Ethan on the shoulder. "Knowing Mama, she'll have the whole town organized by Saturday to get all the necessary repairs done on the Nolan place, and you'll be able to sleep in your own bed again."

Rafe pulled him into a firm embrace.

"I'll miss you, big brother," Ethan said with a solid pat on Rafe's back.

"Nah," Rafe grinned as they pulled away. "It looks like you'll have your hands full." He looked over his shoulder at the spot in the window where Grace could still be seen. "She's real pretty. Just be careful. Neither you nor I have chosen very wisely in the past."

The front door opened and Leah popped her head out.

"You boys coming back in for some pie?" she asked with a quick rub of her upper arms.

"Coming," Ethan responded.

Rafe mock slugged him in the shoulder and Ethan leaned playfully to the side. They skipped up the stairs and into the warmth of the house.

"Pie," Grace said with a smirk, handing him a slice.

"Pie." Ethan nodded.

CHAPTER NINE

True to his word, Ethan had the wagon ready within half an hour—despite his mother's constant additions to their load. Hay for the horses, more blankets than Grace had seen since leaving the Coldhern Estates, and enough food to feed an army for a week.

Jack hadn't wanted to leave Redbourne Ranch yet. He was too caught up in this idea that he was going to find their families ill-gotten treasure and wanted to ask Ethan's father as many questions as he could think of—trying to piece together any clues his stories might garner.

Grace hated the stories—which she was sure had been convoluted over time, but they still carried with them the sting of where she'd come from. Who she was. To think that so much blood had been shed over a few coins of gold or silver ate at her, and her great-grandfather had been the worst of them. She was determined to make a better name for the Nolan family than her predecessors.

"Are you sure it's not too much of an imposition?" Grace asked Ethan's brother, Rafe, who had volunteered to stay behind a short while and take Jack home a little later.

"Don't worry, ma'am. That storm's not going to be here for a few more days yet." He sounded very sure of himself.

"He's rarely wrong," Ethan whispered near her ear as he threw the last of the blankets into the back of the wagon. A tangible tingling sensation travelled down her neck and settled in the pit of her stomach.

"Now, you let my son get that fire started for you, my dear. And stay nice and warm tonight." Leah wrapped a scarf around Grace's neck and looped it together firmly below her chin.

That's exactly what Grace was afraid of. Her son had already started a fire she was unsure she'd be able to quench.

Grace hugged the woman. "Thank you. For everything. I think it was the best Thanksgiving I can ever remember."

And it was.

Leah beamed.

"You ready?" Ethan stood so close to her she could feel the heat exuding from his body.

He helped her up onto the wagon seat and leapt up next to her.

"I'll be back at first light tomorrow. I noticed one of the hinges has come loose on the far gate, and with Tag and Cole heading out to deliver horses in the morning, we'll need to get an early start."

Jameson tipped his hat.

Grace waved at everyone as Ethan pulled the wagon out onto the road toward home. She was glad that she lived only a short distance away from the family to whom she had already grown so close. It gave her comfort to know she had friends, and she pulled a warm, thick blanket up around her shoulders.

It was quiet most of the ride home.

"Look," Ethan broke the silence, pointing to an area in the sky where the clouds had started to disperse and the spattering of stars twinkled in the night.

"Thank you." She'd wanted to tell him how much she appreciated all that he had already done for her and Jack, but the words just didn't seem enough. Before she could say more, they pulled through the gate to the house.

Ethan jumped down off the seat and reached up for her. "I'll be in to start that fire right after I get these horses taken care of." His hands grasped her by the waist and lifted her down with ease. He abruptly let go and grabbed a sack full of food from the back of the wagon and handed it to her. A flicker of light came to life as he lit the wick of a lantern and turned the knob.

"Be careful."

Grace nodded and, without a word, she scampered up the steps and into the house. She held the lantern out and looked about the kitchen, still in complete disarray, and remembered just how much work there was to do before winter set in. Boxes lined the entry with the supplies she had purchased in town, but it was too dark now to do much with them.

Normally at this time of day, her mother would have a ball of yarn she would be working in front of the fireplace and Grace and Jack would be reading their lessons. This was the first time in a while that she really missed her mother. They hadn't been as close as Grace would have liked, but their life had been much different in New York than here. She wondered what it would have been like to grow up in Stone Creek.

Through the window in the kitchen, Grace could see Ethan's dimly lit form moving around the barn. He would be in at any moment and she had no refreshment to offer him. Quickly, she set the basket of food on the kitchen counter, picked up the pail from the hook near the sink, and hurried outside to collect some water. A nice apple tea sounded divine.

Once back in the house, she gathered a couple of the small logs she could use to start a fire in the pot-bellied stove, but the front door opened before she could even obtain a sliver of smoke.

"What do you say we start a real fire?" he asked, a hint of amusement in his voice.

A real fire?

"And just what do you think I am trying to do?"

When he didn't respond, she held up the lantern. He had disappeared. Maybe he hadn't realized she had already collected some wood for the fire. She held the light up in front of her.

"Ethan?" she called hesitantly.

Scratch.

"In here," he said with a grunt.

She followed the sound of his voice, and when she walked around the corner, she was surprised to see Ethan lifting a large cloth covered block away from the inside wall. She hadn't given it much thought, but to her utter delight, hidden behind the object was a large stone fireplace. Bricks surrounded the hearth and extended along the floor. Why she hadn't noticed it before was disconcerting.

"But how did you...?"

"I noticed the grand chimney protruding from the roof when we were here before. It had to be in here somewhere." Ethan hunched down in front of the grate, took off his hat, and set his own lantern on the inner hearth floor to peer inside, up the flue.

"Will you hand me that broom?" he asked, pointing to the other side of the room.

Grace quickly did as she was asked.

Ethan turned it around, so the handle was upright and proceeded to jab the broom up into the flue. Something dislodged, but Ethan couldn't get his head out before a huge cloud of dust and soot powdered his face. When he emerged from the fireplace, it was hard to make out his features. They were blacker than night. He sputtered and spit.

"Well, that was unpleasant," he said wryly as he pulled a handkerchief from his pocket to wipe his face.

Laughter bubbled to the surface, and she placed a hand over her mouth in an attempt to contain it—to no avail.

"You think that's funny do you?"

Grace thought for a moment before nodding wholeheartedly. He rubbed a finger-full of soot from his face, and before she could get out of his reach, he wiped it across her cheek.

She gasped in mock affront, and he tapped her on the end of her nose.

A low, hearty laugh erupted from Ethan's generally serious façade. The rich, deep tones of his amusement seemed to light the otherwise dark room. He brushed the rag over his face, the soot smearing in streaks against the darkened flesh tones of his face.

"Here," she said with a breathy chuckle, "let me do it." She set the lantern on the fireplace mantle and took the cloth from him. She wrapped it around her hand and with one finger reached up to his face, carefully wiping away the smudges.

Ethan's breathing became heavy and he lifted his hand and wrapped his fingers around her wrist, bidding her to stop. Grace knew if she looked up at him she would be lost. They were standing so close. She bit her lip.

Ethan groaned. He raised his hand to her face, delving his fingers into the hair just behind her ear and caressed her jawline with his thumb.

She looked up. Couldn't help herself. The lantern's light flickered in his eyes and his thumb found her lips. Her bosom swelled with anticipation as he slowly lowered his head toward her, his mouth slightly open. Grace curled her hands into the shirt tucked at his hips and closed her eyes, waiting for the moment his lips would meld with hers.

"Don't worry, kid, if it's out there, I'm sure you'll find…" Rafe opened the door, Jack tucked under his arm, "…it."

Ethan's hands fell to his sides and he took a step backward, still holding her eyes captive.

Suddenly the room felt cold, and it took a moment for Grace's thoughts to switch focus.

Ethan bent down to collect his handkerchief, which had fallen to the hearth's brick floor, and jammed it into the pocket of his denims.

Grace could only imagine what she must look like, but took comfort in the fact that she hadn't gotten a face-full of soot like Ethan.

"Will you hand me that box of kindling?" Ethan asked brusquely.

Unbeknownst to Grace, Ethan had already collected enough sticks and dried grasses to start the fire. She recognized some of the planks that had boarded up the window had been broken down in size and a few logs his brothers had cut earlier were stacked next to the newly discovered fireplace. She handed him the box and he reached into his pocket and pulled out something she couldn't quite distinguish in the lantern's dim light.

"I thought you'd have that fire going long before we got here. You're losing your touch, little brother."

On the contrary, Grace mused.

Within moments a fire came to life, flames licking at the large cut logs.

Grace remembered the apple tea and rushed into the kitchen to grab the bucket of water she'd collected. She caught herself on the counter, braced her hands against it, and dropped her head. She breathed in deeply and exhaled slowly. After a moment, she stood up straight and placed one hand on her chest.

"Land almighty."

Apples. Can't have apple tea without the apples. Or a kettle. Grace had no idea where to even start looking for the cooking pots she'd purchased in town. She resigned herself to the idea that her new concoction would have to wait until morning. With the water pail next to the sink, and her breathing in check, she returned to the living area where Jack, Rafe, and Ethan all stood warming themselves by the fire.

"Grace! You'll never guess what I learned today."

"Hopefully, you learned to be gracious and thank these fine gentlemen for all the help they've given us."

"I am real grateful to you," he said to Ethan and Rafe. "And do you know what else I'm grateful for?" Jack turned back to her, intent on telling her his various theories on how they could locate the treasure and what they could do with it once found.

She felt a twinge of guilt that she would deny her brother the excitement of searching for their family's treasure, but her grandfather had spent nearly twenty years in its pursuit and had almost lost everything.

"Jack, I think it's time to turn in for the night."

"Aw, Gracie."

"Don't you 'aw, Gracie' me. It's going to be a full day tomorrow with lots of work to be done. We both need our rest." She smiled and kissed her brother on the forehead. "And I'm sure both Mr. Redbournes would also like to get some sleep."

"All right," Jack said, reluctantly yielding to the idea.

"Can I get you gentlemen anything before I head up?" Grace asked as she reached up for the lantern on the mantle.

"We'll be fine right here, ma'am. Thank you." Rafe pointed at the couch and chaise that had been pulled around the hearth.

"We'll see to it that the fire's out before we doze off," Ethan said with a nod.

"Thank you."

"See you fellas in the morning," Jack said with a wave of his hand.

At the bottom of the stairs, Grace turned to face the men with a closed smile.

"Goodnight."

"Goodnight, Miss Nolan."

Grace retired to her new bedroom, grateful she couldn't

see what lurked in the corners of the room or on the walls. One more night and then she would be able to get to work on the place—starting with their new sleeping quarters.

The door shut downstairs and Grace peeked out the window. Ethan strode from the house and stopped at the water pump.

He wouldn't.

A few hasty pumps of the handle and water spilled from the faucet. Ethan stuck his hands into the liquid and quickly pulled them back, flexing and shaking them. Gooseflesh skittered up Grace's arms as she imagined the cold temperature of the water. He repeated the motion, only this time, he splashed the water onto his face.

Grace gasped.

Ethan scrubbed at his cheeks with his handkerchief. Seemingly satisfied, he pumped the handle again and, to Grace's amazement, he dowsed his entire head beneath the flow. She held her breath and reached a hand to touch the window. When the water stopped, he stood up straight and shook his head free of the excess before darting back into the house.

Grace exhaled slowly, leaned against the window frame, and tilted her head with a smile.

Life in Stone Creek was growing on her already.

Ethan opened one eye and then the other.

Nope. Not a dream.

"It's about time you're up. I'm heading out soon, so if you want me to help you teach these Greenhorns how to shoot before I go, we need to get some targets set up."

Rafe was a better shot with a gun than most of his brothers. Except Raine. Ethan could hold his own, but his skills were no match for the two lawmen in his family.

He swung his legs around the side of the chaise and reached for his boots.

"Have you told Mama you're leaving?"

"No." Rafe set his new Stetson on his head.

"Coward."

"Yep." Rafe laughed and headed out the front door.

Brisk morning air filled Ethan's lungs as he stepped out onto the porch. He was surprised, but grateful they hadn't had much snow. This place was going to take a lot of work and he hoped that his mother would be able to work her magic and recruit a crew or two to come out and help.

Repairs to the inside of the house would be much easier to tackle if they could get the exterior fixed up quickly. The other structures around the house were another matter entirely. Ethan wasn't sure the barn would make it through another winter and it certainly wasn't livable for any sort of animals over any extended period of time. If Grace wanted to keep her horses here and the goat she'd already purchased from Mrs. Day, the entire structure of the barn would need to be rebuilt.

"You start a fire?" Rafe asked, pointing with his nose at the cloud of smoke rising from the smaller stove pipe chimney on the roof.

"They must be awake." Ethan started for the house, but stopped mid-stride to stare at the door.

"What's the matter?"

Ethan didn't respond. He wasn't sure what to say to one very beautiful and intriguing Miss Nolan. He'd gotten very close to her last night, felt like his old self for the first time in a very long time. Hell, he'd nearly kissed her. And, if he were honest with himself, he wasn't sorry.

You're a grown man, Redbourne. Just go talk to the woman.

"Now who's the coward?" Rafe chided with a grin as he led his new horse, Lexa, from the dilapidated barn, and pulled several of his guns from his saddle holsters. He laid a few of them out a good distance in front of the targets.

"Whoa," Jack threw open the front door of the house and ran out into the yard. "Rafe, Ethan, are you going to teach me how to shoot? With a real gun?" Excitement exuded from the kid's voice.

Ethan still couldn't believe that a young man of nearly fourteen had never learned how to use a gun, but he figured that living in the city there wouldn't be as much of a need for one as there was out west.

"Ethan," Jack said, running up to him. "Which one is your favorite?"

With a glance at the door, Ethan walked with Jack over to the display of weaponry Rafe had laid out.

"You carry all this with you? All the time?" He asked his brother, awed at the sheer number of them.

"Not always. But a man in my line of work can never be too careful." Rafe shrugged and pointed at the Winchester. "My little brother has taken a liking to a bow, but if he had to choose a gun, my bet would be that rifle right there.

Ethan hated that his brother knew him so well. He nodded. "I like that you can fire more than one shot without having to reload, and just look at the metal work on that beauty. It's pretty danged accurate too."

"Can I try it?"

Rafe laughed. "That's why we got it out."

Boom.

His first shot landed some twenty yards beyond the intended target, but Rafe showed him how to move another round into the chamber and showed him where to put his feet.

"What in tarnation is going on out here?" Grace had come out the kitchen door on the other side of the house.

She stood on the wrap-around porch with her hands on her hips. Her hair was pulled back up off the nape of her neck, but a few loose tendrils fell down, framing her face.

"Come on down, Miss Nolan. I'm afraid we can't leave here this morning until you and your brother can hit the broadside of a barn." Rafe motioned for her to join them.

Grace disappeared back into the house. When she reemerged, she had two steaming mugs of a liquid that smelled strongly of apples and cinnamon. She handed one to Ethan, meeting his eyes fully before taking the few steps to where Rafe stood next to Jack.

"I found my dishes," she said with pride.

"I can see that," Ethan lifted his mug and pressed it against his lips. He'd never been much of a tea drinker as it didn't seem like anything more than flavored water. However, there was something about this concoction that warmed him from the inside.

"Line up your sights here," Rafe pointed to the sight at the tip of the barrel on the rifle Jack held, "with whatever you are trying to shoot."

"Why don't *you* teach me?" Grace asked without looking at him.

Ethan nodded and motioned for Grace to follow him. He set his mug down next to the line Rafe had drawn with his foot for the second target.

"I borrowed Raine's shotgun. The same one you held that first night we were here. You said you weren't sure how to use it, but it's time you learn." He remembered well the first time she'd held that gun on him after the coyote had attacked the kittens, Bob and Cratchit, and their mother. She'd had no idea how to shoot, but had been prepared to do whatever she needed to in order to protect her and her family.

He admired that.

"Wahoo!" Jack hit the target square in the center.

Everyone laughed.

When the sound of a rider approached, they all looked up to see who would be coming by so early in the morning.

"Ethan!" the huffing rider called as he dismounted his horse. The man looked about as flustered as a long-tailed cat in a room full of rocking chairs.

"Mr. Banks? What are you doing out here? And so early?"

"Another spring broke," he thrust it into Ethan's hands, "and I am supposed to take Myrtle to town in just over an hour for her appointment with the milliner. She *needs* her new Christmas hat. Help me!"

Ethan looked at Grace, standing patiently, shotgun in hand, waiting for him to teach her how to use it. He glanced over at Rafe and Jack, who had now hit three of his targets with some degree of accuracy. As much as he hated to do it, he'd have to let Rafe show her what to do.

"We'll have to head over to Redbourne Ranch, Mr. Banks. But, I think we'll be able to get it fixed up for you. We'll have to make up a spare set for occasions such as this in the future." He patted the older man on the shoulder. "Excuse me a moment."

"Rafe," he said once he'd gotten closer, "I have to go."

Rafe glanced over at Grace and back to Ethan. "Are you sure, little brother?" He tilted his head as if skeptical. "Is there something I can do to help Mr. Banks?"

"Afraid not. His blasted spring gave out and his mother-in-law…it's a long story. Can I take Lexa?" Ethan figured that this way, his brother would have to stop back by the house to switch her out for the wagon before he left town.

"Can you handle her?" Rafe asked with a smirk.

"Funny. Are you okay here?" Ethan nodded toward Grace.

"Get out of here. Help the poor fool with his…problem."

Ethan clapped his brother on his arms and sauntered the few paces between him and Grace.

"I'm sorry," he said, "but I have to go."

Grace's shoulders dropped and she set the butt of the shotgun against the ground, the muzzle pointing upward at an inward angle.

"Oh."

Was that disappointment in her voice?

"All right."

Ethan reached down and took the gun away from her, brushing his fingers across her hand in the process. "The first thing to learn is that the muzzle," he pointed to it, "should never be pointed at something you don't intend to shoot. The last thing we need is for someone to get shot by accident. Especially you."

Flirting? Really?

"Yes, sir," she said with an apologetic smile.

Ethan handed the gun to Rafe. "I'll be back tonight. Hopefully, with a little help. And, maybe we'll be able to get some of the outside work done on the house before the year is done."

She nodded, the corners of her beautiful mouth upturned slightly though seeming half-hearted.

Ethan took a step backward and raised his hand in a wave. "Bye."

She returned the gesture.

Before he had even mounted the horse, Rafe stepped up next to Grace. "I'll bet you're a natural," he said in that smooth voice that always won him attention from the ladies.

All of the sudden, Ethan wasn't so sure that leaving Grace with his brother was such a good idea, but he climbed up into Lexa's saddle and forced himself to turn toward the ranch. They were mere minutes into the ride when Ethan glanced backward.

Big mistake.

Rafe stood behind Grace, his face mere inches from her ear. His hand wrapped around her and he moved her body into the proper stance.

Hell no.

He pulled on the reins and turned back to the house with a slight kick to the horse's flank.

Rafe, Grace, and Jack all turned to see what had happened. Dust kicked up around him as he passed back through the front gate, and before Lexa was even stopped, he slid from her back to the ground and in three determined steps he closed the distance between him and Grace.

"One more thing," Ethan said as he slid both of his hands across her cheeks until he gripped her face firmly between them. He met her eyes for only a brief moment before he lowered his head and captured her lips in his, pleased when a soft moan resonated at the back of her throat and her grip on his shirt pulled him closer.

He broke the kiss only to place another quick peck on her slightly parted lips. With a tip of his hat, he turned back around, grabbed ahold of Lexa's saddle horn and pulled himself up. He didn't look back. Didn't dare.

What did I just do?

CHAPTER TEN

It had been a week and Grace hadn't seen hide nor hair of Ethan Redbourne. She swept another layer of dust from the brick hearth floor in front of the fireplace. She stopped. There it was again—that ticking noise. All this nonsense with Ethan had her losing her mind.

The man hadn't even been to church on Sunday. Hurley Devlin, on the other hand, had been quite willing to introduce her to many of the townsfolk and show her about the small shops along the boardwalk in Stone Creek, but there had only been one man she'd wanted to see.

How dare he kiss me like that and just disappear without a word.

Grace could still feel the warmth of his mouth on hers. She leaned back against the fireplace and raised her fingers to brush across her lips as she recalled the sparking sensation lingering in her memory.

Snap out of it. There was too much still to be done without pining over a man. At least he could have brought the kittens by to see her. She could use a little friend to cuddle with right now.

Each night a different set of Redbournes kept watch at the house, sleeping on the couch and chaise Rafe and Ethan had moved next to the hearth. Grace was still unsure why they were making such a fuss by insisting someone stay with them during the night. Images of the disturbed dust in the cellar staircase and the dead man by the barn flashed through her mind.

Of course, they would insist. The Redbournes were that kind of folk.

Don't look a gift horse in the mouth, her mother always used to tell her. The old adage played through her mind several times over again.

Thank you, Lord, she prayed silently, *for overprotective neighbors.*

The clanking squeal of a wagon approaching jolted Grace to her senses. She pushed away from the rock wall, leaned her broom against the couch, and walked over to the window, pushing her new curtains aside to see who'd come calling.

Leah and Hannah Redbourne.

Grace bolted up straight, her hand reaching up to her hair and smoothing her dress. She was sure she looked a sight. They'd been working on cleaning, sorting, and menial repairs for the last seven days. With a quick glance in the hallway mirror, she licked her fingertips and brushed them across some of the flyaway hairs at her temple before opening the door and stepping out onto the porch.

The sun perched directly overhead. Grace raised a hand to her forehead to block the brightness of the light and allow her to see her approaching visitors. Another wagon came into view, followed by yet another.

"Afternoon, Grace," Leah called out as she pulled her buckboard to a halt.

Hannah jumped down off the tall wagon seat and pranced up the stairs. "Mama's got a surprise for you," she said with a grin.

"What kind of surprise?" Grace hadn't been concerned until she caught the mischievous gleam in Hannah's eyes. "What are you two up to?" Another wagon peaked the small hillside migrating toward the house.

"It took some time, but everyone is finally organized. I figure they'll have this place in prime condition by suppertime." Leah carried two large boxes, a can of paint dangling from her fingers, up the stairs and set them on one of the rocking chairs Grace had placed just outside the door.

"Who'll have this fixed up?"

"Why, everybody." Leah pointed out to the buckboards and horses all headed in their direction.

"They're all here to help *us*?"

"It wouldn't be very neighborly of us to let you freeze to death through the winter, now would it?"

"I suppose not. But…" Grace watched with amazement as one wagon after another pulled up into the yard with men carrying tools and other various supplies. She was speechless.

Women started appearing with all sorts of foodstuffs. Grace directed them into the house. Pies, breads, fried chicken, and other baked goods and vegetables soon lined her table and counter space. Grace was grateful that she'd seen to it that the kitchen had been cleared of cobwebs and scrubbed from top to bottom the moment their bedrooms had been done.

Each of the ladies glanced around her house with a nod of approval. Grace breathed a sigh of relief.

"I was expecting it to be much…worse than this," Mrs. Day said with a wink. "Are you sure you're not hiding a gaggle of servants in here somewhere?" She mocked a brief inspection.

Grace laughed politely. If only they knew. She'd had sufficient experience cleaning a home. The estate had been much larger than this. She'd once thought it would be her home—not just where she'd reside, but as the lady of the house. How wrong she'd been.

"We've brought your new goat. Once the barn is finished, she'll be able to stay in there. But you mustn't forget to milk her every morning." Mrs. Day patted her on the arm and walked out of the kitchen. "It looks like the wood you ordered is also being delivered, dear," the woman called back from the front of the house.

The door smacked shut.

"Mama," a familiar male voice called, "where did you set those nails?"

Grace whipped around and nearly ran into the broad expanse of Ethan's chest. He leaned into the kitchen, still holding the doorframe. His eyes locked with hers and he smiled, standing up straight and tipping the edge of his hat.

"Miss Nolan," he said in a low voice that warmed her insides.

"Mr. Redbourne." She nodded at him, her heart full and fluttering. He looked good. She didn't want him to look good. Didn't want him to smile at her. She wanted to be mad. Wanted to know why he hadn't called on her. Why he'd been avoiding her.

"They're out on the chair at the front, son," Leah said with a smirk, pointing through the house.

Instead of walking back out the kitchen door and around the porch, he brushed past Grace and through the living area to the front door. He smelled good. Like lye soap and ginger. Though, she reckoned, that probably wouldn't last long once he started to sweat. Somehow, the thought of his strong form, doused with perspiration, provided a mental image that started a burning sensation in her belly and rose to her chest. She closed her eyes and exhaled long and slow.

"Ma'am?"

Grace opened her eyes to see a gruff looking man with a greying beard and thick eyebrows as he stepped into the kitchen.

"Miss Nolan?"

She stepped forward. "Hello," she smiled at him, "I'm Grace Nolan."

He cleared his throat, yanked on the front of his hat, and pulled it off, roughly shoving a hand through wavy white and grey streaked hair. "I've got several sheets of glass for replacing windows, if you would kindly show me all of them that are broke?"

Grace had to make a conscious effort not to let her jaw drop. Even the windows would be fixed today?

I must still be asleep, she thought, though decided against pinching herself to find out. If this was a dream, she didn't want to wake for a good long while. With a quick turn around the house she pointed out several areas where the glass needed to be replaced.

"I'll have to remove the frames on a couple of these windows in order to fit the glass. Will that be all right with you, ma'am?"

Grace nodded.

She'd ordered shutters for both the front and back, a large quantity of wood for reconstructing some of the outbuildings—the barn, a water shed, and the smokehouse— and glass that she'd been told would take weeks to get. Yet, here it all was. Everything she had purchased.

"I can't believe you did all this," Grace said, ducking back into the kitchen and capturing Leah by the arm.

Mrs. Redbourne stopped and looked Grace square in the face. "*I* didn't."

Grace scrunched her brows together, then followed the direction to where Leah looked out the large bay window.

Ethan stood out near the barn with planks of wood on his shoulder pointing and giving orders to the men.

Ethan.

Leah nodded and returned to her task at hand—scooping a large wooden spoonful of potato salad on each of the plates that had been set out on the table.

"Come on ladies," one of the women Grace hadn't met yet called as she thrust open the back door to the kitchen, her dark hair pulled back with a blue ribbon that matched her gingham dress. "Hurley Devlin just showed up with a team and they are going to compete with the Redbournes to see who can get their sides of the barn built first."

Leah wiped her hands on her apron, picked up her skirt, and rushed toward the door. Grace followed, as did the rest of the women still lingering in the kitchen. If what she'd seen between these two men last week was any indication of how the two men felt about each other, this just might end in disaster.

When Grace reached the end of the porch, she stopped herself from flying down the stairs by hooking her arm around the tall wooden column at the top of the railing.

Ethan, his brothers, and a few of the other men from town stood on one side facing Hurley and the group of men that she assumed had come with him.

"What are you doing here, Devlin?" Ethan asked, setting down the wooden plank he'd had on his shoulder.

"Heard Grace needed some help building her barn and finishing the repairs on the outside of the house. We came to lend a hand or two to the effort."

Ethan stood there, silent, his jaw flexing as he seemed to contemplate his rival's words. No one spoke. He glanced up at Grace, then back at Hurley.

"The goal is to get this thing built before the sun sets." Ethan tossed something to Hurley. "I guess we could use all the help we can get."

An audible wave of relieved sighs travelled down the porch from the women who had watched with guarded apprehension.

Ethan tipped his hat at Grace and quickly turned back to his work, bending over to retrieve the plank he'd set down. Extending from each side of the barn was a network of boards that had already been nailed together and stacks of wood had been piled at each corner.

"Let's make a race of it," Tag yelled out from his corner of the barn.

A dozen or so shouts of agreement followed from both sides of the invisible line between the groups. Ethan stood up and glanced over at Hurley who nodded back.

"Mama," Ethan said heartily, "seems we're going to make a game of it. Would you do the honors?"

Leah bent over and lifted the hem of her skirt over her boot and pulled a small gun from the strap. She stepped down to the bottom of the stairs and looked from Ethan to Hurley.

"Now, let's keep it clean, gentlemen. No fighting, cheating, or belly aching. Do we have an understanding?"

Both men nodded.

"Now, shake."

Ethan looked at his mother, a look of incredulity lining his features.

"Shake," Leah said again.

Both men reached out a hand and gripped the others. It looked as if they might break each other's hand.

Leah lifted her little pistol into the air, and with a glance heavenward, pulled the trigger.

Men scattered and the sound of hammers pounding against metal filled the courtyard. In a matter of minutes, some of them had already begun to lift the sides. The large building had already begun to take shape.

Grace was awed at how quickly it all seemed to be coming together. This new building was set up just behind the existing barn, which she imagined would have to be torn down, but that would be an adventure for another day. She scanned the work area for the man who'd arranged for all of this and found him, up in what was to be the rafters, hammering some sort of steel brackets to the corners of what would become the roof.

He'd done all of this. For her.

From his location, perched in the frame of the rafters,

Ethan could see the position of every man and woman outside the house. He was surprised to see that Hurley and the strangers he'd come with were actually making a lot of headway on their side of the barn.

"Here, take this," Ethan heard a man say from below.

Ethan looked down to find two of Devlin's men sneaking around the far side of the house toward the cellar with a shovel.

What are they up to?

He had finished securing the steel brackets he had created for the barn and decided he was going to find out. He looked about, but his ladder was no longer leaning up against the main beam. He scanned the interior for any of the other ladders, but it seemed that all of them had been moved.

Ethan placed the hammer in his back pocket and grabbed a hold of the roof joint to pull himself around to the outside ledge.

"Raine," he called to his brother, who was pulling another plank off the pile, "a ladder?"

His oldest brother handed the wood to Cole and Will, who immediately set it up against the framed wall and lined it up with the others below it. It didn't take long before they had the plank nailed in place and Cole was heading for another.

"Lose something?" Raine asked, concern etched on his brow. Ethan thought he'd laugh it off, but as he set one of the make-shift ladders up against the building, he scanned the mob working on the barn.

Ethan quickly climbed down.

"Did you see those men disappear around the side of the house?" Raine asked.

Ethan nodded. "I don't trust them. Hell, I don't even trust Hurley. He's up to something and I want to know what it is."

"Why do you suppose two men, strangers to the area, would be helping to build a barn and then sneak around the back of this house with shovels?" Ethan asked. A part of him was feeling a little facetious, but another hoped Raine, the deputy, would have a good answer.

He thought about Jack's treasure. Certainly, they couldn't believe there was treasure buried in the Nolan's backyard.

"Let's go find out," Raine said.

It was as good an answer as any.

Ethan glanced over the construction and when he saw Hurley busily hammering a plank into place, he hesitated. He did not want Devlin to win this contest—especially because it was for Grace—but the nagging feeling that something was amiss would not relent.

He nodded agreement. "Let's go."

"Ethan?" Mr. Diggle from the telegraph office stepped in front of Ethan before he could follow the men. "I have this telegram for Miss Nolan." He held out a folded yellow slip of paper. "Only I cannot seem to locate the woman."

Telegram?

Ethan held out his hand. "I can see that it gets delivered."

"Would you? I'd be much obliged. Thank you." He handed Ethan the message and quickly turned for the little black buggy parked right in front of the house.

Ethan unfolded the telegram and scanned the brief contents. It was from a Mr. Lee Coldhern. From New York.

Delinquent taxes on Nolan Place?

"Ethan!" Raine pulled him from his thoughts, tugging on the shoulder of his jacket. "We're going to lose them."

Ethan hastily shoved the note into his back pocket and ran to catch up with his brother.

As the two of them approached the back corner of the house, Raine stuck his arm out to block Ethan from moving any farther. Low voices, in mumbled conversation, carried on the light breeze.

Something distracted them and they turned to greet a third to their group. As the larger man of them stepped sideways, Ethan could see Jack clearly speaking excitedly with them.

"What is Jack doing there?" Raine whispered.

"My guess is looking for treasure." Ethan shook his head and stood up to walk away, but Raine caught him on the arm.

"I don't like that the kid is hanging out with Hurley's brutes. Maybe you should warn Miss Nolan."

Ethan had tried to keep their beautiful neighbor out of his thoughts. Rafe had warned him against getting too close too fast, but when he was with her, he didn't want to be anywhere else. He would face her, but he still needed a little more time to think about what he was going to say.

"Jack," he called as if he was just approaching. When he rounded the corner, Jack was already there, but the two men had vanished.

"Just grabbing some...uh," he looked around for something.

"Come on, kid. We need your help or those other fellas are going to win. We can't let that happen, now can we?" He patted Jack firmly on the top of his shoulder and guided him back to the group.

"No, sir."

Odd. He'd called him sir.

"Would you like some help finishing up your side of the roof, Devlin?" Ethan crooned, his arms folded over his puffed chest in satisfaction.

Grace heard the low, throaty growl that came from Hurley. He did not look down at Ethan from his position on the top of the newly constructed barn, but continued to nail the shingles in place. It seemed like before she had time to blink, Ethan and Will were up next to Hurley and one of his friends while Cole, Taggert, and Raine walked the perimeter of the barn, cleaning up scraps and leftover supplies.

She and some of the women folk had hung lanterns throughout the house, put fresh linens on both of the newly formed mattresses in the bedrooms, and had wiped down the walls, swept the floors, and shaken the rugs. Grace had believed she'd accomplished a lot in the last week, but with so many hands to help, the house looked almost new. Almost.

After they had piled up all of the thick dust-laden cloths that had covered most of the old furniture, paintings, and random tools to be burned, Grace had stepped out onto the porch for some fresh air. She had been told to wait for a week or so before attempting to open some of the windows that had just been replaced.

"Can you believe we got it all done in one day?" Jack asked excitedly as he joined her on the porch. "And the sun's still up," he said with pride.

The awe in her little brother's voice brought a smile to Grace's lips. She too was awed by their accomplishment and the man who'd made it all a reality. Her eyes were once again drawn to Ethan. She quickly attempted to push aside the memory of his mouth against hers, but was finding the task more difficult than she'd expected as she watched him climb down from the barn roof.

Instead, she focused on a small group of three or four men who had gathered around the old barn. A couple of mountainous-sized horses stood several yards away from the dilapidated old building. One man fastened ropes to a harness-like contraption that had been secured to the horses, the ends of which had large iron hooks attached.

Ethan strode over to the horses and rubbed each one in turn on the shoulder and neck. Jameson joined them and picked up a sledge hammer that had been resting against a log and with one strong blow had broken a hole in the wood near the corner of the building. One of the other men handed him the hooked end of the rope, and he secured it around something inside the hole.

Grace had a hard time seeing what they were doing.

"Amazing what my boys can do, isn't it?"

Grace turned to see Leah, who came to stand just behind her.

"What *are* they doing?"

"They're pulling down the old barn."

"Tonight?" Grace felt like a month's worth of work had been completed already. She continued to be amazed at the fortitude of the people of this town.

"It's pretty dangerous to leave it standing—especially if you're planning on bringing animals on over."

As she thought of all the women and watched the many men who had worked so hard on her behalf, she was overwhelmed with gratitude and realized that she had been foolhardy to think that they could have made it through the winter without the changes, upgrades, and repairs.

"How can I ever repay you for all of this?" Her emotions were so close to the surface, she had to fight to keep them in check.

"Oh, honey," Leah said as she wrapped an arm around Grace's shoulders, "this life is short. We don't repay kindness, we pass it along."

Grace put her arm around Leah's waist and leaned her head against the woman's shoulder.

"Thank you," she whispered.

"Hi-ya!"

Grace stood upright and watched as the large team of horses started to slowly move forward. The barn creaked against the strain. Ethan stood near the horses and encouraged them to keep plodding steadily forward.

The wreath.

"Wait," Grace yelled as she skittered down the short staircase toward the barn. It wasn't much, but she'd wanted to clean it up and give it to Leah for her kindness. She had to save it.

The whole building started to lean toward her, and instantly she knew she'd made a stupid decision. She willed her feet to move faster, but it felt like she had lead weighing down her shoes.

Without warning, someone slammed into her, uprooting her from the ground and knocking all air from her lungs. She fell to the ground, a great weight on top of her. In an instant she hurt everywhere. Her chest ached. She couldn't breathe.

Crash! The walls of the barn clattered to the ground with a giant thump. kicking up dirt all around it. Still, she gasped for air.

"Miss Nolan," Ethan lifted his body off of hers and turned to loom over her. "Miss Nolan," he called again, this time more urgently than the first.

She couldn't answer him.

He took ahold of her shoulders and leaned down close to her face. "Grace. Breathe, damn it!" he demanded quietly.

Air filled her lungs and she gasped as relief flooded her chest. Ethan rolled away from her and she sat up, trying to take in another gulp of air. Ethan sat with his arms resting on his knees, head bent, and jaw pulsing. He exhaled slowly.

"I'm okay," she told the small crowd that had now gathered around her—though her body defied her every word. She lay back down. "Ouch."

CHAPTER ELEVEN

Ethan's heart pounded fiercely in his chest. Fool woman. What had she been thinking running out into the yard like that when the barn was about to fall?

She's okay, he told himself as he closed his eyes.

"Ouch," Grace said in such a way that a trickle of laughter bubbled up from somewhere inside of him. He bit it back. He should be angry. And she should be scared, not full of humor. Did she have no idea what a collapsed building would have done to her small frame?

"You all right?" Tag asked, his hand extended.

"Fine," Ethan said, brushing the dust off his clothes once he was standing upright.

"You are a marvel tonight, little brother. How in the world did you get over to her so fast?" Raine asked as he joined them.

"The Lord only knows," Ethan replied, glancing over to where Grace was also now on her feet.

She caught his eyes with hers. "Thank you," she mouthed to him as Leah, Hannah, and Mrs. Day all escorted her toward the house.

"You're quite the hero, Redbourne." The disdain was overly dramatic and dripping from Hurley's words.

Ethan had thought for a brief moment that, just maybe,

they would be able to put their past behind them. He shot Devlin a look that he hoped would quell the man's desire to continue any conversation.

"Let's get this mess all cleaned up and we can go home."

"I'm afraid we have other matters to attend to, but I am sure the biggest toad in the puddle will be able to finish up right fine." He strutted toward the house. "I'm just going in to say goodbye to Grace." He raised his eyebrows and licked his lips. "Think she tastes as sweet as Victoria?"

Crack!

With one short stride, Ethan's fist connected with Hurley's jaw, sending him sprawling backward to the ground.

"Finally!" Will shouted, fists up and ready to fight as he turned to face Hurley's men, who all stood still as if awaiting instructions.

Damn, that felt good. It had been a long time coming.

"Have a little respect for the lady, Devlin."

Hurley shot to his feet, but before he could pull his apple peeler from his boot, Raine had drawn his gun.

"We'll have none of that here tonight," he said, leaving no room for argument.

Hurley dabbed a finger at the small trickle of blood that lined the corner of his mouth. "Give *the lady* my respects," he said to Raine, then motioned for his friends to follow.

"Thanks, Raine, but I was ready for him."

"Are you as addlepated as you sound?" Raine holstered his gun, but took a menacing step toward Ethan.

"He had it coming."

Raine relaxed his stance some. "Yes…" he paused. "Yes, he did. Just don't go getting yourself killed. After all the hard work Rafe put into fixing up that shoulder of yours, he'd kill me for sure."

"If Mama didn't beat him to it," Cole piped in.

Ethan retrieved an ax from the pile of things they pulled from the barn before toppling it. He figured they could chop most of it up and Grace and Jack would be able to use it through the winter.

"Let's get to work."

Luckily, several of the menfolk from town and the surrounding farms had stuck around to help out. Ethan was proud to call Stone Creek home. He'd heard stories from Rafe and Raine, who'd both lived in other places, about some towns where the people didn't care about each other and refused to pull together when times required it. Ethan wanted to show these men, mostly farmers, just how grateful he was that they'd been willing to give up an entire day to help.

As they were pulling the last of the wood from the pile, Ethan stumbled over something lodged in the dirt.

"What in tarnation?" He reached down with his gloved hand and found what looked like the edge to a wooden doorframe. He followed the edges, usurping dirt and clay by the handfuls until he'd uncovered the entire perimeter of what looked like a door leading into the ground.

It wasn't uncommon for people to build cellars or underground rooms, but he'd never seen anything quite like this. He brushed off a few inches of dirt from the top, revealing a circular iron handle. He wrapped his fingers around the metal piece and tugged. The door opened, but was filled to the brim with a mixture of dried mud and hay. If there was something in there, it looked like it had been filled in a long time ago. Still, he couldn't very well risk being wrong and having Grace or Jack or one of the animals fall into an unstable hole in the ground.

"Charcoal," he used the family's nickname for his only little brother as he called him over.

"You find something?" Cole asked.

"Do you remember when you and Alaric found that old mine shaft over by the Cooper's place?" Cole and his best friend had been exploring a few years back and uncovered an abandoned mine shaft that had appeared to be caved in.

"How did you guys get in?"

"Like this." Cole lifted his foot as if he was going to stomp his way into the opening, but Ethan stopped him.

"We have no idea how long this has been blocked off and I would hate for you to break a leg right before sledding season," he said with a wry grin.

"Good point. Hold on," Cole held up a finger before disappearing into the new barn. When he returned, he had a sledge hammer in his hands.

Ethan nodded as he took the tool from his brother. He swung and hit the caked dirt with blunt force. The edge of the doorframe popped up higher through the dirt, sitting awkwardly against the ground. It looked as if it could be pried loose. He handed the hammer back to Cole and gripped the corner that had risen out of the ground. He pulled.

Nothing.

"Hit it again," Cole suggested, handing the sledgehammer back to Ethan.

"What you are doing?" Jack asked, peeking over Cole's shoulder at their find.

Ethan hit the bottom corner, hoping to pop up the protruding side even farther.

It worked.

A crack in the mud also revealed the metal corner of something akin to a metal lockbox of some sort. Ethan stood on the far end of the door and gripped the edge one more time. He pulled as hard as he could, his muscles straining tightly against his shirt. Finally, it gave way, and what had appeared to be a doorway, was in actuality a hidden compartment.

"Whoa," Jack exclaimed, now kneeling next to the box with keen interest. "What's this?" he asked eagerly, pointing to the metal piece that extended from the dirt.

It took a little coaxing, but soon the small metal box was freed from its hole.

"It looks like a safe box—you know, the kind that people

used to keep their valuables in." Ethan said as he rotated the case, studying the hinges and lock. It had a large dent in one side. He guessed that he'd done that when he hit the dirt with the sledgehammer.

"How do we open it?"

"I'm no locksmith, but I think we can still get into it," Ethan said. He turned to Jack. "Go get your sister. She should be here when we get it open."

Jack nodded and scampered away into the house.

Ethan looked around, satisfied that none of the other neighbors seemed to care about the box he'd just unearthed. He doubted that Grace would want it to be opened out here with everyone watching, so he tucked it up under his arm. With so little left to do, and the sun just beginning to dip beneath the horizon, he thought it was time the townsfolk all got home to be with their families. He removed his gloves and with a firm handshake, he thanked each one of the men personally for coming and participating.

It wasn't long before the last of the wagons had disappeared over the hill. Ethan grabbed some basic tools from his kit and headed toward the front steps. His family had lingered, curious to see what this mysterious box kept hidden inside its confines.

Grace and Jack sat on the top step watching, waiting.

Ethan studied the box for a few moments. He determined that the lock side would be harder to open. He thought it best to attempt to remove the plates along the back. With a screwdriver and a hammer, he set the box down on the porch step and fixed the long, metal shaft of the flathead against the hinge and tapped it slightly with the hammer. It didn't give way immediately like he'd thought it would. However, the screws shifted, loosening the space between metals.

He wedged the screwdriver down in between the steel box and rounded iron plates and tapped it with the hammer on the side instead of the top, driving the small hinge farther away from the edge of the container. With a few more well-placed hits, the first piece fell away and Ethan immediately moved to the second. Within a few minutes, the box was ready to open.

He picked it up and set it on Grace's lap.

She looked up at him, and he could see the trepidation in her eyes. There was no way of knowing what was inside, although the container wasn't overly heavy, so Ethan didn't think there was a mound of gold coins waiting to be found.

Grace took a moment, fingering the cool metal in small patterns.

"Come on, Gracie. Open it!" Jack wailed with scarcely concealed excitement.

She set the box on its side and with both hands attempted to pry the box open. It didn't budge. She giggled nervously and tried again. Still, the box would not open. Ethan handed her the screwdriver and the hammer.

"Thank you." She set the tip of the screwdriver into the crease and gently tapped the top with the hammer and it immediately cracked open. She handed the tools back to Ethan and pulled the sides open as far as she could. With the lock still intact on the other side, the opening was still fairly small.

"Allow me?" Ethan asked, sitting on the step just below Grace.

She nodded.

Ethan donned his gloves and slid his fingers inside the box and pulled the sides in opposite directions. The lock busted free and the container laid open for all to see. Leah held up her lantern, lighting a deep green velvet cloth that seemed to wrap around the contents of the box.

Grace moved down across from Ethan, reached in, and ran her hand over the soft material that had been protected, for who knew how long, in its sealed home. She pulled back one side of the cloth and then the other. A black pouch sat atop a worn old book. It looked like some sort of diary or journal.

"Well, what is it?" Jack asked, his impatience becoming more apparent in his voice.

Grace picked up the pouch first and with a deep breath emptied the contents into her hand. An intricate golden key with a large fanciful top that resembled a key all on its own, and two long, slender green gems of different shapes spilled onto her palm.

"See! I knew it," Jack shouted. "The treasure is real!"

"Are those diamonds? Emeralds? Rubies?" Will asked, nudging his way in for a closer look, but effectively blocking the lantern's light.

"Sorry," he said after Ethan shot him a look of warning.

"Dad?" Ethan looked up at his father, a distant expression on his face. "Are these emeralds?" He looked at Grace, silently asking her permission to take one. She nodded and Ethan picked up the cylindrical shaped gem from her palm and handed it to Jameson.

It certainly wasn't impossible. After all, some of the Redbourne fortune had come from the precious gems that had been discovered in his grandfather's mines. However, that was a secret that the Redbournes didn't want to let get out. Granddaddy Redbourne had been very specific about who would be privy to that information. He'd always said that people got crazy when it came to money. And he was right.

Jameson lifted the cut and polished jewel into the light of the lantern. "It's hard to tell in this light, but it looks genuine to me."

Grace's eyes grew wide and she looked back down at the other gems in her hand. Quickly, she opened the pouch and returned the contents to its protective casing and pulled tight on the strings. She set the bag back into the metal container and pulled out the book. Carefully, she opened the cover and gently flipped page by page.

Tears welled up in her eyes as she read some of the passages.

"It's our grandfather's journal," she said quietly.

"Why would Grandpa Nolan lock up his journal with a couple of emeralds?" Jack reached for the book, but Grace closed it and placed both hands over the top.

She wiped away the lone tear that had found its way down her cheek. "What a treasure you've found for us, Mr. Redbourne," Grace said as she looked once again over at Ethan. "I don't know what else to say, but thank you."

Ethan didn't know what to say either, but there was something holding her back. Something that scared her. What was in that journal?

Grace pulled the green cloth and pouch from the metal box and hugged them close to her as she stood up.

"You have to believe me now, Gracie," Jack exclaimed, holding her with both hands by the arms. "When can we start looking for the treasure?"

She looked her brother in the face. It took a minute before she spoke. "There is no treasure, Jack." She shook her head. "Grandfather wasted his life and means looking for something that just isn't there."

"But Gracie, you saw it. Proof. Right there in your hand."

"Proof that Granddad was a fool," she spat.

This was the first time Ethan had ever seen Grace so...so bitter. Angry.

"If these were real, do you think our family would have ever left Stone Creek and moved to New York? Do you think we would have had to work so hard to live? To survive? Do you really believe that wasting your life looking for treasure will make you happy?" She stood up and started for the door, but turned back around. "It won't. And the sooner you learn that, the better."

Jack ran up the stairs, into the house, and slammed the front door.

"Excuse me," Grace said with a visibly forced smile. "It has been a lovely day and I can't tell you all how appreciative I am of everything you've done here today. If you don't mind, I think I am going to turn in now."

"Of course, my dear," Leah said with a brief hug around Grace's shoulders. "Repairs are done on the house, so as long as you'll promise to lock those doors when we leave, you won't have to put up with my boys on your couches anymore."

Ethan hadn't really thought about that. He should be happy that he'd finally be able to work out in the smithy on his own projects and finish up some of his overdue client orders, but something akin to disappointment settled in his gut.

"I promise," Grace said softly. She glanced over at Ethan, then to all of his brothers. "Thank you all. Now, if you'll excuse me, I guess I should go talk to my brother." She opened the door to the house, but turned back as if in afterthought. "Mr. Redbourne?"

Jameson, Will, Tag, Cole, Raine, and Ethan all turned back to look at her.

Leah and Hannah both laughed out loud, and Grace smiled.

"Thank you."

Grace closed the door and leaned up against it, the book, pouch, and cloth still clutched in her arms against her chest. Maybe they should have never come here. She glanced at the staircase, then closed her eyes.

Give me strength.

Jack could never know the contents of that journal. If he had any idea that her grandfather had written every clue, dead end, and possibility in its pages, she would lose him for sure. She couldn't let him throw away his life like Horace Nolan had.

Grace closed her eyes and allowed a few fat tears to escape down her face. She wanted answers to the questions she'd posed. With these two very large precious stones alone, their grandfather could have seen to it that his family had lived comfortably. Instead, his only daughter had worked herself into the grave and his grandchildren had become all but indentured servants.

She could not be bitter. Would not allow it to bring her down. It was what it was and there was no use dwelling on what could have been. At least they would have something to fall back on if the money ran out before they could make a go of the farm.

Opening her eyes, she glanced at the staircase again, assuring herself that Jack could not see her, and she proceeded to the stone in the wall where she had hidden their money. It gave way a little more easily this time. She eased the stone from its position and set it on the floor, careful not to make much noise.

Chimes.

Grace stood up straight. There were definitely chimes coming from somewhere in her house. She walked a few steps over to the old grandfather clock, but it still sat with its hands set at seven minutes past three. Same as before.

With another quick glance at the journal and the small bag holding the gems, Grace placed the pouch in the hole next to her funds, but the book simply would not fit—no matter how she tried. Finally, she replaced the stone cover and with the book held to her chest, walked over to the chaise and sat down, pulled her feet up onto the end, and lay back against the decorative pillows.

Where could she hide it?

Then, the idea hit her and she bolted upright.

I know just the place.

CHAPTER TWELVE

Snow fluttered playfully to the ground. Ethan sat in the window seat of his shop watching it fall. The light flurries brought a smile to his lips as he thought about spending time with his family finding the perfect tree to bring home and decorate for Christmas.

He'd spotted several wonderful trees at the edge of their property on the way into town just over the bridge, and the pines growing in the copse separating Redbourne Ranch from the Nolan place had some definite possibilities.

"Ethan, are you ready?" Hannah giggled as she opened the door to the smithy.

He stood up and pulled off his thick apron and hung it on the rack where his scarf, hat, and coat all sat on their respective hangers. Glancing over at his cooling pad, he smiled. He'd almost finished his Christmas projects.

"It's snowing," she exclaimed, twirling about in front of his door, allowing the flakes to land on her face. "Isn't it wonderful?"

Ethan thrust his arms through his coat, donned his hat, and hung his scarf undone from his neck. He shut the smithy door and wrapped his arm around his little sister's neck and pulled her, giggling, alongside him.

"Stop." She said with a snort of laughter as he lifted her off the ground and over his shoulder. It was much easier to do when she was wearing riding britches.

The Redbournes had been blessed. While winters were often harsh, Mama and Dad had always worked throughout the year to store up enough food, warm clothing, and other supplies to keep them safe and happy. They'd also made sure that their children knew the importance of helping those who were less fortunate—especially during the holidays and through the winter months.

Ethan let go of Hannah and she ran over to her horse, untied him from the front hitching post, and climbed up.

"Before long, we're going to have to switch out the wagon wheels for your metal brackets," his father said, looking up at the snow riddled sky. He tossed a couple of tarpaulin sheets onto the back of the wagon along with an axe, a saw, and some rope.

Ethan was sure the whole town thought he was a little cracked, but if he had to continue to be only a blacksmith, he wanted to use his skills to make life better and easier for his family. Creating sleigh tracks and adapters for the wagons was just one of the ways he could do that. They were one of his favorite inventions.

"Why are there two wagons hitched? Aren't we just going to ride the horses like usual?" Ethan asked.

His brothers all pulled up on their horses. All except Raine. Ethan had wondered if Raine would join them this year. Christmas had been hard on his oldest brother over the last few years. Ever since his wife, Sarah, had died. He'd been a mess that first year, but had seemed to cope with his loss extremely well over the last few years—except during the first couple of weeks of December.

Ethan started for the barn. Storm had been itching to go for a ride and he was sure the horse would appreciate the opportunity to stretch his legs. Ethan had let him out to run and graze in what was left of the fields every day, but it wasn't the same.

"Oh, Ethan, honey," his mother called out to him as she pulled her woolen mittens over her hands. "Would you mind driving the other wagon? We need to stop by and pick up the Nolans."

The Nolans?

He'd been so busy catching up with his commitments and trying to complete his own work that he hadn't seen or spoken to Grace since they'd had the barn-raising. Cole and Will had taken over the horses she and Jack had selected from their herd, and Raine had been out to check on them a few times—being the deputy and all.

Ethan felt like a coward. But, hopefully he'd be able to make it up to her soon enough. Thoughts of her parting lips—warm, moist, inviting—had haunted him since that day, right after Thanksgiving, when he'd been so bold as to sample the taste of her sweet kiss. Truth was, he'd ridden out to her place more than once over the last week, but he hadn't been able to bring himself to confront her.

"Ethan?" Leah called loudly.

He cleared his throat.

"Yes, ma'am. I'd be happy to."

The nicker of an approaching horse turned everyone's attention to Raine, who sat astride one of the new Quarter horses.

"Glad to have you join us, son," their father said as he pulled himself up onto the first wagon next to their mother.

When Ethan climbed up into the second wagon, he smiled to see his mother's favorite denim quilt in the space beneath the seat. He shook his head with a laugh. My mother—the matchmaker. He gathered the reins and with a quick snap, they were on their way. It had been a long time since he had looked forward to seeing a woman, but he enjoyed Miss Nolan's easy company and ready smile.

Ethan had only seen a glimpse of the challenges that she had faced in her life, but found that he desired to know more about the woman who'd travelled across country just before winter to start a new life with her kid brother. Grace had such hope and an innocent belief that everything would be all right.

He would make sure it did.

Grace stood by the window, pulling aside the curtains every few seconds watching for the Redbourne wagons to appear over the peak of the hillside.

"Why are you so nervous?" Jack asked, lounging on the couch, shoving a piece of peppered jerky into his mouth. "They'll be here soon enough."

Ever since she'd spoken to him about their grandfather and the reasons she didn't want him searching for that old treasure, he'd seemed to have lost his excitement for everything—including Christmas.

"Jack, don't you remember the huge trees we had at the Coldhern's every year at this time?" she said with awe in her voice. "The silver bells and blue ribbons? The peanut brittle and honey cakes?"

"Yeah, and I remember washing hundreds of extra dishes and linens, and all the parties we were never invited to. No thanks."

"The Redbournes have been very kind to request that we come along." Grace moved to sit next to him on the couch. "Hannah was quite insistent that you be there. She sure is a pretty girl, isn't she?"

Jack sat up a little taller against the back cushions of the couch. Grace suspected a smile hid just beneath the surface of her brother's semi-indifferent façade.

"Can I at least pick it out?"

She patted him on the knee. "Of course, Jack. It'll be the

first tree all our own."

Movement caught her attention out the window. Two wagons were making their decent upon Nolan Place. She liked the sound of that. Nolan Place. It was home. Finally.

Jack grabbed his coat and gloves and headed out to the back yard to collect his horse. Hound had already been saddled and was ready to go. Her brother was seeming more confident astride the gelding every day.

The moment Grace caught sight of Ethan, her heart skipped a beat. His eyes were shadowed by his hat, but he smiled. His brown leather coat, with the wool lining, was open at the neck, exposing his red plaited shirt. He lifted a hand and tapped his hat in greeting. When he pulled up next to the stairs, he jumped down off the wagon and held out his hand for her.

"Are you ready to find the perfect tree for Christmas, Miss Nolan?"

He certainly seemed to be in good spirits today.

As Grace descended the stairs, her foot caught on one of the boards and she pitched forward into Ethan's arms.

Jack's loud laughter barely registered above the sound of her heart pounding wildly in her ears. When it was joined with Ethan's deep baritone, she looked up at him.

"I hadn't meant for you to jump," he said with a raised brow, "but I'll take it." He lifted her up and set her in the front seat, then hopped up after her.

"I don't know what it is when I am with you, Mr. Redbourne, but I seem to be quite clumsy."

"Really? I hadn't noticed." He looked forward, but Grace didn't miss the smirk that played with the corners of his mouth.

She sat back against the seat with a smile of her own.

When they passed by the thicket that divided her property from the Redbournes, she glanced over at Ethan. She'd thought they would just collect one of the pines trees growing there and they would be done, but apparently, they had other plans.

Snow fell all around them, but Grace wasn't cold for now. She looked down at her long strands of hair cascading from her shoulders. Light flakes accented her brown waves like little glittering crystals. Rays of sunlight filtered through small breaks in an otherwise cloud covered sky.

"I think we'll just head up the ridge beyond the river there." Ethan pointed to a thickly wooded area just beyond the bridge ahead.

New York had plenty of snow, but the landscape didn't look like this. A light breeze swirled around her and she huddled a little closer to Ethan. She was surprised when he moved the reins into one hand, wrapped his arm around her, and pulled her close into the warmth of his body.

"Better?" he asked without looking down at her.

"Much," she replied.

In a clearing not too far from the road, the others had come to a stop and dismounted.

"Do you own all of this land?" she asked without thinking. She'd been taught from a very young age that it was presumptuous and not polite to ask about a person's financial holdings. "Excuse me. I didn't mean to pry."

"There's nothing to excuse yourself for. We've been very blessed." Ethan said with an air of gratitude. "My dad bought land from a lot of settlers who'd given up on the westward dream. He gave them a fair price on their property, but when all was said and done, we owned most of the land for miles in every direction."

"And ours? Why didn't your dad buy our land?"

"From what I've been told, your granddaddy didn't want to sell, but he needed to be able to feed his family. Since there wasn't a mortgage on the house and he owned the property outright, he simply closed up shop."

Thunk.

Shards of lightly packed snow splattered against Ethan's chest, sending powdery ice crystals into Grace's face, down her neck, and into the top of her dress.

Laughter filled the small gulley.

Ethan stopped the wagon, jumped down, and had a snowball in his hand before Grace had even realized what had happened. Balls of snow flew in every direction. She ducked low as she climbed down off the seat. The onslaught didn't last very long as the snow was hardly thick enough to pack.

Ethan held his hands up in the air.

"Truce," he yelled. He looked down at her and jerked his head sideways.

Grace raised her hands as well and stood up next to him.

Jameson's laugh was loud and rich. "Come on. Let's find us a tree," he called to everyone.

As she lowered her arms, Ethan reached out, fitting her gloved hand into his, and started to run. Her feet nearly slid out from beneath her on several occasions as they maneuvered the newly wet ground, so Grace gathered the material of her skirt with her free hand to keep up.

After a moment, Ethan slowed to a casual pace and they admired the different shapes, sizes, and colors of the multitude of pines. Grace inhaled deeply, the sweet and musty scent of the woods in wintertime imprinting on her memory. It was perfect.

"You realize you need to choose one, right?" Ethan said after a while.

"Actually, I told Jack he could have the honor of selecting our first ever Christmas tree."

"You've never had a Christmas tree before?"

"The Coldherns always had the most beautiful trees, adorned in blues and silvers, so, I guess we did have a tree. In a way."

"The Coldherns?"

"They were like family in many ways. We had lessons with them, played with them, but then we cleaned up after them, did their laundry, made their meals…"

"And?"

"And what?" She didn't want to talk about the Coldherns anymore. She hadn't thought about them, or Lee, practically since she'd arrived in Stone Creek.

"It sounded like there was something else you were going to say."

"Nothing. That was it. We worked for them. That's all."

"Come on, Ethan. Grace. We found it. The perfect tree." Hannah motioned for them to follow her.

The Redbournes all stood around a perfectly shaped pine, colored a deep rich green void of the overly blue tones of some of the trees. Grace hoped Jack would be able to find a tree just like it.

"Isn't it wonderful?" Jack asked, eyes wide, and a grin from ear to ear.

"Yes," she said. "It is a lovely tree. But I'm sure yours will be even better."

His smile drooped. "But, Gracie, this is the one I chose."

Grace squealed with excitement. "I was hoping you would say that. I think it is the most perfect tree I have ever seen." She threw her arms around her little brother, glad he was acting more like himself.

"But where is the Redbournes tree?" Grace asked with a new level of curiosity.

"Right over here," Ethan called.

Standing not ten yards away was a tree similar in color and shape, but stood a good foot or more taller than theirs.

In less than an hour, they had both trees cut, banded with a tarpaulin sheet and rope, and had them loaded into the wagons. Grace didn't want to leave. She wanted to soak in the memory of this little adventure. She stood in the center of the clearing, closed her eyes, and smelled the fresh woodsy air. The city definitely didn't smell like this.

"It's time to go," Ethan stood behind her and whispered in her ear, his hand resting lightly just above her hip. He completed her moment.

Grace wanted to melt into him. To feel his arms encircle her completely. Was the line of propriety the same in Kansas as it had been in the city? She'd been down this road before and wasn't sure she wanted to travel that path again.

She turned her head to look at Ethan and nodded toward the wagon.

"Let's go."

The Coldherns and the Redbournes both had money, but that was where their similarities ended. The Redbournes were a warm and loving family, who had accepted her and Jack without hesitation. So, why was she still comparing Ethan to Lee Coldhern? In her heart she knew Ethan was different, but her heart was having a hard time convincing her head. Money married money. It was as simple as that. And Ethan Redbourne had money.

She didn't.

CHAPTER THIRTEEN

"If you don't mind my asking, ma'am, why don't you want Jack looking for that treasure?" Ethan knew he was overstepping, but he also understood the kid's need to connect with something bigger than him. To have a little adventure in his life.

It took a long time for Grace to respond. She fidgeted with the yarn of his denim quilt covering their legs, and she shifted on the seat, but did not move away from him.

"I've heard stories about that treasure my whole life." Her voice was quiet, distant somehow. "It was all my grandfather ever talked about. He spent so much time focused on what he'd lost by moving to New York that he failed to see what he had right in front of him—a family who loved him, a warm home to live in, a life…worth living."

Ethan remained silent.

"When I was a little girl," a smile touched her face, "I used to sit on grandfather's knee and listen to countless tales of his adventures along with the other children. He even had this old pocket watch with a compass inside of it that he used to say would lead to the treasure if he could just figure out where to begin."

Ethan's brows crowded together. He'd seen a trinket just

like that recently.

"After grandfather passed away, it disappeared. Silly, isn't it?"

"What if I told you that Hurley Devlin has a watch just like that?" Ethan asked as they rounded the hill toward Redbourne Ranch.

"I would say that you two need to make peac—"

"Whoa," Jack called out anxiously as his horse stamped his feet and pranced about a good hundred feet ahead.

Ethan looked around to see what could be agitating the gelding. He smelled it before he saw it.

"Jack," he called in a low voice so as not to startle the skunk crossing the trail. "Try to back the horse up and let the varmint pass. You don't want to scare it now."

"Scare *it*? Come on, Hound," he said, distress evident in Jack's voice.

Without much warning, the gelding's front two legs came off the ground, sending Jack sprawling backward onto the ground, before bolting toward the north corral.

"Arggg," Jack bellowed.

The little skunk had sprayed him and then scampered off into the lightly dusted brush.

Grace gasped.

"What do I do?" Jack bellowed, his nose scrunched and plugged between his forefinger and thumb. "This is awful. I can taste it."

Ethan chuckled. "He's fine," he told Grace. "But unless my mama has some bottled tomato juice and one of her special lye mixtures made up, he may have to sleep out in your barn for the next few days."

"What is that smell?" Grace's nose scrunched up and her mouth moved into a disdainful pucker.

"You don't have skunks in New York?"

"Not that I've ever seen. Or smelled."

Ethan laughed loudly.

"I'm afraid you're gonna have to walk the rest of the way out to the ranch, kid" he called out to Jack as he took a wide swing off the road. "Luckily, it's not that far." Ethan pointed at the house.

Jack started to run, trying to catch up to the wagon, but Ethan wanted no part of that. The smell this far away was bad enough without having the culprit right in the back of the wagon. He slapped the reins.

Raine met them at the front of the house. "So, Hound is running in the north field. Any idea where his rider got off to?"

"Skunk," was all Ethan said.

Raine tsked. "Ack. Better go tell Mama so she can get the tomato bath ready."

Ethan nodded and started for the house.

"Mr. Redbourne?"

Ethan, he wanted so badly to correct her.

He turned around with raised brows, trying to keep the scowl from his face.

"I was wondering if I might borrow a book from your Dickens collection?"

"Of course." He pointed to the smithy. "You know where it is." And he headed in to prepare his mother for the disaster that was about to descend.

She took the news better than he had expected she would—especially after what happened with the twins last time.

"That poor thing. Not even a month here." Leah removed her mittens and set them on the table behind the door. "Go get the basin, would you, son?" She headed into the kitchen. "Oh, and Ethan? Don't forget to take that box for Miss Nolan when you leave."

Poor kid was right. He might lose a layer of skin, but when Leah Redbourne was finished with him, he would smell of leather and lye.

"Yes, ma'am."

When Ethan approached the smithy, he caught sight of

Grace through the window taking his Dickens book of his shelf. What he hadn't expected was for her to put another book on the shelf in its place. He opened the door and she whipped around like a startled rabbit.

"Sorry," he said as he pulled the large metal tub down off the top shelf against the wall. "You found the book okay?"

She placed a hand over her heart and held it up. "Thank you. Nothing like '*A Christmas Carol*' to get you into the holiday spirit."

"Mama said she has a jug of apple cider for you to take home. And she's got a box full of cranberries, ornaments, and ribbons for your tree."

Grace smiled. "What's that for?" she asked, pointing to the tub.

"Your brother."

"Oh." It took a minute. "Ohhhhhh."

It was only another few minutes before Jack tromped into the yard. Leah and Lottie, both with wooden clothespins pinching their noses together, met him at the gate before he could get to the house.

Ethan didn't miss the exchange between Grace and her brother—as if she was apologizing for his predicament. She held her nose closed with her thumb and base of her forefinger and shook her head.

His mother motioned for Lottie to continue to the back, and pulled the pin from her nose. "Get this gal on home, son," Leah said. She turned to Grace. "And don't you worry about your little brother. He'll be right as rain soon enough, and then I'll send him on home to help you decorate that tree of yours. No use waiting around here."

"Shall we?" Ethan said with a sweeping motion toward the wagon.

"It's been a long time since we've had someone taking care of *us*," Grace said. "Thank you."

The ride back to the Nolan's place was quiet. Ethan could

not stop thinking about Hurley's watch. As much as he hated to admit it, what if there was some truth to the old legends?

When he pulled up in front of the house, he jumped down and reached up for Grace. The action had become natural, comfortable. He placed his hands about her waist and lifted her down easily.

She met his eyes briefly, then looked away. "I think it will look lovely in the living area across from the fireplace." She walked to the back of the wagon, the back already unlatched, and slid the box from his mother until she could get a good hold on it.

"You got it?" he asked, just a hint of skepticism in his tone.

She narrowed her eyes at him and proceeded to carry the box up the stairs and into the house.

Ethan pulled the wrapped tree from the wagon bed and hoisted it over his shoulder. For its size, it was fairly light and with the sheet tied around the boughs, it was easy to get through the open doorway.

Once the bindings were removed, the tree bounced back to its full, exquisite shape, prompting Grace to clap her hands and giggle with excitement. Her hair fell over one side of her face and when she turned to look at him, her smile faded into a soft curve of her mouth. Her beautiful, supple mouth.

"So, what did my mother put in there?" he asked, forcing himself to look away.

Grace removed her coat and gloves and placed them on the table next to the box. She shook her shoulders back and forth in a little shimmy. "Brrrrr," she sounded, rubbing her hands together before delving into the carton. "You said apple cider, right?" Grace replied as she pulled the glass jug from the box and held it up for him to see.

"The best, I might add."

"Hard to beat my grandmother's recipe." She eyed him with speculation. "I can't wait to try it."

Grace pulled out a canvas bag that, from the purplish color staining the bottom, contained the fresh sprigs of cranberries. A needle and thread and a bolt of cut burlap, fashioned into ribbon, were the next things to be drawn from the box. Subsequently, she pulled out several willow branches that had been molded and dried into balls.

"These are...beautiful."

Once everything was laid out on the table, the look of utter confusion on Grace's face told Ethan that she had no idea what to do with most of the items his mother had sent. In most cases, as he'd done in the past, he would tell his mother he didn't need a woman to make him happy, but in this case, it seemed one already had.

All right, Mother, he said as if she would be able to hear the thoughts in his mind. *I'm here. I'll help. And yes, I'm falling.* He hoped his feelings were not one-sided. She seemed to enjoy his company, but he needed to hear her say it.

"Well, I guess I'll leave you to it." He tugged lightly at the front of his hat and opened the front door.

"Mr. Redbourne?" Grace closed the space between them with just a few steps.

When she looked up at him, her green-flecked eyes wide and alluring, he groaned inwardly, unsure it was wise for them to be in her house. Alone. Together.

"Don't leave," she whispered.

"Why?"

She bit her bottom lip.

Stop.

"Honestly," she took a step backward, a wicked grin lighting her face, "I'm not tall enough to reach the top of the tree."

Ethan laughed. It had been a long time since he'd felt like laughing, yet since he'd met her, it seemed to happen a lot. He glanced at the pine, its fragrance now pleasantly filling the air, and then at the near empty box.

"Come on, shorty," Ethan said, stepping back into the house and shutting the door. He paused. "Right after I put the horses in the barn with some hay and water."

Grace clapped again.

When he returned, he removed his hat and placed it on the old rack next to the clock. His coat was next, but he simply laid it across the back of the couch. As he crossed the room toward the table, he rolled up the sleeves on his shirt.

"I'll just go heat some of this up on the stove." Grace picked up the jug of cider and disappeared into the kitchen.

Ethan strode out to the small lean-to where they had stacked the wood from the old barn and retrieved a few pieces. He thought he could get a fire going to take the chill off. He chided himself for not thinking of it sooner.

Within minutes, a roaring fire blazed in the fireplace. Ethan moved the half-full water bucket away from the heat and stood there a moment to warm his hands before heading back over to the table.

He proceeded to select a few items from the table—two pinecones, cranberries, some ribbon and one of the ornamental balls he and his brothers had fashioned out of willow branches earlier in the year. He'd done it many times throughout the years, around the Redbourne table as they'd prepared the holiday decorations.

Ethan shoved a sprig of cranberries into one of the willow balls and secured it with some ribbon. Just yesterday they had finished all of the decorations for the ranch. He was all too familiar with what needed to be done. He just wished that he had thought to bring some of his copper sleigh bells. They would have made a nice addition to her tree.

Leah and Jameson Redbourne had always taught their children how to do all the tasks required on the ranch. The boys had all learned how to cook, wash dishes, and darn socks, while Hannah had learned how to wrangle horses, mend fences, and muck out stalls.

Every year his family would string the cranberry garlands with popped corn, tie cinnamon sticks and dried orange slices with tiny red ribbons to pinecones, and gather a bunch of interesting looking twigs to give variety to the tree. One of his favorites was when his mother would string a small wreath of pinecones together and fill a glass jar with water to place in the middle with cranberries floating on top. The centerpieces had always turned out beautifully and added so much to the ambiance of the season. She truly had an eye for designing beautiful things and for making their house into a home.

This year, they'd even finished making a kissing ball Hannah had seen in one of her Christmas catalogs, complete with pinecones, cranberries, and pine boughs tied atop one of the willow branch ornaments with mistletoe dangling beneath it. Now, he just needed a few more hours in his shop and his own Christmas projects would be complete.

"Here you go." Grace emerged from the kitchen with a mug of warmed apple cider, a light steam rising from the brim.

Just as she reached out to hand it to him, her foot caught on the edge of the rug. As she lurched slightly forward, Ethan prepared himself for the steaming contents of the cup to splash all over him. Thankfully, she caught herself without spilling a drop.

"Not this time," she said with a smile.

Ethan breathed a sigh of relief.

"Fire!" Grace's eyes were wide in surprise.

He smiled. *She likes the fire.*

Grace quickly set her mug on the table and rushed toward the fireplace.

Ethan turned around. A thick ember had fallen from the hearth and had started the woven rug on fire.

"Ah, hell!"

He bounded over the top of the couch to grab the rug and haul it outside.

Splash.

Gasp.

Ethan was soaked and, with one eye open, he could see Grace standing in front of him with a hand over her mouth, eyes even wider than before. He shook his hands free of some of the excess of water that dripped down the front of him, and wiped the rest out of his eyes.

"The fire's out." Grace pointed at the rug in his hand.

He looked down. A trifling chortle threatened. Ethan tightened his jaw, but when Grace folded her lips together and moved the bucket up to her eyes in an attempt to hide a giggle, he couldn't stop the laughter that followed.

"Fire's out," he confirmed and dropped the rug.

"You're soaking wet," she stated the obvious.

Suddenly, all laughter was gone. Ethan's senses were on fire. He wanted to be near her. Wanted to touch her. To kiss her. He reached out and grabbed a hold of her, tossing the water bucket aside, and pulled her tightly against his chest.

"Now, you're wet too."

There was fire in her eyes. Lord, help him, but she was the most intoxicating creature. He bent down and captured her lips with his. She still tasted like warm cider. He lifted a hand and twined it into her hair, cradling the back of her head with his palm.

"Mr. Redbourne?" she breathed even as she returned his impassioned kisses.

He slid his arms down to encompass her waist, pulled away enough to look at her, and gently placed another light kiss on her lips. "Don't you think it's about time you start calling me Ethan?"

"Ethan?" she whispered, her eyes open and alight, searching his.

He kissed the tip of her nose.

She bit her lip. His undoing.

If Ethan didn't leave right now, they were both going to be in a whole heap of trouble. He needed air. And someone to knock some sense back into him. What had he been thinking coming here alone?

Lord, give me strength.

He had to go. Now. With great restraint, he let go of her supple form and rushed out to the wagon bed. The cold air assaulted his damp skin. Just what he needed. With a few deep breaths, he began to think clearly again.

It didn't take long before Ethan started to shiver, despite himself. He needed to get this wet shirt off and put on his coat. How was he going to do that without Grace seeing his scars? He contemplated hitching up the horses right now, climbing up onto the wagon bench, and heading for home without another thought.

"Coward," he said aloud. Besides, that wouldn't be fair to Grace. His forearms rested against the sides of the wagon. He sank his head.

Tell me what to do, he pleaded.

His skin puckered into gooseflesh as a cold afternoon breeze swirled past him. Ethan pushed away from the wagon and strode over to the lean-to, pulled out a few long sticks from a bundle he'd placed there to keep dry, and turned back for the house.

Control, Redbourne.

CHAPTER FOURTEEN

Grace's feet wouldn't move. Glued to the floor, she stood there, staring at the fireplace, her chest heaving with deep, full breaths. Ethan really had to stop doing that. His hot mouth had seared her lips and every inch of her felt alive. Lee's kisses had never made her feel like this.

When feeling seemed to return to her legs, she walked over to the window and pulled back the coverings. Ethan leaned against the wagon, shaking his head low between his arms. She backed away.

At least he hadn't left. Again.

The mess on the floor wasn't going to clean itself. She retrieved a towel from the wardrobe in the hallway where she kept all of her new linens. As an afterthought, she opened the doors again and pulled out one of the new shirts she'd ordered in for Jack.

As she walked back into the living area, the door opened and Ethan walked inside looking like a drenched cat. He walked up to her, but kept his distance.

Grace wasn't sure whether to be disappointed or grateful.

"Miss Nolan…"He set a small bundle of sticks up against the stones of the fireplace. His head was bent. She could barely see his eyes. "Grace…" he started again, reaching down to take her hand in his.

He'd used her Christian name.

Breathe, she reminded herself.

"No gentleman would have been so forward. You are just too damn beautiful." He cleared his throat. "Forgive me?"

Beautiful? Her heart did a little flip at the word. *What did he ask?*

She thought for a moment.

"Will you stay and help me with the decorations?" she asked, her head tilted slightly as she raised one brow.

"Of course."

"Then, you're forgiven," she said with a smirk.

Ethan nodded. "Here," he said, reaching out for her towel. "Let me get that."

"You're still wet. Why don't you go change?" she asked, holding out Jack's shirt. Before he took it from her, she held it up to the wide expanse of Ethan's chest. "So, maybe you and my fourteen-year-old brother are not exactly the same size. I'm afraid I don't have anything for you to change into."

"It's all right. I brought my coat."

Grace had nearly forgotten about the leather jacket with the wool lining that fit him so perfectly. Heat rose in her cheeks.

"Go!" she said, still holding the towel and the shirt.

Ethan snatched his coat from the back of the couch and retreated to one of the vacant rooms down the hallway. He was definitely one of the more modest men she'd ever met. Lee and his friends had always taken every opportunity to show off their bare-chested physiques.

She sat down at the table and attempted to imitate what Ethan had started with the willow balls. Ethan walked out of the room and over to the fireplace, where he laid out his shirt to dry.

"Am I doing this right?" she asked, holding up the ornament she'd been working on.

"Honestly, I don't think there is a right or wrong way to do it. It's your tree. What do *you* want it to look like?" He took the seat at the end of the table.

"Can we put the ribbon in the tree? I think I need to see it before I'll know what we need to do next."

Ethan pushed his chair away from the table and picked up the bolt of burlap. "Just tell me where you want it."

Grace bit her bottom lip again.

"One thing," he said, turning to face her. His eyes boring through her and into her soul.

"What is it?" she asked innocently.

"You have *got* to stop doing that."

"What?" she asked, trying to think of what she had possibly done to aggravate him.

"That!" he pointed at her mouth.

She released her lip.

"Do you have any idea what you are doing to me, woman?"

"I'm sorry. I didn't reali—"

Ethan turned around and placed the end of the burlap ribbon toward the top.

Grace felt lighter than she had in a long time.

"Why did you become a blacksmith?" she asked, wanting to learn more about the man who'd already made such a big impact on her life.

"It was something to do." Ethan shrugged. "Dad wanted to make sure that all of us had respectable skills that could be put to use if we needed them. I liked working with metal and had a lot of ideas to make improvements on the ranch with things I could design and make."

"I've seen your work. You are very talented."

"Thanks. But I'm not going to be a blacksmith forever. One day, I am going to show my father what I can do with horses, and I'm going to run Redbourne Ranch."

"What about your creations? Your tools?"

"Running the ranch doesn't mean that I can't have

hobbies. Mama has encouraged all of us to develop talents. Cole draws, Rafe crafts pottery, Will fights. I'm not sure Mama considers that a talent though." He laughed. "I'll still do my fair share of working in the forge."

"Well, *that* was unpleasant." Jack walked through the door, his skin bright pink, she guessed from scrubbing.

Grace sniffed. That awful stench he'd carried with him before was gone.

"Ah, Jack. You are just in time," Ethan called from behind the tree.

"Your mother works miracles," she said with awe in her voice.

"Just don't let her hear you say that," Ethan snorted. "She'll never give any of us any peace."

From the way his lips upturned, and a small dimple appeared just below his eye, she knew he jested with her. He loved his mother. It was easy to see.

"There are so many great things we can do with the tree. You should see theirs, Gracie. It had little metal ornaments all over—sleigh bells, miniature lanterns, these balls made out of bended sticks—"

"You mean, like those?" Grace asked with a laugh, pointing to the table.

"Yeah," Jack exclaimed. "Just like those." He rushed over to the table and began to fiddle with the pieces.

After the burlap had been woven throughout the tree, Grace stood back, and in an instant had a vision of what she wanted to do.

While Ethan and Jack attached sprigs of cranberries, dried oranges, pinecones, and ribbon to the willow ornaments, she gathered a few pieces at a time and started placing them in the tree. She used the twigs Ethan had brought in from outside, a few of the cranberry vines, and the newly decorated ornaments to fill the tree in in all the right places.

Within no time at all, it was done.

They all stood on the fireplace bricks in awe of their accomplishment.

"You're just missing a few little candles and it will be perfect."

"I don't think we'll use candles on this tree," Grace said.

Jack shook his head. "The year the Coldherns' decided to put candles on the tree, they left it lit up all through dinner. The tree and all the paper ornaments caught fire, which jumped to the curtains in the hall, and they nearly lost the entire west wing of the estate."

"They're pretty and all, but I rather like the tree the way it is." She didn't just like the tree. Grace loved the tree. It was everything she had hoped it would be.

"Okay," Ethan said. "No candles." He walked over to the fireplace and picked up his shirt. "It's getting a little warm in here now and this is dry, so I think I'll just go put it on." Ethan excused himself to the back room.

Grace picked up the shirt she'd purchased for Jack and walked down the hall to return in to the linen wardrobe. Her eyes were drawn to the broad crack in the door that exposed Ethan's now bare back. She knew she should look away, but couldn't help herself. He was such a handsome man and his back looked so strong and firm.

He stretched his arm back, rotating his shoulder. It was then that she noticed his reflection in the very large mirror hanging on the wall and the horrible mangled scars that covered his chest just below his shoulder.

She gasped.

His eyes met hers in the mirror and his expression grew steely and cold. Immediately she looked away. It was as if she had intruded on something very personal with him.

Stupid girl.

Her heart hurt for the unimagined pain Ethan must have experienced to retain scars like those.

When Ethan returned, his whole demeanor had changed.

"I've overstayed my welcome," he said gruffly. "I best be getting home. I still have chores to finish up and a lot of work to do."

"Please, Ethan," she said, rushing toward him, placing a hand on his forearm as he retreated.

"I have to go," was all he said, but he stared at her hand, his jaw pulsating, until she snatched it back as if she'd been burned.

Ethan grabbed his hat from the rack behind the door, placed it on his head, and headed outside with purposeful steps.

Grace watched from the window as he retrieved the horses from the barn and hitched the wagon. She debated following him, but figured he needed some time. She had a feeling his scars were not only on the outside.

Every day she discovered more layers to that man, and she wasn't surprised to realize that she wanted to know more.

Ethan needed to work. He needed to pound out his frustrations on a chunk of metal. He'd been wrong to think that scars like his wouldn't matter to the right woman. Grace was the right woman, yet she'd reacted just as he'd feared she would. Horror. Disgust.

What had he expected?

Being a blacksmith suited him. It meant he could seclude himself in his own space. His cave. He glanced over at the newly formed blades still lying on his cooling rack. He wanted to punch something. Anything. But in his shop he would only do more damage than good.

It had already been two days since they had decorated her tree, and still he was angry. At himself mostly. For daring to hope things would be different this time. He had allowed himself to get too attached far too quickly.

Never again.

Ethan donned his gloves and with his tongs, pulled the metal from the forge. He placed it against the anvil and grabbed the mallet dangling from its hook on the edge of the countertop.

Clank. Clank.

Something about the repetitive action soothed him and he could feel his resentment start to flow out of him.

Who was he kidding? He couldn't get the woman out of his head. He'd overreacted.

Clank.

The door to his shop opened and his mother poked her head in. "We're heading out in half an hour, son. I'll be expecting you to be dressed proper."

"I'm not coming." Ethan couldn't remember a time when he'd flat out defied either one of his parents, but he didn't think he carried the right spirit to be sitting at church in front of God and everyone.

"What's gotten into you?" His mother asked as she stepped all the way into the smithy and removed her bonnet. She took down the stool that hung from the overhanging hook in the far corner of the room. "Did something happen with Miss Nolan?" She sat down, crossed her legs, and put her hands in her lap.

He couldn't look at her.

"Ethan," she called his name quietly.

Clank.

He hit the metal again, but this time with less vigor.

"I'm such a fool, Mama." He hung his tongs back in their place and left the metal on the anvil to cool on its own, without shaping it. He leaned back against the counter behind him and folded his arms across his chest.

"Now, why on earth would you say something like that? You're a Redbourne. A bit stubborn maybe, but not a fool. What's happened?"

"I think I love her, Mama."

Leah chuckled. "Honey, if love makes you a fool, then I am the biggest one of them all."

"I thought I could be happy working out here in the shop and staying far away from women, but…"

"But, that girl has brought out something in you I haven't seen in a long time. Laughter. Courage. Life."

Ethan nodded.

"So, what's the problem?"

He didn't want to say it. Barely wanted to admit it to himself. "I'm…"

"Scared?"

How did she always know?

"We all get scared, Ethan. It's what we do with that fear, the actions we take, that will define who we are." Leah stood up and walked over to her son. "Don't let fear get in the way of your happiness. You are what you make of yourself. And, from where I'm standing, you're one of the best." She nestled herself momentarily into his arms. "I love you."

"I love you too, Mama."

She pushed away from him. "Now, get those ridiculously large muscles into your Sunday best and meet us out front. We are going to church. As a family."

She winked.

"Yes, ma'am." He pushed himself away from the counter, picked up the hunk of metal with the tongs, and dropped it into his water bucket.

Ethan needed to apologize, but he wouldn't be surprised if Grace Nolan didn't want to speak to him. Ever. He'd been a dolt.

The book.

Ethan suddenly remembered she'd borrowed a book from his Dickens collection and he'd seen her replace it with her grandfather's journal. He quickly put away the tools he'd been using and walked over to the bookshelf.

It was gone.

Someone had been in his shop, but who else would have known it was there?

Impossible.

Grace looked a little closer. Jack stood in the far corner of the church's courtyard speaking with Hurley Devlin. His back was to her, and there, protruding from his rear pocket, was her grandfather's journal.

How?

Grace looked around for Ethan. He was standing near the church steps in a seemingly deep conversation with Raine. She glanced back to Jack, who spoke with animation to the rough-looking men. He kept reaching behind him and tapping the journal. Grace wished she could hear the conversation, but at this point had no doubt about the topic.

He wouldn't.

"...and that's why I believe you should. What do you think, dear? Will you do it?"

Grace glanced back at Mrs. Day, who had been speaking to her for the better part of fifteen minutes. She'd hardly heard a word.

"If you'll excuse me, Mrs. Day." She smiled and dipped her head. "There's something I need to attend to."

She'd only taken two steps toward Jack when Ethan accosted her arm and gently moved her in the direction of the church gardens.

"I don't have time to grovel right now. Or to explain why I..." How could she tell him how sorry she felt for intruding on his privacy? "I need t—"

"Shhhh." He spun her around to face him and placed a finger over her mouth. "You need to listen to me very carefully."

"But I—"

His mouth covered hers in a brief kiss. His hands clasped each of her arms at the shoulder. When he pulled away and steeled his eyes on hers, he had her full attention.

"Hurley has your grandfather's watch."

"How do y—"

He cocked an eyebrow and she cut her question short.

"I know you think it's crazy, but that treasure is out there, Grace, and Jack is determined to find it. So is Hurley." Ethan's hands slid down her arms until he captured her hands. "You have to make a choice. If you don't let your brother find your family's legacy, someone else will."

Grace lifted her jaw and started to open her mouth, but thought better of it. She wanted to hear what else Ethan had to say.

"Do you remember the man we found dead out at your place?"

Like she could forget.

She stared at him, eyes narrowed.

"Sorry."

"What about him?" she asked.

"Raine and the sheriff found out that his name is Walden Shivley. A letter addressed to him came into the post office yesterday from New York, from a man by the name of…Lee Coldhern. I know you said you worked for some Coldherns in New York. Do you know him?" his voice had become little more than a whisper.

Do I know him? How was she supposed to answer that?

"Grace? What is it? You *do* know him, don't you?"

She nodded slowly, not trusting herself to speak. She'd left her life in the city to start over. Why then, did it seem that Lee was following her? He'd made his choice. She had to admit she hadn't expected the connection between her past and her present.

"What did the letter say?" She wasn't sure she wanted to know.

"Raine's over at the sheriff's office right now. They are getting ready to open it—along with a few members of the town council."

"Let me get Jack, and we'll come with you."

He nodded. She was surprised he'd agreed to allow them to go along.

Hurriedly, she rounded the corner to where her brother had been speaking to Hurley and his group of rough-looking friends. He now held the journal is his hands and looked as if he was getting ready to hand it over to Ethan's rival.

"Jack," she exclaimed as she rushed toward them.

He shoved the journal back into his pocket.

"Mr. Devlin." She bowed her head slightly. "Mr. Giles. Gentlemen." She had no idea the names of any of the other men who surrounded her brother. "If you'll excuse us a moment."

"Grace," Hurley said stepping forward. "It is so good to see you. Jack has just been telling us about the adventures of moving into your granddaddy's old place."

Grace looked at Jack, trying desperately to think of what she might say in response that would not encourage further conversation. She lifted her chin.

"We discovered a hidden fireplace, tore down the old barn, found a dead man out on our land…yes, I'd say we have dealt with some very interesting things." She put her arm around Jack's shoulder and firmly tried to pull him away from the menacing crowd.

"It's real sad about Shiv," Hurley said as he took a step in front of them. "He was a good fella." He reached out his hand and placed it on Grace's arm. "I haven't had a chance to come a callin'. How about allowing me to escort you to the Christmas Festival?"

"She already has a date." To Grace's relief, Ethan appeared behind her.

"I didn't realize you'd staked a claim, Redbourne."

Grace could feel the tension mounting between the men. She grabbed Jack's hand and pulled him out of ear's reach of the others.

"Jack, where on earth did you get that journal?"

"But how did y—"

"And you were going to give it to Mr. Devlin? Of all people. You know how the Redbournes feel about him."

"Grace, I…"

She could see the conflict in his eyes, and she thought of what Ethan had said. *That treasure is out there…if you don't let your brother find your family's legacy, someone else will.*

"I was wrong," she finally admitted, "in not allowing you the chance to read grandfather's journal. Just promise me you will not turn it over to Hurley."

He nodded.

"How did you get it anyway?"

His smile grew wide. "Cole found it on Ethan's bookshelf and gave it to me. His friend Alaric is supposed to be back from visiting with his grandpa in Colorado tomorrow. Cole says he's real good at deciphering clues. Says we'll find that treasure in no time. Only…"

"Only what?"

Jack looked down at his shoes. "We needed grandfather's compass."

"Jack, you know that disappeared a long time ago. When he died."

"But, Gracie, I remember the compass and Hurley has one just like it. I thought if I could get real close to him and all that, well…"

"He might let you borrow it?"

"Not exactly."

"Jackson Oliver Nolan. Were you planning on stealing Mr. Devlin's watch?"

"Shhh. Keep your voice down, Gracie. He might hear you."

Grace looked up. Hurley and his brutes were still all

standing at the far edge of the church courtyard talking and laughing amongst themselves. Ethan, who was speaking to his father near their wagon, caught her stare and motioned toward the sheriff's office.

This was it. The time had come for her to make a decision. Steeling herself, she decided that if someone was going to find the treasure from her grandfather's stories, it needed to be a Nolan.

"Listen, Jack. The Redbournes may have found a clue, but you have to know that if Ethan is right, one man has already died in the name of finding this treasure. We have to be careful."

"Does that mean we're going to look for it? That you're going to help?"

His eyes had regained the light they'd lost over the past few weeks. She heaved a resigned sigh.

"Yes."

CHAPTER FIFTEEN

Mr. Shivley,

Dear Sir, as of your last correspondence, you have not yet discovered the location of the treasure I hired you and your company to locate, for which purpose I have entrusted valuable items, such as Mr. Horace Nolan's compass, into your care. This delay is unacceptable. Please note that if I do not receive word of your success by year's end, I will send replacements and will deny all moneys previously agreed upon.

Please be advised that after my brief romantic involvement with Mr. Nolan's granddaughter, I have learned that while she is something to look at and quite intelligent, she is also gullible and of poor status. I do not desire that Miss Nolan, nor her young brother be harmed. A sincere, gentle word will gain you her trust. I am certain Mr. Nolan's journal will be found somewhere on the premises of the old farmhouse. Find it before she does.

Miss Nolan is never to be made aware of our arrangement. This is of the utmost importance. I know *that you and your company will not fail me. Your contact in Stone Creek has been a valuable resource. Use him.*

As agreed upon, you will send word once the treasure has been located. It is not to be disturbed. You will be very well compensated for your efforts upon my arrival and purchase of the Nolan property.

With Regard,
Lee B. Coldhern

"Your company? He couldn't have just written a name? Someone we could question?" Raine looked tired. He and Ethan had been up all night re-reading Coldherns' letter and now, with the sun barely rising over the hills, they were already riding up in front of Nolan Place.

Ethan smiled at the name Grace had given to her new house.

"Why don't we just catch the train to New York and confront Mr. Coldhern face to face?" Ethan could see his breath as he spoke. He figured the temperature had dropped a good twenty degrees through the night and was surprised at the thick snowflakes that continued to fall. If it didn't let up soon, they would have to postpone their plans for the day.

"Ah, you're just sore because of his *'involvement'* with your girl." Raine pulled his coat tighter around his scarf-laden neck.

He wasn't too far from the truth. Ethan didn't like the idea of another man being romantically involved with Grace—especially a man with so little concern for her well-being.

"I don't know how the dolt thinks he is going to be able to convince Grace to sell her pro—"

Raine threw his finger to his lips and dismounted, his hand hovering lightly over the handle of his holstered gun. Ethan followed suit, grabbing his rifle from his saddle holster, but as he looked around, he didn't see anything out of the ordinary—until he looked down.

A dozen or so booted tracks made their way up to the house and the front door was slightly ajar, swaying lightly with the cool morning breeze. He looked back down the road, chiding himself for not noticing the tracks coming from the direction of Devlin's place.

Grace.

Ethan's heart started to race and his jaw clenched. If anything had happened to Grace...he didn't want to think about that. He had to find her. He started up the front steps. Raine stood beside the doorway, his gun drawn. He motioned for Ethan to go around the porch to the back.

Raine pushed against the already open door and it swung wide.

"Miss Nolan," he called inside.

Ethan peeked in through the back door to the kitchen. Nothing looked out of place. He grabbed the handle and tried to open it. It was still locked. He continued around the porch, peeking in through the windows as he went, but nothing.

Grace would have been expecting them. Where was she?

When he reached the front door, Raine was already in the living area.

"Miss Nolan?" he called again.

Enough of this pussy footing around. He was not going to sneak around. If someone other than the Nolan's were in the house, they would have both him and his brother to contend with. He stepped inside the door and strode toward the kitchen.

"Grace!" he yelled in a booming voice.

"Ethan?"

He whipped around, heaving a huge sigh of relief.

Grace came running down the stairs, fully dressed for the day, a look of sheer panic strewn across her features. "Ethan, he's gone." She ran into his arms, threading her own under his coat and around his waist, her palms flat against his back, and buried her face into the soft wool at his chest.

Ethan squeezed her, closing his eyes and inhaling the fresh lavender scent of her hair. She was safe.

"Who's gone?" It took a moment for Ethan to realize it had been a stupid question. Who else would it be?

Jack.

Grace pulled away from him and looked up into his eyes. "The journal is missing too."

"Where would he have gone?" Ethan asked.

"He wouldn't have gone without us. We had a plan. He wanted our help."

"I don't think he was planning on leaving so early."

Grace's head snapped toward Raine. He pointed to the trampled snow leading up to the house.

"You mean, somebody may have taken him?" She glanced back at Ethan for confirmation. "Not Mr. Devlin?"

Ethan wished he could tell her more. He was glad Raine was here. He'd be able to ascertain some information, but Ethan couldn't help but wish Rafe hadn't been called away. Rafe was a tracker. He had a real talent for following and finding people. That's what made him good at his job.

"They'll be after that treasure," Raine said assuredly. "I'll ride into town and get the sheriff. Maybe we can get a group together to go after them. Someone will know where they've gone."

"That'll take too long, Raine, and you know it. If Hurley's desperate to get to that treasure, there's no telling what he'll do with the kid. Those men he's been associating with aren't exactly the church-going types either."

Grace's eyes opened wide. "You think they'll hurt Jack?" She shook her head. "No. This isn't happening."

"Never thought I'd say this, but we're lucky it snowed last night." Raine pointed outside at the tracks leading away from the house. "There will be a trail to follow. We'll have to hurry though, if the snow gets any heavier, we may lose them before we even get started."

"I'll follow the tracks," Ethan said. "You take Grace home and get the others."

"I'm not going to let you go after them on your own, Ethan," Raine told him with a firm set to his jaw.

Ethan had expected no less, but it had been worth a try.

"Then, what do you suggest, big brother? We're wasting time sitting here jawing about it."

Unfortunately, they had no idea if the treasure had been hidden in a mine, or a cave, or simply buried under some random tree in the middle of nowhere. Without the journal, or the compass for that matter, they may be simply running a wild goose chase.

Ethan realized that his dad might have an idea where to start, but he and Tag had been heading out to the west pasture first thing this morning to mend a downed stretch of fence bordering the Cooper's property.

"You're right. Redbourne Ranch is closer than town and we've got a built in posse of our own."

Ethan snorted. Two men down, they were still a force to be reckoned with.

"I wish I'd gotten a good look at that journal—not that it would help us know where to start." Ethan turned back to Grace. "Didn't you say that your grandfather had had the compass for a long time and never found the treasure?"

Grace nodded.

"I would like to know what's changed that these ruffians would chance being caught out in a snowstorm to go after it this morning.

Grace backhanded him on the arm. "When I asked Jack how he'd gotten the journal, he said that your brother had found it and given it to him."

"I'll beat him within an inch of his life," Ethan's hands balled into fists.

Cole. It had to be. He was always the one looking for a

new quest. If Alaric had been in town, they would probably have already set off to find the treasure on their own. Luckily, he was still in Colorado visiting his grandpa.

"Apparently, somebody named Alaric is coming in on the train today, and is really good at deciphering maps and clues. Do you think he might be able to help?"

Ethan threw his hands up into the air. Of course.

"Only one problem," Raine said. "We don't have the journal."

"Maybe not, but if I know my little brother, he will have memorized the thing before giving it back to Jack." He looked over at Raine.

"Well, what are we waiting for?"

They hurried out to the stable. Ethan swung Grace up onto Storm and climbed up behind her. He didn't dare have her attempt to ride in this weather, as inexperienced with horses as she was, and taking the wagon would not be a good option with the heavy snowfall. It felt right to have her here, leaning against him, depending on him. He sure as hell wasn't going to let her down.

By the time they reached Redbourne Ranch, the tracks they'd left this morning had all but disappeared. Ethan lowered Grace to the ground.

"Go inside and tell my mama what has happened. I'll be back as soon as I round up my brothers and a few of the hands."

"Don't leave me here," she asked, desperation lacing her words.

"I won't."

"I'll ride out to the west pasture to see if I can find Dad and Tag. We're going to need all the help we can get." Raine looked up into the sky. "Lord, help us all," he said before pulling his mount around and heading out to the fields.

With conditions like these, there was little they would be able to accomplish on the ranch. The barn door was closed, but a small lantern's light shone through the window. Ethan figured Cole was probably still out there milking Joey.

Without bothering to dismount, Ethan tugged open the barn door and rode Storm inside. A bluster of snow and wind whirled into the doorway and Cole looked up from the stool.

Ethan slid down off the horse's back and pushed the large wooden door shut to stop the chill from getting to the rest of the animals.

"Ethan, can you believe this snow? As soon as my chores are done, I think we shoul—"

"Give me one good reason why I shouldn't beat the tar out of you right now," Ethan growled as he lifted Cole off the stool and held him against the wall of the barn.

"Because your father is standing right behind you." Jameson's low, firm tone seemed to reverberate in the hollowness of the room.

Ethan didn't let go.

"Ethan," his father warned. "Let him down."

Ethan raised an eye at Cole and with a firm shove, let go and turned around.

"You got back quick," Ethan said to his father as if nothing out of the ordinary had transpired. "Tag here too?"

Jameson nodded. "We figured the fence would keep for today. The horses aren't going to be out running and the Cooper's cows have all been moved to the other side." He lifted a rope off a hook on the wall and pulled a lantern down off the shelf.

"Did Raine find you?"

"He's out talking to Marty and a few of the others. Will's grabbing some extra blankets and filling the canteens."

"What's wrong?" Cole asked. He hauled the milk can over next to the door and turned to face them.

"What do you know about Grace's granddad's journal?" Ethan asked pointedly.

Cole shrugged and looked away. "I might have read a bit

of it. Why?"

Ethan took a step toward him, but his father extended his arm, preventing him from getting far. "Because Jack's gone and gotten himself kidnapped by Devlin and his men. They wanted that journal and now, because of you, they have it. And him."

"Wait. They're out there right now? In this?" Jameson asked, concern lacing his voice.

"We didn't mean any harm, Ethan. Alaric is coming home today. You know how he loves a good mystery. I just thought—"

"You didn't think, Charcoal. That's the problem," Ethan said harshly.

"Sorry, brother," Cole said quickly, "but maybe I have something that will help."

Ethan eyed him speculatively.

"I'll finish getting the wagon loaded, but I don't know how far we'll get—even with the new attachment blades," Jameson called as he started toward the shed.

"Wait. Come with me." Ethan marched out of the barn and toward the smithy with his father and Cole on his heels.

He walked around to the far side of his shop and gripped ahold of the iron handle of the barn-sized door. It had been a while since the extended entrance had been opened and with the snow quickly piling up, it was harder to open than Ethan had expected.

He'd been grateful for the large quilt that had hidden his large project from view. Even though it had been finished for near a month, he'd wanted it to be a Christmas surprise for his family.

Ethan reached for the edge of the blanket and pulled it back to reveal the intricately designed sleigh with two separate expanded attachments. He'd wanted something that would carry the whole family.

"Oh, Ethan...son, this is incredible." Jameson ran his

hand across the finely carved metal designs in the side of the sleigh."

Ethan stood up a little taller.

"Whoa, can we take it out for a ride?"

"Help me get it out of the shop," Ethan said.

He walked around to the other side, toward the back of the sleigh. Cole and his father pushed on the front to turn the direction and Ethan pushed from behind.

"I'll go get Matilda and Clyde," Jameson called as he darted out of the shop and ran back toward the barn. The two Clydesdales their father had taken as payment from a Scottish settler a few years ago were strong and highly capable.

"I'll be right back," Cole said.

It wasn't long before Jameson was back with both of the giant horses and they made quick work of hitching the team. Ethan climbed into the front seat and snapped the reins. The jingling sound brought a smile to his face as he watched his father's face light up.

"Come on," Ethan encouraged his father to jump up onto the front seat. He handed him the reins.

The snow still had not relented and Ethan mused that he should have made some type of covering for the top.

A project for next year, he determined.

Ethan went into the house to find Grace. He didn't have to go very far as she had been waiting by the fireplace and stood up as soon as he walked into the room.

"Are we ready to go?" She asked, her voice a slightly higher pitch than usual.

"Just about," Jameson said from the doorway.

Cole came down the stairs three at a time. He held his drawing notebook and some loose papers in his hand.

"Ethan," he called, motioning to the dining room table.

His mother, father, and Grace all followed him into the room. The door opened again and in filed the rest of them— Will, Tag, Raine, and a snow crusted Hannah.

Cole spread out a few of the papers on the table. They were maps. He looked up at Grace.

"I am sorry for all the trouble, Miss Nolan." He glanced over at Ethan. "I wasn't thinking."

"It's quite all right, Cole. What do you have here?"

He hunched down over the table. "I had a couple of days to look at the journal, so I mapped out each of Horace Nolan's attempts and jotted down some of the clues he found."

Ethan was amazed at the talent his little brother had at drawing. His maps were detailed and showed considerable thought.

"Nice job, Cole," Ethan said, patting him on the back.

"Thanks."

"This will come in handy if this storm ever lets up, but maybe we can figure out where they would have even started."

In less than a quarter of an hour they had a plan. Each of them had retrieved and set their pocket watches to the same time so they could meet back at Nolan Place every hour. The treasure had become the last thing on anyone's mind. They needed to find Jack before something bad happened, and with the wintery conditions, sight would be limited. Each of his siblings—including Hannah, his parents, and a few of the ranch hands would be on horseback. He and Grace would be in the sleigh.

As they were getting ready to head out into the cold, Ethan decided to make one more little stop in the smithy. He retrieved an umbrella, a torch and matchbox, and his copper compass—the one his own grandfather had given him when he'd started his internship at the blacksmith shop in town. It may not be the special compass they needed, but with the course Cole had plotted out, he figured it couldn't hurt.

CHAPTER SIXTEEN

It was the most beautiful thing Grace had ever seen. The sides of the sleigh gleamed red between the mounds of clustered snow now accumulating on the sides and edges.

She had seen sleighs in the city, mostly black in color, but none were so unique in shape and design. This had to have been what Ethan had kept hidden in his shop.

She waited patiently by the door while everyone else filed out and mounted their horses.

Where was Ethan?

She'd scarcely asked the question when he appeared out of the smithy and ran to the door for her. He popped open an umbrella and escorted her quickly to the sleigh. Before she sat down, he wiped off the front seat with a towel and laid a blanket in its spot.

"Let's go find your brother."

They set out into the cold, unsure of where to look. They had decided to split into groups and cover all four sides of the Nolan property.

Luckily, Grace thought, *the Nolan lands aren't nearly as extensive as the Redbournes'.*

It was still early yet, but the clouds and heavy snowfall blocked the sun enough that, on occasion, Ethan would stop and light the lanterns on either side of the horses to illuminate their way.

"Stop!" Grace screamed to be heard, though Ethan sat only inches from her.

She squinted, and there, on a low-hanging branch, hung a long piece of material blowing roughly in the wind. Jack's scarf. She knew it was his. It had to be. She rushed from the sleigh—propriety be blamed—and ran toward their first clue that her brother had passed through this way. She brought it up to her face. It crunched, caked with frozen snow. She pulled it back a little to look at it, and her heart sunk. Blood splotches adorned the edge.

"What is it?" Ethan asked from directly behind her, holding his hand up in front of his face.

She held it out, refusing to let her tears show. "We have to find him, Ethan. Now."

Grace shoved the scarf into his arms and marched toward the sleigh, ignoring the chilled assault on her face.

Ethan hopped into the seat next to her, but instead of grabbing the reins and starting out again, he turned until his knee was on the bench between them, and they were facing each other.

"Grace, we can't keep looking like this. It's time to check back in. We all agreed that we would meet back at your place every hour."

"But—"

"If the snow wasn't coming down so hard, we could extend the check-in time, but the last thing we need to do is lose someone else and have two or three people to find instead of just one. Besides, the horses need water and a few minutes to rest."

In her mind, Grace knew that what Ethan said made sense, but her heart wasn't ready to turn back in. She scanned the ground for any sign of the direction they may have headed, but the wind had blown away and the snow filled any tracks that had been there maybe even as little as an hour beforehand.

"The faster we check-in, the faster we can get back out here, right?"

"Right," Ethan confirmed.

"Okay, then. Let's check-in. Maybe somebody else has found something too."

It was cold. It seemed to cut through to her bones, but Grace didn't care. Jack was out there somewhere, and for the life of her, she couldn't even remember if she'd seen his coat at the house. She prayed he was warm. And safe.

Ethan's little brother, Cole, had scoured her grandfather's journal for clues as to where the treasure might be. He'd analyzed every dead end and every possible clue her grandfather had found over the time he had lived here. But they were missing something.

On the quick ride back to Nolan Place, Grace mulled over all the stories Grandfather had told them over the years, trying to draw out any details that might offer some hint of where to go. She revisited the box that had contained the journal and the gems and the key.

The key.

"The key," she repeated, this time aloud.

She tried to remember what it looked like. Tried to think of why it had been important to her grandfather. What it might have opened. If only she had taken more time to have read the entries in his journal, she might have had a better idea of what it meant. Grandfather had put that key in the pouch along with those jewels, so it must mean something. But what?

"What key?"

"The one that was in with my grandfather's gems and journal. There was a gold key."

Ethan seemed to ponder the idea for a moment.

"Hi-ya!" he exclaimed, urging the Clydesdales to move faster through the onslaught of snow that now fell upon them.

Seven horses and riders awaited them in front of the

house. As soon as Ethan brought the sleigh to a stop, Grace jumped out, the hem of her dress catching on something. She nearly fell, but quickly regained her footing and tore her dress away from whatever held her. Though her feet were freezing, she scampered up the stairs to the stone where she'd hidden the pouch.

Grace pulled off her gloves with her teeth and threw them down at her side. She yanked the loose brick from its place in the wall and patted around inside the hole for the pouch. When her fingertips grazed the velvet bag, she pulled it out and immediately emptied the contents into her hand again.

There it was. The key.

"What do you think it opens?" Ethan stood behind her, his deep voice spreading warmth down her spine.

There was something about it. Something familiar. Grace just had to think for a moment. She traced over the large intricate gold-patterned top with her fingertips. It was beautiful in design. That was it.

The grandfather clock.

Grace pulled herself to her feet, ducked around Ethan, and stood in front of the old grandfather clock in the entryway. The same intricate design of the key ornamented the perimeter of the clock's face. Grace stared at the keyhole for a long time. Once she opened this door, she didn't know if she'd be able to close it again. And that scared her.

"Jack," was all Ethan had to say to pull her out of a darkening abyss of fear.

Grace delicately placed the key into the hole. It fit. She turned. When she opened the etched glass door, nothing happened. There was no sudden revelation as to where the treasure might be. No clue even as to where to begin. Her heart sank. She'd failed her brother.

Ethan moved behind her. She could feel his presence, even before the warmth of his hands touched her sides. He kissed the back of her head. What were they going to do? Jack was out there in this storm and she felt helpless to do anything about it.

"What are these?" Ethan's breath was hot against her neck as he leaned forward, pointing to one of the three holes in the face of the clock.

Of course.

While the key didn't look anything like other windup instruments she'd ever seen, it was the right size. She didn't waste a moment before carefully pushing the tool into the hole as far as possible. She exhaled as she slowly turned the key. Once. One of the weights began to rise. Twice. It lifted higher. She repeated the process until she'd rotated it thirteen times.

The weight sat up against the seat-board, but nothing happened.

Grace moved the key into the hole directly across from the first and repeated the steps.

While another weight also lifted to the seat-board, still nothing else happened.

Her breaths had become shallow and she had to force herself to inhale deeply and exhale. The final hole was toward the bottom, forming a perfect triangle with the other two. Grace placed the key inside and wound the last point.

"What is taking so long in here?" Cole opened the front door and stepped inside, shaking off the snow that had accumulated on his hat and coat before moving closer. "We wanted to compare findings."

Grace peered over her shoulder at him, then returned her focus to the clock.

"That's the key from the pouch," Cole said, an excited edge in his voice. He huddled closer around the clock.

The weight had risen to an appropriate height, but still, nothing happened. Grace held her breath as she tapped the pendulum and it started to swing. Nothing.

"Maybe you need to set the time," Ethan said quietly in her ear.

"Oh, yes. What is the hour, please?" she asked, the clock still reading seven minutes past three.

Ethan and Cole pulled out their respective pocket watches.

"A quarter of nine," Ethan said.

Grace's fingers shook, but slowly, she moved the intricately carved gold minute hand with one finger. As she hit four o'clock, she stopped to allow the chimes to sound, but they didn't. Refusing to be discouraged, she started moving the hand again. Suddenly, the chimes sounded.

Odd.

She waited for the ringing to finish before moving the hand again until it was five o'clock. She paused once more, waiting for the chimes. They didn't sound. As she started winding again, there they were.

Something was definitely off.

She repeated the process until she reached eight o'clock, but this time, instead of stopping on the hour, she spun the hand slowly past eight until the chimes sounded. The hands read seven minutes past eight.

They all held their breath.

With a few loud stomps up the front steps, the door opened.

"I'm afraid we're not going anywhere until that snow lets up," Jameson said from the doorway. He took off his hat and brushed the snow from his shoulders. "After you, my darling." He took a hold of Leah's hand, kissed his wife lightly, and saw her into the house. The rest of the family followed.

Grace turned, but it took a moment for her to register what Jameson had said.

"What about Jack?"

"Hurley knows better than to stay out in a storm like this," Jameson offered. "They will have found shelter by now."

"Don't worry." Ethan spun her to face him. "We'll find him."

"We sent the others home. A man can hardly see past the

end of his own nose out there." Raine rubbed his hands together after he shut the door. "We put the horses in the barn. I hope that is all right with you, Miss Nolan."

"Of course."

Grace didn't know whether to scream or cry. Her little brother was out there somewhere and there wasn't anything she could do right now to find him. Truth be told, they didn't have the faintest idea where to look. Or, even where to start. And neither did Jack. That was one of the most frustrating parts. If Hurley Devlin knew enough about this treasure to be out looking for it in this weather, why did he need Jack? She shook her thoughts free of what she couldn't do right now and tried to focus on what she could.

"Please, everyone, come in and rest awhile."

She looked back at the clock. Why the key? With no answers, she shut the glass door and locked it again, quickly returning the key to the black velvet pouch with the gems and setting it on the table behind one of the couches.

She glanced over the chaise at the Redbournes, who now sat, attentive in deep conversation. Cole had laid his map down on the table and rolled it out, pointing to various spots where the journal had indicated possible points of origin. Grace just couldn't stay. She went into the kitchen and quickly started a fire in the stove. The least she could do was to offer these men and women something warm to drink for their efforts. She hoped that the soothing scents of apple and cinnamon would calm the banging in her head.

Bong.

Bong.

Bong.

It wasn't in her head. A faint tolling sound seemed to be calling out to her through the floor.

"Grace?" Ethan leaned into the kitchen.

She looked up. "You heard it too?"

He nodded.

"But where is it coming from?"

"Is there a basement in the house?"

"Just the old…"

"Cellar," they both said at the same time.

Grace pulled the hot apple cider from the stove. Ethan pulled a lantern from the top shelf in the kitchen. He opened the door on the stove and plunged a stick from the small woodpile on the floor into the fire and burned the end. Once the lantern was lit, he grabbed a hold of Grace's hand and, without taking the time to don their coats, hats, or gloves, they ventured out through the kitchen door, down the short steps, and over to the large cellar access.

Even though the lock had been cut through, the Redbournes had restrung the cellar's door handles with a heavy chain. Ethan set the lantern on the ground and yanked on the thick iron links until they were clear. He reached down and took a hold of the metal grips and threw the flaps open with one swing. Grace was momentarily taken aback by Ethan's strength. His back looked like taught cords of rope straining against his shirt with the effort of lifting the heavy wooden doors.

Ethan locked eyes with Grace.

"Are you ready?" he asked as he picked up the lantern and held his hand out to her.

She breathed deeply and placed her hand in his.

"As I'll ever be."

CHAPTER SEVENTEEN

Clocks.

Big clocks. Little clocks. Wooden clocks. Clocks made of metal. Ethan had never seen so many clocks in one place. The cellar reminded him something of his own shop, and he realized this had been the place that Grace's great-grandfather had built the timepieces that he had become so known for—especially in Stone Creek and the surrounding towns.

"This is incredible," Grace said as she perused the room that was significantly bigger that Ethan had expected it to be. "Which one do you think chimed?"

"I wouldn't be surprised if they all chimed." The ticking sound of the working clocks filled the room.

A sudden darkness washed over the amazement he'd seen in her eyes just moments before.

"Somebody had to have wound these clocks for them to even be working. Within the last week." It was as if she had just realized that she indeed may have been sharing her home with strangers. Or, villains.

He walked over to her and bent down to look her in the face. He lifted her chin with his finger until she glanced up at him. "Whoever was here is gone now."

"But what did they want down here? Why was this room

so important to them?"

Ethan didn't have an answer. Yet.

A couple of make-shift cots had been constructed in the room, and Ethan wondered why they had chosen to sleep in the cellar, instead of the house where there had been comfortable couches and beds. He glanced at the low, long table just beneath the stairs and wondered why a clockmaker would choose to have his workshop where the light would be so difficult to come by. He guessed there were some answers he would probably never get.

The sound of something heavy and wooden scratching against the floor drew his attention to where Grace was attempting to move one of the larger clocks. He was across from her in a moment and lifted the timepiece to the side.

"Did you find something?"

"I don't know. Can you shine the light over here a little closer?"

He did as she asked.

A large clock face had been carved into the wall and two ornately designed metal bars had been fastened to the center as hands. Ethan had to look closer. It was hard to tell with only one light, but it looked real. Like it could really work. The time was not correct, so he guessed that the intruders had been too busy winding the other clocks or looking for something else that they missed it completely.

"Ethan, look," Grace said as her fingers glided over two small holes placed in the same position as those in the grandfather clock upstairs, and a narrow slit, just wide enough for a thin metal file, made up the third point just below the center where the two clock hands met.

"You don't think…"

"Where can we find another crank? There has to be one around here somewhere. Although, I've never seen a clock that would require three different pieces to wind it."

The more Ethan stared at those openings, the more

familiar the shapes became.

"What if it didn't? Need three different pieces to wind it, I mean."

Grace's brows furrowed together as if trying to concentrate on his words. She shook her head a little and shrugged her shoulders. "What do you mean?"

"Hold that." Ethan shoved the lantern into her hand and quickly ran up the wooden steps.

"You're going to leave me down here? Alone?" he heard her call after him.

He pushed open the kitchen door and ran through to the living area where Grace had left the small pouch on the table in front of the chaise. He slid Cole's map aside and snatched up the bag.

"We may have found something," he told the others as he ran back through the kitchen and out to the cellar. "Bring your lanterns."

When he reached the bottom of the stairs, Grace was holding the lamp close to the engravings.

"Look at these," she said without turning around. She caressed several small tick marks carved on the inside edge of the numbers. "There are too many of them to mark seconds." Her focus moved from the slashes to other crude designs that adorned the perimeter and face of the clock. "Is this a crack in the stone?" Grace pointed to a long, curvy line that crossed from one side of the clock to the other.

Ethan pondered the markings for a moment. Grace was right. There was more to this clock than what they were seeing.

Cole and Will were the first to reach the bottom of the stairs—one lantern between them.

"Whoa," Cole exclaimed. "There's nothing like this in our cellar."

"Somebody sure liked clocks," Will said with awe as he scanned the underground room.

"My great-grandfather was a clock-maker." Grace smiled,

then turned back to the wall. "What do you think they mean?"

Will and Cole huddled closer and peered over Grace's shoulders. Will pushed Ethan to the side. Apparently, he was too tall to see over.

"It's a compass," Cole blurted out with elation. "See." He pointed to the directional letters that had been carved into the stone. However, they were not in their usual positions. The N, just beneath the minute hand, was positioned just after the one on the clock at the tick mark representing seven minutes past the hour. The S inside of thirty-seven, and E and W were laid out respectively at twenty-two and fifty-two.

What good would a compass be without some sort of map they could use to tell them where to begin? Especially, a giant compass that had been built into the side of a wall. The map Cole had drawn was great and detailed, but based solely on speculation from the many failed attempts of Horace Nolan. They needed something concrete, a solid clue that would direct them where to go.

"The chimes always sound at seven minutes past the hour," Grace said, a new light forming in her eyes. "If the seven actually represents..." she ran her fingers over the tick marks, "forty-three degrees, and forty-three degrees signifies north, then we would need to alter our direction forty-three degrees east. Right?"

Damn. Smart too.

"Grace," Ethan said, remembering the pouch in his hand.

She brought the lantern down to his face.

Ethan took the lantern from her and set it down on the edge of the worktable. He placed the small, soft pouch into her hands. "Not three separate keys or cranks. Place holders. One key."

She scrunched her eyebrows together again. "We already know that this key opens and winds the grandfather clock upstairs." She dumped the gems and the key out into her open palm.

As the rest of his family joined them, their lanterns alight, the giant watch face carved into the wall seemed to come alive with a life of its own.

"Incredible," Raine whispered.

Ethan placed a hand in the small of Grace's back and turned her around to once again face the clock. He bent down, eye-level with the first two carvings.

"May I?" he asked, reaching into her palm for the emeralds.

"Yes, but…"

He looked at the stones and placed their unique shapes into the openings.

"Ah," Grace's quick intake of air spread satisfaction through his chest and limbs.

They fit perfectly, gleaming brightly in the fill of the light of the four lanterns now focused on the clock in the wall.

"And the key?" Grace asked, holding up the small end.

Ethan took it from her and turned it around, gently sliding it into the open groove below the center of the adjoining hands. Once it felt like the key had locked in place, Ethan pushed gently against the emeralds. Something clicked and he stepped back, motioning for Grace to take over.

"Wind it up. Let's see what happens."

She looked at him, then down at the key. Gingerly, she reached out for the long, slender end of the golden stick and braced the teeth between her thumb and forefinger.

Ethan forced himself to breathe.

She tried to turn the key, but it wouldn't budge. Ethan placed his hand over hers and pushed down on the protruding end of the key and to everyone's surprise and delight, it moved. They pumped the lever twelve more times—with each round, it sounded as if the very foundation of the house were being wound.

Grace pushed the key until it was flush with the rock face and reached up to grab onto the minute hand. It was time to set the clock.

Ethan took a step backward to give her plenty of room. As she came around the top of the hour, Ethan could feel the anticipation coat the room. She passed the twelve slowly. The one. The two. Until, finally, she reached the seven. With a loud click, the clock hands began to move themselves. Grace's head bobbed up and down as she watched them.

Ethan reached out and pulled her back next to him. When the clock stopped at seven minutes past ten, it sounded as if the gears had come to a grinding halt.

"Some clock," Tag said, pulling his pocket watch from his vest. "It's only nine-thirty."

"It's a clue," Cole said, smacking his brother on the arm with the back of his hand.

Suddenly, the room rumbled. Dirt fell from the ceiling above them and a few crumbling rocks tumbled down the walls.

Ethan drew Grace closer to him.

"Quick," Jameson called to his wife and children as he guided them all toward the stairs.

Whoosh.

Everyone froze.

A whisper of cold air surged into the room as the wall slid open, leaving an open space just large enough to fit a foot through.

"It's a door!" Will cried as he tried to push it open farther. "It's stuck."

"It can't be that simple," Grace said, shaking her head in disbelief.

Simple? What part of their venture so far had been simple? Ethan was not generally one who sought adventure in far-away places like some of his brothers. Still, his heart started to race at the prospect of the legendary treasure being just on the other side of the wall. He glanced at Grace, whose eyes were wide with anticipation. She was biting her lip again.

Ethan smiled. He joined with his brother and father, and together they were able to slide the stone door behind the wall. He retrieved his lantern and stepped inside the room.

Empty. There was nothing there. Ethan's hopes sank. He looked over at Grace. She was blinking rapidly, her chest heaving with deep, but quickened breaths, waiting for him to say something.

He shook his head.

Grace ran into the room, followed by his brothers. The small chamber was barely big enough to fit them all.

"Nothing?" Will said loudly. "There is nothing here? I thought we'd found it." He shook his head. "I think I need some air."

Tag and Cole followed Will out into cellar.

"If it's not here," Jameson said, leaning into the compartment, "then where is it?"

"We're missing something," Raine said what Ethan had been thinking.

Grace spun around inside the chamber, scanning the walls, the floor, the ceiling, seeming to search for something they may have missed. She stopped and tilted her head at Ethan. Only, he realized, she wasn't looking at him, she was looking past him. He turned around and saw the object that had drawn her attention.

A large rotting box, Ethan guessed contained the inner-workings of the stone clock, protruded from this side of the wall just beyond the edge of the door they'd opened. Weights dangled from the bottom, but there was no pendulum.

"May I have a lantern, please?" she asked, lifting it from his hands as she moved past him.

"What are you looking for now?" He followed her.

Grace scanned each side of the box on the wall. "A way in," she said.

"What makes you so sure there is something under there?" Ethan asked.

"Call it a gut feeling," she said with a wry smile.

Yep. She fits right in.

"I thought you might want these." Taggert dropped an old toolbox at Ethan's feet. "I found it in that room under the work table. Thought they might come in handy." He looked at the box and a perplexed Grace. "Guess I was right." He smiled.

"Nothing crazy is going to come popping out of this box when I open it, right? Tag?" Ethan had experienced far too many of the twins' practical jokes to know for sure. It just seemed too coincidental.

"Ethan, I swear, if something comes out of that box, it wasn't my doing."

That was good enough for Ethan. His brothers were jokesters, not liars.

He opened the toolbox. Trappings of all sorts stared back at him. The hammer caught his attention first. He applied the back end to the edge of the large wooden box on the wall. With a few well-placed taps, he pried the planks away from each other and the box came off. A large metal casing now protected the clock's innards.

It would be simple enough to remove, Ethan just needed a screwdriver.

"It's my great-grandfather's signature," Grace said, her fingertips caressing those perfect, plump lips of hers. "Look." She pointed to the engraving in the bottom corner of the casing.

G.U.N. 1822.

Ethan did look. Closely. The depth of the grooves and the smooth, rounded edges of the letters meant the clock maker had signed the cast before the metal had cooled completely.

"Your great-grandfather's initials spell gun?" he asked, trying to keep the amusement from his voice.

Grace raised a brow and looked at him through narrowed eyes, as if challenging him to say another word. "Gerald Ulysses Nolan," she stated. "Eighteen twenty-two. That was just two years before he disappeared."

Ethan was impressed. Not many people knew the names of their own grandfathers, let alone their great-grandfathers, or their histories. Of course, not everyone's great-grandfather had been a thief who'd stolen a fabled ancient treasure from a not so extinct Incan priest either.

It only took a few moments for Ethan to remove the screws. He set down the tools and gripped a hold of the metal plate. With a little twisting and shaking, the casing came loose enough that he could remove it. To Ethan's amazement, there, dangling from a bar above the gears, was a black velvet pouch, identical to the one they'd found in her grandfather's lock-box.

Grace reached up and slid the small bag from the post. "There's only one way to find out." A clear, thin slab of glass slid out into her hand, framed by a wide, brass wire with thin metal threads encasing the disc. A thick metal bar, rounded with one flat side, extending from the bottom like a handle.

"It's a lens of some sort," Grace said as she held it up to the lantern's light.

"But where does it go?" A nagging feeling settled in Ethan's gut. It was right in front of them. He could feel it.

Grace handed it to him. It resembled a magnifying glass, but as he moved it back and forth it didn't distort the object of his focus or magnify it.

"Ethan," Cole called from the other room. "Come quick."

Ethan and Grace hurried from the small chamber to where Cole stood, staring at the clock.

A huge grin spread across his face. "It's the map," he said with unwavering confidence. Cole walked up close to the clock and pointed to the center where the hands met. "Look at the base of the top hand."

Ethan and Grace both scrunched down to the look at the metal connector. It was marked with an X.

"Do you remember when we went to that museum in Boston when we went to visit Rafe at school?"

"Yes," Ethan said slowly.

"Remember that painting when you first walked in that had a map laid out of all the wax figures, art pieces, and the location of the live musical theater?"

"Yes," Ethan said again, vaguely remembering the map. Then it hit him. At the bottom of the painting, a red 'X' marked where the entrance of the museum had been depicted.

"The X," Ethan said proudly.

"The X meant the beginning. We found the start. It's here."

"What are you talking about?" Grace asked.

Ethan picked her up and whirled her around. "Your house. This is where we start."

Grace looked back at the clock. "Well, where do we go?"

They stood back and looked at the clock, this time with a different perspective. The designs that, moments ago, looked like simple patterns and etchings suddenly took on new meaning.

"This is the river," he said pointing to the crack that Grace had discovered earlier.

"Yes, and these," Cole pointed to one set of triangular markings, "are the woods between the Nolan property and ours. And these," he pointed to another set, "represent the copse where we cut down our trees."

"Then this," Grace pointed to the scratches above the minute hand, "is the church in town." She stood up straight and glanced over at Ethan. "The clock in the tower of the church was built by my great-grandfather. That's where I think we should go."

"Go!" Cole said with urgency in his voice. "I'll try to draw the rest of the map and then I'll meet you in town."

"What if it's still snowing?" Grace asked hesitantly.

Ethan took her face in his hands, he didn't care who was watching. "We know where we're going and it's only ten miles into town from here. We'll make it." He planted a light kiss on her lips, ignoring the whistles and comments of jest from his brothers.

"What do you think we'll find there?" His father asked with a raised brow.

"There's only one way to find out." Ethan held out his hand to Grace. When she slipped her hand into his, he reveled in how good it felt there.

"Tag," Jameson turned to his son, "you and Will see to it that your mother and sister get home safely. We'll be back as soon as we can. Cole, since you seem to have a good feel for this treasure hunting business, you'll come with us. Raine, you too. You need to collect the sheriff and let him know that Jack's been taken."

"Jameson," Leah said quietly.

Ethan watched as his mother rushed toward his father. Jameson pulled his wife into a tight embrace and quickly found her lips. Showing affection was not an uncommon thing in the Redbourne household. Ethan had seen his parents kiss on many occasions. He turned to look down at Grace. Her hair spilled over her face and, in this light, it shone with several varying shades of wood, wheat, and honey. She was beautiful. And loving. And courageous. What more could he possibly want in a woman?

Right then and there he made a decision. Once they'd found Jack and all was put right with the world, he was going to do something about it. Ethan squeezed Grace's hand and she snuggled a little closer to him, resting her free hand on his arm and her head against his shoulder.

"Be safe, my love," Leah said quietly. She then blew kisses to her sons and winked at Grace. "Bring that boy home safe."

Ethan looked up the stairs to the door overhead.

"I intend to," he whispered just loud enough for Grace to hear.

CHAPTER EIGHTEEN

Snow blanketed the ground and flurries still swirled in the air. Stone Creek was quiet, except for the music coming from the Broken Pony and the sound of metal clanging against metal at the town smithy. It was still early yet, but Grace imagined that most folks wouldn't chance the snow today.

Mr. Pierce, the town's blacksmith, stepped out of his shop, his mallet in hand, and waved a greeting. They reciprocated.

Grace felt torn between her fear for Jack and the enjoyment she experienced being next to Ethan. She reveled in the delight she'd felt when he'd captured her hand in his or when he kissed her lightly on the mouth. Ethan drove the sleigh to the livery, jumped out, and knocked on the door. He clapped his hands together and shoved them under his arms.

Mr. Phillips, the liveryman she'd met last Sunday, opened the door and motioned for them to come inside. Ethan climbed back into the sleigh and drove it indoors, out of the cold. Raine, Jameson, and Cole followed on horseback.

"Thank you, Mr. Phillips," Ethan said, extending his hand to the man.

"I'll go find the sheriff," Raine said. "Now that the storm has let up, we may be able to gather some men to go looking for Jack and the others."

Ethan nodded.

"Now, let's head over to the church. I'm sure the good reverend will let us in."

When they got outside, Grace looked up at the clock in the tower. It looked much bigger from this angle than she'd remembered. She wondered if it was the pastor who kept the clock wound or if the job belonged to someone else.

The reverend didn't think twice about letting Jameson, three of his sons, and Grace into the church's clock tower—which was much smaller than she had expected it to be. She was surprised that they could all get in there and have any room at all to move with all the exposed metal rafters and chains hanging everywhere.

"Take as long as you need," the white-haired pastor said before descending the staircase.

A metal ladder style staircase led up to the face of the clock. She trailed her eyes up the thin, black iron staircase that wound up the corner of the room to the attic. The open door displayed the inner-workings and gears housed up there. Grace glanced around, feeling a little overwhelmed, when something caught her eye. A stream of light created a beam extending from a hole in the center of the massive iron clock hands to the floor near the staircase leading down to the chapel.

Fascinated, she climbed up the metal stairs that took her to the edge of the clock face. Grace reached into her pocket and retrieved the lens they'd found in the basement chamber behind the wall. It appeared to be near the same size as the hole in the hands, but she was just a little too short to inspect the opening.

"Did you find something?" Ethan asked, climbing up the metal stairs behind her.

"Don't you think it odd that there would be an opening where the clock hands meet? Isn't that where there is normally some type of fastener holding them together with a nut?"

"You're right."

Grace handed him the lens. "I thought this might fit there."

"You are brilliant. Cole," Ethan directed his attention to his brother, "hand me that step stool on the floor over there."

Once he'd placed the short wooden ladder on the floor, he held a hand out to her. "Go on," he said. "See if you were right."

Just the feel of her hand in his made her feel more at ease. Quickly, she climbed the three steps until her face was level with the opening. Ethan handed her the lens by the handle, and she placed it up against the space. The glass was the exact same size, only the metal extension of the lens would not allow her to fit it into place.

"This is the right place," Grace told the others. She could see that there was a place for the extension to fit, but the angle would not allow her to place the lens inside.

Think.

She took a step down, looking at the bottom frame of the opening. There were seams cut into the metal where it appeared a piece had been fitted in place. Two tiny buttons protruded from either side of the seams. Grace pressed them, and the center piece sprung open far enough that she could slide the metal portion of the lens into the slot. It sat at an odd angle, but after everything else she'd seen today, she didn't question it. She simply pushed it until it clicked.

Pop.

A small drawer popped open in the brick below the clock face. Ethan pulled out another velvet pouch—this time, much larger than the other two. He handed it up to Grace. The top of a two-tiered telescope had been nestled neatly inside the bag. She pulled it out to examine the find.

"Look," she said, "there's an inscription at the bottom. *Only when the sun's at its peak can the paragon of fortune be unearthed.* What do you think it means?" she asked.

"That you'll only find the treasure when the sun hits noon," Cole provided his interpretation. It sounded good to Grace.

She fingered the brass-trimmed bottom and discovered bare threads. It took only a moment for Grace to realize that the lens and scope went together. So, she screwed the top of the telescope onto the lens and pushed the entire contraption back into the opening.

Clank.

The sound had come from just on the other side of the clock. She peered through the window, but it looked as though the glass had not been cleaned in a century, and now, snow blanketed the bottom rim and over the numbers.

"Something's happening," she warned.

All of a sudden, the hands of the clock began to wind. When they finally came to a stop, there was another popping sound. A glint of gold glittered in the sun as it peeked from behind the clouds. Its contrast against the black iron of the hands was stunning. She glanced over at the stairs leading up to the utility door that would grant access to the iron balcony resting just beneath the clock.

"We need to go out and see where the hands stopped. And I think there is something inside of one of the clock hands."

"One clue at a time, love."

Did he just call her, love? She could get used to that.

Grace climbed the last step again and quickly looked through the eyepiece. It looked out over some rather large hills amidst a heavily wooded area. It was almost as if she were looking at a snow-covered garden—similar to the one she and Hannah had worked on in her backyard.

"Well, what do you see?"

"Trees. A lot of them. And some steep hills, jagged hills. There might be a cave, but it's hard to tell through all the snow." She turned to look down at Ethan. "I don't recall seeing hills like that around here."

Ethan pondered for a moment, then he closed his eyes, a knowing smile touching his lips.

"I know exactly where it is."

"And where might that be?" someone with a deep, scratchy voice asked.

Grace and Ethan both turned to look at the man who'd spoken. The town blacksmith stood at the top of the staircase, pointing a gun at them. Jameson lay sprawled on the floor at his feet.

Grace's eyes opened wide and her hand shot to her heart. *Please don't be dead*, she pleaded. *Please don't be dead.*

"Mr. Phillips?" Ethan asked, surprise evident in his voice. "What have you done?"

"Aw, Ethan, it's unfortunate, really," the man said. "You was always such a good kid. I'm sorry you had to get mixed up in all this."

Ethan took a step forward, along the short metal walkway. "What exactly have I gotten myself mixed up in?"

"You should probably just wait right there, son." Mr. Phillips aimed the gun a little higher.

Grace's attention was drawn to Cole. The smithy hadn't seen him approach from behind. Ethan must have seen him too as he tried to keep his old friend focused on him.

"Don't play games with me, Redbourne. I know you're looking for Uly's treasure."

"How do *you* know about the treasure, Sal?"

It was the first time Grace had ever heard anyone use the man's first name.

"I know enough. Hell, I was younger than you when Nolan came looking for someone to pour his locks, and mold his keys. Just a boy. Who do you think fashioned the parts for his clocks? For his hidden compartments?"

"Come on, Sal. It's me, Ethan." He could hardly believe what was happening. This man had been like a father to him. "We've known each other a long time. You've taught me almost everything I know about blacksmithing." He took another restrained step toward his old friend. "Why are you doing this, Sal?"

"I want what's been coming to me for near fifty years," he said with a firm set to his jaw. "Nolan promised me a share of his beloved treasure if I would help him in secret. Even after he'd stolen my gal, Ethan, I still agreed to help him. For her sake." He shifted his stance, his expression becoming cold. Rigid. Soulless.

Grace stepped closer to Ethan, sliding her hand into his. He squeezed it.

"Then," Mr. Pierce continued, "he up and left her in the middle of the night with nothing but his kid and a broken heart. She lost her laughter that day, and the music from her heart stopped." His broad shoulders and muscular arms reminded Grace a lot of Ethan.

Cole looked up at his brother right before he reached for Pierce's gun. Ethan shook his head, but it was too late. The blacksmith was too strong. With one fierce blow, Mr. Pierce sent Cole flying backward, down the long staircase to the chapel.

Ethan bolted forward.

Grace's hand flew to her mouth.

"Why you s—"

"I wouldn't." Mr. Pierce pointed his gun at an unconscious Jameson's head.

Ethan stopped in his tracks, mere feet from the man now threatening his family.

"Cole?" Desperation hung in Ethan's voice like a solitary storm cloud on the sky as he called down the stairway.

No response.

"Cole!" he yelled his brother's name this time. "Sal, let me go see if he's all right."

"I'm sorry, Ethan. What's done is done."

"You won't get away with this. The deputy will be here any moment with the sheriff," Grace blurted out.

"Then, I guess we best get a movin'. Come on down here,

son. Real nice and slow."

Ethan put his hands up in front of him. "Sal? Please?" he appealed to the man.

"Sit right here, next to your pa." Mr. Phillips relieved Ethan of the gun that was tucked into his belt and took a step toward Grace, climbing backward up the stairs, his gun still trained on them. "And Ethan," the man whispered loud enough for Grace to hear, "if you move, I'll shoot her."

CHAPTER NINETEEN

Ethan hung by his feet from the rafters of the tiny church attic with all the gears clicking and turning in rhythm. Pressure mounted in his head. If he stayed like this much longer, he was going to be in real trouble.

Mr. Pierce had taken Grace.

How could I have let that happen?

Mr. Pierce had held all the cards, especially with a gun he'd threatened to use on Grace or his father, leaving Ethan with no other choice but to comply. He'd allowed the man to string him up to protect them. Now, he needed to get down to do the same.

There wasn't a lot of room to maneuver in this little room, but he didn't need much. Ethan bent himself in half at the torso and wrapped his tied hands around the chain that suspended him. After a few attempts, he was able to push the hook, holding the chains together at his ankles, through the thick iron link to which it had been anchored, effectively freeing his feet.

Slowly, he straightened out his body, gripping the chains in his hands, until he was confident he would be able to drop without killing himself. Sweat dripped down Ethan's face and neck.

He let go. When he hit the floor, shooting pains pulsed through his foot and leg. He took a moment to rub the throbbing from his leg, then worked quickly to free his hands.

Ethan had worked alongside Sal Pierce for the better part of seven years. How had he not known the man had cracked? Now, he had Grace and was headed for the hills and the treasure. In his newly crafted sleigh. He'd never catch up in time.

Ethan tugged on the handle of the flap in the floor. It didn't budge. Something was holding it shut and Ethan had a feeling it wouldn't be opening any time soon. He scanned the gear room for anything he could use as leverage, but short of breaking the clock, there was nothing. The only other way out was through a short service door that stood a few feet off the floor and led out onto the roof. It was crazy. He knew it, but what choice did he have?

At least, he consoled himself, he didn't have the same fear of heights as Rafe. He laughed incredulously. Who would have ever guessed that *he,* of all his brothers, would have gotten himself into such a predicament?

Ethan opened the little door, the width of which looked barely large enough to fit his shoulders through. The cold air slapped his face with a winter's warning. Without thinking any more about it, he turned onto his back and, with a little maneuvering, pulled himself out through the door and onto the roof. He just needed to get to the north side, to the wooden step ladder that had been constructed as a part of the church's exterior.

He took a step. Then another, slipping only a moment before he was able to regain his footing. With both arms up for balance, he took the next step, but could not maintain enough traction to keep him upright, and he fell onto his hip, sliding toward the ledge. He scrambled with his feet, but to no avail. As he slipped over the edge, his hands caught on the snow-packed gutter, but he just could not hold on.

He landed in a bed of snow on the balcony just below the clock.

Thank you, Lord.

"What in thee hell are you doing up there?" Raine called up from the street below. The sheriff, looking even more grumpy than usual, stood behind him.

"Raine," he peered over the edge, "it's about time you showed up. Dad and Cole are both hurt."

Ethan took a moment to catch his breath, then headed for the utility door that would get him back into the clock tower room. He stopped short when he remembered what Grace had said about there being something inside one of the clock hands.

He leaned his back up against the glass, but the hands were just too close to the clock for him to position himself in a place to see what was there. However, he reached behind the minute hand and, sure enough, a compartment had opened. Ethan felt for the unfastened latch and pulled. The door opened. Ethan pressed his face against the clock window in attempt to see, but to no avail.

As he pulled back, he saw it in the reflection of the glass.

Gold. It looked like a fancy wide-tipped blade.

Impossible.

Ethan glanced up to the tip of the minute hand and noticed the edge had not been sealed. He guessed it had opened at the same time as the small compartment. He wasn't tall enough to pull it from the metal casing, so he did the only thing he could think of. He jumped up and grabbed ahold of the minute hand and pulled it downward. Metal slid against metal. When the shiny object of his curiosity fell free from its iron home, Ethan reached out and caught it just before it tumbled to the ground below.

The metal was slick against his palm. It felt every inch a weapon. Ethan pulled it in front of him and set the end on the balcony. A spear. A true, honest to goodness, golden spear. The head of it reached Ethan's chin. It was ornamented in three different colored stones, all the size of a five dollar gold coin. Ethan guessed them to be an emerald, a ruby, and a sapphire. This spear alone was probably worth more than the whole Nolan farmhouse. Confident no one else had seen his acquisition, he climbed through the utility door and into the clock tower.

"Are you all right, son?" Jameson asked, still lying on the floor rubbing his head. He glanced around the room. "Where's Grace?"

"Pierce took her," Ethan said with a quick shake of his head. His jaw flexed at the thought. He didn't have time to explain. He had to go.

"Raine, I think I convinced him to head out to the old Cooper mine—the one Cole and Alaric came across a few years back."

"The treasure?"

"He wants it. Says Nolan owes him."

"Mr. Pierce? Our Mr. Pierce knew Uly Nolan?" Raine asked in disbelief. He recovered quickly. "Where did the clue really tell you to go next?" The question was more like a knowing statement.

Ethan hated that his big brother always just…knew.

"The gardens at cave junction," Ethan said with a smirk.

Raine helped their father to his feet. "Nicely played."

"You okay, Dad?" Ethan asked.

Jameson nodded his head. "Go," he said. "Grace needs you."

At that thought, Ethan headed for the stairs.

"What you got there?" Raine asked, pointing to the golden lance in Ethan's hand.

Ethan held it out. "*The* spear," he called back as he made his way down the staircase, not waiting for this brother's reaction. "The one the priest used to kill one of Uly's partners in the stories." He called loudly, skittering down the steps to the chapel. He had to find Grace. And her brother.

And, he thought, looking at the spear, *the treasure.*

When Ethan reached the bottom, he found the good reverend helping his little brother sit upright on the last row of pews. Cole's eye was swollen and his face bruised. It looked like he was favoring an arm and was having a hard time getting comfortable. Ethan breathed a sigh of relief. He threw his arms around his brother's shoulders.

"Ow." Cole shied away with a groan-like laugh. He looked up. "Sorry, I couldn't stop him, Ethan."

Ethan looked at his little brother, grateful he was breathing, let alone sitting up and speaking. "You're...alive." He shook his head. An image of Cole, reaching for Mr. Pierce's gun, etched his memory. "You almost got yourself killed." Ethan ruffled Cole's hair. He would have smacked him too, but thought better of it. "What can I do?"

"Sheriff went to get Doc Cooper. I'll be fine. Go!" Cole practically yelled the last word.

Ethan didn't need to be told twice. With the spear firm in hand, he rushed to the livery. He may not have the sleigh, but Cole's horse, Maverick, would get him there in half the time. He glanced down at the spear still wrapped in his hand. It was highly conspicuous. He pulled Cole's extra blanket from his saddle bags and carefully rolled the weapon inside and strapped it alongside the rifle holster.

Mr. Phillips had not emerged from his office, which Ethan thought odd. He finished strapping the saddle to the black stallion's back. The liveryman wouldn't have just sat back and allowed Sal to take the sleigh and Ethan suddenly feared the man's fate. He breathed a sigh of relief as he rounded the corner to see Mr. Phillips sleeping on a cot against the back wall of his office. The rise and fall of his chest told Ethan he was all right.

Dark clouds once again covered the sky and a light smattering of snowflakes tumbled down around Ethan as he urged Maverick faster. Once he crossed the bridge, it was a straight shot to the garden, which was on the far edge of the Nolan property. Luckily, Pierce had had less than a thirty minute head start.

Ethan's hands stung from the cold. He remembered shoving his gloves into the pocket of his coat. Without slowing the horse, he reached back and was able to retrieve them quickly. The woolen insides felt soothing against his newly chaffed skin.

When he caught sight of the sleigh, he pulled back on Maverick's reins and slowed his pace, ducking behind a cluster of trees. A man, who Ethan recognized as one of Hurley's brutes, stood next to the sleigh holding Clyde's reins.

Hurley and Sal were working together? It didn't make sense. Sal hated the Devlins—especially Hurley. They must have believed that the Cooper's mine was the entrance all along. Ethan was glad he could confirm it for them. He sniggered at his fortuitousness.

Neither Grace, Hurley, nor Mr. Pierce were anywhere to be seen. He figured they must have already gone into the mine shaft. That worried Ethan. That old mine had been prone to cave-ins. The last time he had been there was to dig his brother and his friend out.

He had to think for a moment how he would get past the guard.

Crack. The muffled sound of a gunshot loosened the embankment of snow that had accumulated just above the mine's entrance.

A loud, fearful scream echoed through the mine and out into the open. The man holding the horses jerked his head toward the sound and yelled down the shaft. After a moment, he turned back and spit into the ground with a satisfied grin.

A few yards beyond the mine's entrance, an improvised corral contained several horses—Ethan guessed the same ones Hurley had purchased from Mr. Phillips a few weeks back. He also recognized Hound, Jack's horse. If Ethan could just get over to the corral without being noticed and open the gate, he may be able to create enough of a diversion to get inside of the mine undetected.

He could hear Raine's voice in his head—*'Why didn't you wait for me?'*

There was no time. If someone down there was getting trigger happy, it would only be a matter of time before Grace or her brother got hurt. He needed to get down there. He pulled himself up onto Cole's horse and pulled on the reins to guide him toward the corral.

"Going somewhere?"

"Raine," Ethan said exasperated, "you ought not to sneak up on a man like that." He nodded at the man with his brother. "Sheriff."

"I've got to get inside, Raine. There was a gunshot. I have to make sure she is all right. We need a diversion." He nudged his horse forward a few steps. "I figure if we can get those horses out of that corral—"

"How about we just arrest him?"

Ethan nodded. "That works too."

Sheriff Fogarty drew his weapon and rested it atop his saddle horn, while Raine's new Winchester rifle lay across his lap. They started toward the mine, the sheriff in the lead and Ethan bringing up the tail end. When they approached, the man raised his head in greeting. Ethan stayed hidden behind his brother.

"Nice sleigh you have there," Raine said to the man who'd only been in town a few weeks.

"Just trying her out on the new snow," the thug replied casually.

"I'm wondering though," Raine continued, "how you got it out of the livery where my brother left it."

Ethan urged Maverick forward a few more steps until the man could see his face. He glanced to the rock where his gun leaned.

"I might rethink that if I were you," Raine said quietly, his rifle cocked, aimed, and ready.

The sheriff placed a finger against his lips as he dismounted.

"Now, they'll be no yellin' or funny business." The sheriff clamped his cuffs on the man's wrists. "Why don't you just have yourself a seat right over here, Mister...uh... Come to think of it, son, what is your name exactly?"

While the sheriff spoke with the new prisoner, Ethan turned to Raine.

"What are you staring at me for? Let's go."

They opened the gate on the corral and led their horses inside. The animals would be safe there for the time being. As they approached the mine's entrance, Ethan glanced into the darkness. It would be impossible to see anything in there without a light.

Of course.

"I'll be right back," he said to his brother and ran to the sleigh. He remembered that he'd grabbed a torch and match box from his smithy before they'd left and he'd placed them inside the seat bench to keep them dry. When he lifted the bench, he breathed in relief. They were still there.

Ethan lit the torch and held it in front of him.

"You never cease to amaze me, little brother," Raine said from behind him.

"Let's just hope it lasts."

"I said, let—me—go!" Grace did not appreciate being tugged around like a little rag doll. She yanked on her arm once again, and, this time, he released her. She could not let him see the fear that threatened to show its ugly head at every turn.

When they'd first pulled up to the mine entrance, several men—many of them who she'd seen earlier with Hurley

Devlin—had been standing around, apparently awaiting instructions. They'd built a temporary corral to house their horses, and all of them were armed. With lanterns, ropes, and a variety of what looked like digging instruments, they'd all headed into the cave.

If these men had Jack, she would go with them without a fight. She needed to know her brother was safe. They hadn't gone too far, when they came to a divergence where three more men had been waiting. Hurley Devlin turned around, but his face fell when he saw her.

"Grace? What are you doing here?" He sounded genuinely surprised.

"Where is my brother?" she responded coldly.

"Why is she here, Sal?" Hurley ignored her question.

"Leverage," was Mr. Pierce's reply.

"He said neither she, nor the boy, was to be harmed."

"Where's Jack, Hurley? Is he all right?" she asked, but he wasn't listening.

"You think I care about any of that now? I'm not taking orders from him anymore. This treasure belongs to me." Something in Mr. Pierce's eyes grew wild. Angry. Desperate.

"Let her go, Pierce. She doesn't need to be here." Hurley stepped in front of Grace in a protective stance, which surprised her. "It was enough that you brought the boy into this, but this is where I draw the line."

Crack.

Hurley dropped to the ground, clutching his leg.

Grace screamed.

"And I certainly am not going to listen to you." He spat on the ground near Hurley.

"Run, Grace," he yelled, but it was too late.

The man she'd heard them call Giles, grabbed her from behind, both arms locking around her. She kicked and squirmed.

"Stop, Miss Nolan," Pierce snarled between gritted teeth,

"or your little brother will meet the same fate." His breath was like a melting pot of sewage and meat. She looked away, but stopped struggling.

"String him up," Mr. Pierce directed his men. "The coyotes will find him soon enough."

Giles carried her a few more steps, then dropped her with a shove. She glanced back over her shoulder at Hurley. He met her eyes and she understood his apology.

Hurley screamed out in agony as they lifted him by his feet and dangled him from one of the wooden supports.

Grace closed her eyes, forcing the tears to withdraw.

Ethan's coming.

Even the idea of him gave her strength. And, something within her told her it was true. Ethan was going to come.

As they walked deeper into the mine shaft, the colder it became. Grace wrapped her arms around herself and briskly rubbed. No one spoke, but she could hear the low murmur of men's voices up ahead. She guessed they'd only been walking for ten minutes when they came to a stop at the end of the tunnel.

"Have we found it yet?" Mr. Pierce asked one of the men hunched over a gaping, rutty hole in the ground, glowing with light, a rope extending from a support beam in the corner through the gap in the rocks.

"The kid says there's nothing down there, except another mine shaft."

Jack? Where?

"He says he can see light at the end of the shaft. We're guessing there is another entrance somewhere on the other side of the hill."

Grace rushed to the hole and peered inside. *Jack climbed through there?* A rope threaded a crevice so small, it was a wonder that her fourteen-year-old brother had been able to fit through it.

"Jack?" she called down, desperate to hear his voice.

She waited. Nothing.

She opened her mouth to call again, when he came and stood beneath the hole. He was so far down, she could barely see the whole of him through the opening. He held up a lantern.

"Gracie? Is that you?"

"Run, Jack," she yelled. "Get out of there. They're—"

"That's enough," Pierce yanked on her arm until she was in a standing position. He turned to the others. "Pull him up. I want a full report."

"Yes, sir."

"And you, young lady," he walked with her a few steps and shoved her to the ground, "can wait over there."

Grace hit hard against the rock protrusion in the mine wall and bounced onto the ground on her hands and knees. Her elbow throbbed and her knees stung, but she turned onto her bottom and leaned back against the offending outcrop.

"Stay put," he said, turning back to the men attempting to pull Jack from the tunnel below.

Four lanterns, that she could count, lined the ceiling. Grace looked around for anything she could use as a weapon, but all of the tools were within reaching distance of the men. She couldn't run. Not until she knew that these men would not be able to pull Jack back up through that hole.

"Grace." Someone called her name in a low whisper.

Ethan?

"Don't turn around, love."

It *was* Ethan.

"Listen to me very carefully, okay?"

She nodded slowly.

"Can you walk?"

She nodded again.

"What is taking so long!" Mr. Pierce yelled at his man.

"He seems to be fighting it, sir."

Pierce looked at her. "Then, shoot him."

"No!" Grace screamed and pushed herself to her feet. "Run, Jack!"

The old blacksmith lifted his arm, gun in hand, and aimed. "You've both outlived your usefulness."

Crack!

CHAPTER TWENTY

"Change of plans," Ethan said as he stepped out from behind the side overhang on the wall, and shot out one of the lanterns.

Fine shot. Rafe would be proud.

"Why can't you shoot like that at the Thanksgiving competition?" Raine asked dryly. "Pierce!" he called out to their old friend. "Put down your gun, Sal, and we can all still walk out of here."

Raucous laughter erupted from the man.

The two men behind Pierce dropped their weapons and raised their hands in the air.

"Fools." His face lost all amusement.

The rope anchored around the vertical support beam at the end of the shaft tightened, causing the base of the post to slide a few inches toward the hole it was strung through. A loose cascade of rock debris and dirt showered down upon them.

"Ethan," Raine called urgently. "We have got to get out of here."

"No!" Grace cried. "Jack is down that hole. He's on the other end of that rope."

"Take her," Ethan said, not taking his focus off of his old

master.

The men behind Pierce ran toward them in retreat.

"I won't leave you," Grace said, grazing his arm with her fingers.

Raine pulled her out of his view.

"Ethan," she called. "I love you."

Ethan's heart swelled, but he forced himself to keep focused.

"The treasure's not here, Sal. I lied."

"I don't believe you. You've never lied to me before. Besides, everything we learned led us here. And you confirmed it." He sounded desperate.

"You hurt my family, Mr. Pierce. I knew you weren't thinking straight, but this?" Ethan swiped his hand across the air. "This is too far." He paused. "I lied."

Click.

Ethan exhaled. Sal's chamber was empty.

Mr. Pierce tossed his gun aside and charged. "Aaaaaaaaaaa."

Ethan couldn't shoot the man who'd been like a father to him. Didn't want to fight him either. But when Sal reached him, fully intent on taking him down, Ethan instinctively dropped and rolled backward, his feet against the man's chest, and lifted him from the ground, over his head, onto the dirt floor behind him. Growing up with six brothers had its advantages.

Sal groaned and coughed.

He pulled himself to his feet, waiting for the old man to attack again, but he didn't arise. He lay there, still as stone.

"No!" Ethan screamed. He scrambled to his master's side. "Mr. Pierce, get up!" he demanded. "Sal."

Boom.

Pain shot through Ethan's jaw and he tumbled backward onto his backside. He hadn't expected the force behind the blow. His mind clouded and black crept in around the edges of his sight.

Focus, Redbourne.

"Should have seen that one coming, Ethan."

Ethan fought to clear his head as Mr. Pierce slowly approached, breathing heavily.

It seemed that punch had taken a lot out of him. Sal grabbed Ethan by the hair and lifted, forcing Ethan to rise. He stared into Ethan's eyes. Ethan saw anger and greed burning brightly in them.

"I don't want to fight you, boy." Pierce's voice was raspy. Tired. "But I will if you don't stay out of my way." He let go of Ethan's hair and slammed a fist into his stomach.

Ethan doubled over, unable to believe the strength of his old master.

Sal brought both fists down on Ethan's unprotected back.

Ethan's face banged against the floor. He coughed hard, tears welling up in his eyes.

"For fifty years, I've waited. Fifty. Years!" Sal screamed into the rumbling darkness. "The treasure belongs to me, not to some spoiled rich money-grubber from New York. Me!" The mine shaft continued to drop rocks and dust down on the men.

Ethan knew they were running out of time. He had to do something fast, or both of them would be buried under the earth. He forced himself to his feet, facing Mr. Pierce. Sal frowned and grunted as he swung a meaty fist at Ethan, barely missing.

"Sal, listen to yourself." Ethan dodged another blow, then another. "This isn't you."

"Then who is it, my boy? Tell me." Mr. Pierce continued to strike out at Ethan, each punch slower than the last.

Sal drew back and forced another jab at Ethan.

Now! Ethan screamed in his head. He grabbed onto Mr. Pierce's wrist and twisted with all his might. Sal shrieked in pain and surprise as Ethan bore him to the floor, his arm twisted sharply behind his back.

"I see a man who has lost all hope. I was like that for a long time. We need to get over our fears, Sal. We need to overcome our weaknesses and allow ourselves to love and be loved." Ethan released Mr. Pierce's wrist and stood. "Now let's get out of here before we both die."

Mr. Pierce stood, hunched over, his hands on his knees.

The post bearing the rope slid a little farther outward and more rocks tumbled to the ground. The cord suddenly fell limp. Jack. Ethan closed his eyes for a brief moment with gratitude. The kid had to have gotten free of the line, but the damage had already been done. This end of the tunnel was going to collapse and they needed to get out. Now.

"Sal," Ethan said with the sudden urgency he felt, "we have to go."

Rocks started to crumble and the ground began to shake. Sal looked up and shook his head.

"I can't." He breathed heavily. "Go," he whispered.

"No." Ethan closed the distance between them in moments and heaved his master blacksmith up onto his shoulders.

They would make it back. Both of them.

Large boulders crashed down behind them, but Ethan didn't look back. Couldn't. His head pounded. His face and jaw throbbed. And he staggered under the weight of his friend. But he had hope. An image of Grace's smiling face stood before him like a carrot dangling in front of a mule.

When the ground stopped shaking and the sound of rocks crashing to rubble had ceased, he stumbled, but did not fall. His knee nearly touched the earth, but he pushed hard against the ground, straightening his back. Ethan could see the light of the entrance and strength washed over him. He heaved Mr. Pierce out into the light of day, lifted him off his shoulders, and onto the ground.

"I need some water over here," Ethan called, motioning to Mr. Pierce. He breathed in the cold air deeply.

Grace ran to him and threw her arms around him. She felt so good in his arms. He bent his head down, his face nestling into the curve of her neck. He didn't want to ever let go. She pulled back and looked to the entrance with hope written all over her features. After a moment, she turned to him.

"Where's Jack?"

"You told him to run, didn't you?" Ethan remembered the slack in the rope just before the rocks began to cave. The only way it could have done that was if he'd gotten free of it. At least that is what he chose to believe.

She smiled. "So, where does the second tunnel lead?"

The garden at the cave junction. It had to be linked to the caves, there was no other explanation. He raised a brow, a smirk forming on his lips. *Ow. That hurt.*

"Redbourne," Hurley called out to him before he'd had a chance to voice his thoughts. His old rival lay in the back of a wagon holding several of Stone Creek's new prisoners.

Ethan bent down and kissed Grace lightly on the tip of her nose. "I'll be right back."

He wondered if any of the men with Hurley had bounties on their heads. If so, maybe it would bring Rafe back into town for Christmas. He approached the wagon, thrilled to see his father in the high seat.

"Thought you could use a little help," Jameson said with a wink.

"And Cole?" Ethan asked.

"Banged up a bit, but the doc says he should heal up real nice. He has a broken arm, but nothing any boy of mine couldn't handle. Looks like you got a beauty there yourself." He pointed to Ethan's jaw.

"It's nothing." Ethan said with a smile.

That hurt.

"Ethan." Hurley reached out his hand from the back of the buckboard. He was lying down with thick blankets pulled to his chin. Ethan eyed him speculatively. Making peace with

Hurley Devlin was like tempting the devil himself, but Ethan was ready to move past the hurt and bitterness he held from the accident. He stretched his shoulder in a backward circular motion before taking Devlin's hand.

Hurley placed something cool and metal into his palm. "Thank you," he said.

Ethan looked at his longtime rival. The color had all but drained from his face, still streaked in blood, but Ethan could see it in his eyes. He'd meant it.

"About the accident…"

"Don't," Ethan said, not wanting to go back there.

"I…I didn't know the forge would tip, Ethan. I swear. I never meant for you to get hurt. Not like that." Hurley's voice grew faint. "Please forgive me."

Visions of hot coals falling down on top of him from the portable forge in the smithy, glowing embers searing the flesh of his chest and shoulder, the smell…

Enough! He had to let it go.

"We've all done things we're not proud of, Devlin." Ethan suddenly remembered something his mother told him. "But it's what you do from here that will define who you are."

Hurley tightened his grip on Ethan's hand.

"Keep it safe."

Hurley had been lucky Ethan and Raine had come upon him when they had. He'd been near unconscious. Left for dead. They'd cut him down, bound his wound, and carried him out to the sheriff. He was lucky to be alive.

And to think, the day was just beginning.

The faint jingling of bells on the sleigh filled the frosty air with a warm sense of anticipation. Grace needed to see Jack. To hold him and know that he was safe. A part of her still worried that he would be lost somewhere underground, but she trusted Ethan. More than she cared to admit.

She wrapped her arms more tightly around Ethan's arm as he drove. Showing any type of affection in public had been frowned upon in New York. Especially at Coldhern Estates. Especially with Lee. But here, everything was different. Ethan was different. And she loved him.

"It's just over the bridge and through that cluster of pines." Ethan pointed to an area just beyond the next hill.

Grace glanced up at him, wanting to soak in his strong, handsome features.

"What's wrong," she asked, noticing the tight crinkling of his brow.

He didn't respond. He just looked at her, offered a tight-lipped smile, and returned his eyes straight ahead. As they pulled into a clearing in the trees, he narrowed his eyes and scanned the area.

"Whoa," he said in a low, smooth voice that sent tingles down Grace's back. She shivered, but it wasn't from the cold.

He got out of the sleigh and moved to the center of the garden, where a large mound of snow protruded from the ground.

She joined him. From that vantage point, the openings of three different caves were visible.

"This is wonderful," she said, gazing at the snow frosted pine trees and the white rolling hills, soaking it all in.

"Grace, I…"

She could sense the hesitation in his voice.

"Which one is connected to the mines?" she asked, rushing toward the one in the center. She glanced back at him, the furrow returning to his brow.

Fear slipped in, and a part of her realized that Ethan didn't know. She turned back to the center cave, then moved to the right, and the left. Where was Jack? Grace ran down a small slope to the cave closest to the direction they'd come. She ran inside. It only went back a few hundred feet, but with the light of the sun that had now burst through the heavy weave of darkened clouds, she could see all the way to the end.

A part of her broke inside. What if Ethan was wrong?

Don't throw yourself into a fit of hysteria. Jack is fine. Jack is fine.

"Jack is fine," she said aloud.

"Grace." Ethan met her at the brink of the center cave. "I..."

"Don't."

He reached out to touch her arm, but she impulsively pulled it away.

"You made me believe that...that..." Tears formed in her eyes and this time she could not stop them from falling. "You made me believe that Jack was all right. That he would be here, in this place."

"Grace, I..."

She didn't want to hear it. Didn't want excuses or apologies.

Ethan pulled her into his arms. She struggled against him at first, but quickly succumbed to the warmth of his embrace, and she buried her head into his shoulder and let the tears flow.

"Gracie? Are you all right?"

Grace snapped her head up, hope refilling the emptiness that had carved out a section of her heart. There, walking up out of the center cave, was her brother—coal-smudged and shirtless. Grace ran to him, nearly knocking him off balance, giggling through her tears. She thrust her arms around him and kissed his head and face over and over.

"Perfect," she said, glancing from Jack to Ethan. "Everything is unquestionably perfect."

"I'm sorry I didn't find the treasure," Jack said with a lowered head as he set his lantern down on the ground. "I really thought the legends were true. I wanted to believe that grandfather was right."

"About that," Ethan said as he turned back toward the sleigh.

"Where is your coat? You must be freezing."

"Yes. It's a little cold out here."

"A little co..." She shook her head.

When Ethan returned, he carried an object wrapped in a big, thick blanket. It rested across his arms and he held it out to them.

"What is it?" Grace asked. She glanced at Jack, standing there half naked, his shirt torn and dirty. *He must be freezing.*

She quickly folded back one side of the blanket and then the other.

"I can't believe it." Jack's eyes grew wide as saucers. "It looks like..."

"The spear?" Ethan filled in for him. "From the stories."

Jack nodded with vigor. "He *was* right. Can I touch it?"

Grace dipped her head in affirmation.

Jack picked it up with reverence, his fingers tracing the jewels that adorned the top.

Grace grasped the blanket from Ethan's arms and wrapped it around her little brother's shoulders, then turned to Ethan. "But where did y—"

"The clock hand in town."

"Ah. And you didn't tell me."

"Well, you were a little preoccupied."

They both laughed.

"There's another blanket in the sleigh," Ethan told Jack.

"In the clock tower, you said you knew exactly where the clue would lead. Was that true?"

Ethan pulled her into his arms and planted a soft kiss on her lips. "It's right here."

Grace thought about it for a moment. Trees. Jagged hills. Caves.

"But where?"

Ethan shrugged and let go of her as she turned in circles, scanning the clearing.

"Jack," Grace motioned for her brother to join them.

"Ethan believes the treasure is here, in this garden. Are you up for a little more treasure hunting?"

"Here? What makes you think so?"

"That's a long story. One to be told in front of the fireplace with a steaming cup of your sister's apple cider." Ethan winked at her. It warmed her from the inside out.

"I don't think there is going to be a clock way out here," Grace said thoughtfully.

"Why do you need a clock?" Jack inquired.

"Don't ask," both Ethan and Grace said at the same time.

They laughed again.

There was only one cave left to check. Jack retrieved his lantern from the floor of the center cave, although the light was now barely a flicker. They walked inside the small entrance, hidden slightly by years of undergrowth, and it opened up into a large room that went back a hundred feet or so. At first glance, it looked very similar to the first one Grace had seen.

As they were about to leave, she noticed an odd ridge in the dirt and she took another step toward it. The ground gave way and she started to fall. Grace's heart felt like it had flown into her throat, but then Ethan's strong hands wrapped around the flesh above her wrist and he pulled her up into the safety of his arms.

She smiled in relief. "Thank you. Best be more careful on these ventures."

He released her and immediately she missed his warmth.

Ethan pointed to a gradual slope that appeared to lead to the bottom of the cave. With careful steps, they followed the would-be trail until they reached the lowest point in the room.

Jack held up the lantern and looked around. Rocks and other debris covered the floor. Light glinted off something at the bottom of the ledge she'd almost fallen from. Grace took the lamp from Jack and held it up in front of her.

The lanky fingers of a human skeleton rose from the dirt in the ground. She turned away.

"What is it, love?" Ethan asked, venturing forward.

"It's a...a person."

Ethan crouched down around the skeleton. Grace held the light above his head, but she remained behind him.

"I'm afraid it's not just any person," Ethan said, pulling something from the dirt and holding it up in his palm for Grace and Jack to see.

An emerald.

"There are four or five of them here. This...person, is your great-grandfather."

Grace needed to sit down. For years her family had believed that Uly Nolan had abandoned his family. Grace looked up to the ledge. But he'd fallen to his death.

"When we get back into town, we'll call on Mr. Collins and he can bring a few of his men down here to excavate the bones." Ethan finished collecting all of the gems he could find. There were six in all.

That treasure had to be close. *Why else would Uly Nolan have been here?*

They climbed back up the slope and out into the cold fresh air. Grace took a deep breath. It felt good in her lungs.

"So much for finding a clock," Grace said, trying to lighten the suddenly morose spirit.

"Wait a minute." Ethan narrowed his eyes and skimmed the area opposite the caves. "That's it." He rushed to a large mound of snow covering what looked to be a well at the far edge of the garden.

With a few finely-placed sweeps of his hand, Ethan had cleared the snow from the top of the structure. Only it wasn't a well. It was a sundial.

"Uly must have wanted to pay tribute to the Inca somehow. See this?" Ethan pointed to the center of the sundial where a giant sun had been carved into the stone. Will said something about the Inca worshipping the sun or something. I honestly didn't pay a lot of attention."

Grace had seen a sundial before, but wasn't really sure how they worked. She kicked at the base of the structure and more snow fell away, exposing stone very similar to the wall at home where she'd hidden her money.

"What did that telescope say?" Ethan asked.

Grace thought for a moment trying to remember the exact words. "Only when the sun's at its peak can the paragon of fortune be unearthed."

"Sun's at its peak? What time is it?" He reached into his denims and pulled out a pocket watch. "A quarter of twelve. We have fifteen minutes to figure this out."

Jack pulled the blanket up tighter around his neck, the spear still held firmly in his hands.

"Maybe there is a hole somewhere on the dial that it will fit into," Grace said, pointing to the primitive weapon in Jack's possession.

Ethan immediately brushed more snow from the top of the sundial. Grace ran her hands over the stones and the idea hit her. She quickly felt for any loose stones. Sure enough, one of the stones just below the face of the ancient-style clock budged under her touch. She wiggled it and dug snow out from around its edges until it finally came out in her hand.

There was a symbol inside the hole. It looked like the outline of a pocket watch. Or, a compass. Grandfather's watch. Maybe Ethan's pocket watch would suffice.

"May I see your watch?" Grace asked, her palm open.

Ethan reached into his pocket and placed a watch in her hand, closing her fingers over the top of it. "Maybe this is what you are looking for."

She looked down. It was her grandfather's watch. "But how?"

"Hurley."

Grace quickly placed the closed watch into the mold, but nothing happened.

"Maybe you need to push it in farther," Jack suggested.

It was already in as far as it would go.

"It's not quite noon yet. Maybe we have to wait for the sun to hit the right spot on the dial." Grace was getting anxious. It had already been a very long day, but she didn't know if she would appreciate another day, let alone week, month, or year of hunting for this treasure. If this treasure was here, they were going to find it. Today.

Ethan clicked open his watch. "Three more minutes." He leaned against the tall stone piece in the middle that cast the shadow and it shifted. Ethan threw his hands up as if not sure what he'd done.

"You pushed it toward the twelve. Do it again."

Ethan pushed the piece as far as he could and Grace pressed the watch into the stone.

Click.

The entire top of the stone sundial moved.

"Here," Grace said, "Jack, help me." She pushed against the sides of the stone, but it wouldn't move.

After a moment of letting her try, Ethan stepped forward and grasped the edges of the large plate in his arms and rotated it outward, revealing steps leading down into some sort of hidden chamber.

"Jack, where's that lantern you had?" Ethan asked.

Jack ran to the entrance of the cave where he'd left his light, but the flame had gone out.

"Well, there is only one way to find out," Ethan said, swinging a leg over the top of the opening. He climbed down, followed by Jack—who would not relinquish his hold on the spear—followed by Grace.

When she reached the bottom, she squinted into the darkness, hoping her eyes would adjust quickly.

Whoosh. A fire came to life as Ethan held a torch up to the very empty room.

"I still had the matchbox in my pocket," he said, "and this, was hanging there." He pointed to an iron sconce on the wall.

It had all been for nothing. Someone could have come across the treasure a long time ago and no one ever knew about it. She tried to ignore the nagging feeling that she was missing something. The chamber looked completely undisturbed.

"Check the walls," she said, unwilling to give up.

"Here," Ethan called out. He'd found a large circle that had been carved into the wall. Two rows of several small squares had been placed around the bottom half of the inner perimeter and a wide slit opposite them at the top.

"That's not exactly what I was expecting." Grace stood back, but could not make it look like a clock.

"Jack," Ethan said, then glanced up at Grace, "may I see that spear?"

Jack readily handed it over and Ethan placed the arrowhead tip into the slit. He pushed it until it clicked, leaving only enough of the spear to expose the three jewels at the top. Ethan handed the torch to Grace.

"Now, if you were the sun at its highest point, where would you be?" he asked.

Grace thought about it a moment. A rather large stepping stone jutted from the ground at the back of the edge of the chamber. She stepped on top of it and held the torch level with the center of the circle.

"Ethan Redbourne, you are a brilliant man."

The spear acted like the piece of a sundial that cast a shadow on the vertical stone. The shadow pointed to the twelve.

Ethan moved his fingers over the twelve, then clenched them into a fist.

"Do you trust me?" he asked her.

"Undoubtedly," she said firmly.

He pressed the button just above the twelve that had no number labeled.

"Seven minutes past the hour."

The chamber wall unsealed. Ethan reached his arm through the wide ravine between the door and the wall, and, with one good shove, it opened completely.

Six large wooden chests filled the space, glittering in the firelight as flames danced with gold and silver. Grace stepped through the doorway and with one deep breath, bent down to unlatch one of the chests. It creaked in protest as she raised the lid.

Both hands rose to her mouth, open in awe.

"Wahoo!" Jack screamed as he reached into the chest and ran his fingers through hundreds of magnificent gems.

When all the chests had been opened, Grace stood back against the door next to Ethan, awestruck and amazed.

"Thank you, Ethan. For everything." She glanced over at him and he pulled her into his arms.

"Thank *you*." He bent down and placed a light kiss on her lips.

She laid her head against Ethan's chest. "We found it, Grandfather," she whispered. "We found Uly's treasure.

CHAPTER TWENTY-ONE

Christmas Day

Small flurries of snow swirled about the sleigh as Ethan pulled up to Nolan Place. Grace's tree stood in the center of the window. The bright reds of the cranberries and rich browns of the twigs and pinecones gave it just the right amount of warmth framed against a glittering winterscape.

"Merry Christmas, Ethan," Jack called as he ran out the front door and down the stairs. "Merry Christmas, Clyde. Merry Christmas, Matilda," he said, holding an apple out in his hands for each of the horses. He laughed as the animals happily chomped down the sweet treat.

"Jack," Ethan called. A light fluttering churned in his stomach. "May I have a word?"

The boy climbed up next to him on the front seat. "Sure, Ethan."

"I know your father's been gone a long time, and your grandfather too, so I think that makes you the man of the house."

Jack sat up a little taller.

Just ask.

"Jack, I love Grace."

"Anybody can see that," he said with a smirk.

Ethan breathed a laugh.

Do it.

"I'd like to ask your permission to marry your sister." It came out faster than he had intended.

Jack narrowed his eyes at Ethan and did a quick mock assessment, bringing his hand to his chin and rubbing in contemplation.

Ethan had never considered that her little brother might say, no. He shifted uncomfortably in his seat.

After a few moments of appraising silence, Jack's face broke into a wide grin. "That'd be great!" he exclaimed, then a concerned look replaced the excited one. "Wait. Does that mean Hannah is going to be like my...my sister?"

"Not exactly." Ethan laughed.

"Then, yes. You can marry Grace."

The front door clacked shut and Ethan looked up. Grace stood at the top of the stairs holding a few boxes and bags. She was stunning. Her honey colored hair had been twisted into a loose rope-like cord that hung down one side of her neck. Her cheeks were pink and her lips plump and full.

Ethan sprang from his seat and up the stairs to relieve Grace of the packages. He promptly loaded them into the back of their winter carriage next to Jack, then held out a hand to her.

"You look lovely this morning, Miss Nolan."

She blushed, a soft smile rewarding him for noticing.

"And you look quite dashing, Mr. Redbourne," she replied, slipping her hand into his and climbing up onto the front seat of the sleigh.

Jack groaned from behind them. "Can we go now? Please?"

Ethan and Grace both laughed.

Grace slid close to him on the seat.

Ethan reached down and drew the thick denim quilt he'd received for Christmas a few years back, up onto Grace's lap.

It was his favorite.

"So, Jack," Ethan called back to him, "what did Santa Claus bring you for Christmas?"

"Ah, Ethan, I don't believe in Santa Claus anymore. I'm fourteen you know."

"So," Ethan said with a grin. "I'm twenty-one and the jolly old elf still visits my house every year. You can't be a Redbourne and not believe."

"Really?"

"Really."

"Well, what did you get for Christmas?" Jack asked with a hint of skepticism.

Ethan reached down and squeezed Grace's hand.

"Everything."

Garlands of pine boughs and cranberries decorated the rooftops and railing of the homestead at Redbourne Ranch. Grace reveled in the feel of family and home that emanated from the place.

Ethan picked her up at the waist and lifted her from the sleigh. He looked good with his white twill shirt and black suspenders, barely visible beneath his black leather coat with the wool lining. He smelled good too. Grace couldn't have asked for a better Christmas.

"I'll be in as soon as I take care of the horses," Ethan said with a reassuring smile.

Grace nodded.

The wonderful smells coming from the house made Grace's mouth water. She imagined a turkey in one of Ethan's large Dutch ovens, and Lottie's rolls were sure to be on the menu. It took everything she could do not to lick her lips.

"Look," Hannah said to Jack as Grace walked into the house.

The pungent aroma of the pine tree in the family room filled Grace's mind with memories of the day they'd chosen that tree and how Ethan had helped her and Jack decorate their own.

"There's also one for you," Hannah pointed.

"What is it?" Jack asked, picking up the box labeled with his name. "It's real heavy."

"I don't know. Ethan made us promise not to open them until after the two of you arrived. I think he's..."

Grace didn't hear the rest of Hannah's sentence.

Leah pulled her aside and helped her remove her coat. "We're so glad you could join us, my dear. You have certainly put the sparkle back into my son's eyes. That's the best Christmas present any mother could receive. Thank you."

Grace didn't know what to say. She threw her arms around the woman. "Thank *you*. For welcoming us into your home and your lives."

The door opened and Ethan walked in with the packages she had prepared for the Redbournes. Grace hoped they would be well received. The past few days had given her some time to finish up the last of the gifts. Ethan set them down in front of the tree.

"Ethan," Hannah said pulling on the front of his shirt. "You've made us wait all day. Can we please open them now?"

Ethan laughed richly as he bent down face to face with his only sister. "Yes, Hannah, you can open it now," he said, tapping her lightly on the nose.

She clapped her hands and immediately ran to her box. The rest of the family sat on the floor, in chairs, and on the couch as Ethan picked up the gifts and passed them out to each of them. When he handed a beautifully decorated box to her, Grace couldn't help but beam up at him.

Slowly, she tore away the paper and lifted the lid. Two metal blades with latches and straps stared back at her. She wasn't sure how to respond. She had no idea what it was, but she didn't want to appear ungrateful, so she smiled at Ethan. "Thank you?" The words sounded pathetic, even to her.

Ethan laughed loudly at her response.

"They're ice skates," he said. "For skating on the pond." He pointed toward the far end of the house.

Grace wasn't sure her expression changed much at the news. She'd never been ice-skating before and the thought of venturing out onto the ice with sharp blades attached to the bottoms of her shoes didn't do anything to bolster her confidence.

"Don't worry," Ethan laughed again, "I'll be right there with you."

She bit her bottom lip.

Ethan leaned over and whispered in her ear. "I thought I told you not to do that."

Grace looked up at him, trying to look apologetic, but she could not keep the smile from lifting the corners of her mouth. "Sorry."

Her presents were passed around and everyone quickly opened the loosely wrapped packages.

"These are great, Grace. Thank you," Tag said as he pulled the knit cap over his head and wrapped the matching scarf around his neck. "We can wear them out on the pond."

Heat rose in Grace's cheeks at their words of appreciation and excitement over their gifts. She could feel herself beaming at their praise.

"Let's go try them out," Will suggested, picking up his skate box, his hat and scarf already donned.

"Shall we?" Ethan asked, his arm crooked in invitation.

The rich, deep brown color of the wool she'd chosen for Ethan made the sage green of his eyes stand out brilliantly against his tanned face. He was the most beautiful man she had ever seen.

Ethan carried both of their boxes in his other arm as he led her out to the gardens where the large pond had completely frozen over.

"Are you sure it's safe?" Grace asked skeptically.

"Yep," he replied as he strapped the blades to his feet.

"And you've done this before?"

"Uh-huh," he said, fastening the last blade to her boot.

"Well…"

"Come on, Gracie." He used her familiar nickname. "It'll be fun." He lifted her up from the bench where she'd felt perfectly content.

Gingerly, she tested one foot on the ice, then the other. When she didn't immediately fall on her face, she attempted to take a step. Her foot slipped a little, but Ethan's firm grip on her hands prevented her from falling.

He guided her out into the middle of the pond.

"How are you doing that?" she asked, amazed that he could skate backward when she could barely keep herself upright.

"Practice."

Grace looked around the nature-made rink. Some of the Redbournes were better than others. Hannah held Jack's hand as he tried to maneuver on the blades. Jameson zipped past them, chasing Leah, who moved equally as fast on her skates. When he finally caught up to her, they both tumbled sideways into the snow bank, smiling and laughing.

Everyone else laughed too.

"Hmhmm."

Grace turned to look at who had cleared his throat and froze. Lee B. Coldhern stood at the end of the pond, briefcase in hand, and brow raised. She glanced at Ethan and back at Lee. The stark differences in the two was amazing. Even the way they carried themselves was different.

"Can I help you?" Jameson asked, skating to the edge of the pond.

Why was he here?

"I'd like a moment with Miss Nolan, if I might."

Jameson looked at Grace. "Might he?"

"Who is that?" Ethan asked quietly.

"That," she said, not bothering to mask the sudden disdain in her voice, "is Lee Coldhern." Grace felt Ethan go rigid.

Before she could stop him, Ethan had skated away from her and without warning, landed a punch in the man's kisser, sending him sprawling backward. His satchel slammed against a stone in the garden and papers flew in every direction. Grace bit back a satisfied smile.

"Ethan," Jameson grabbed a hold of his arm, "you better go on inside, son, and take a breath."

Lee hastily gathered his papers together and shoved them back into his leather case.

"You'll excuse my son, Mr.?" Jameson held out a hand to the man and helped him up.

Ethan sat on the bench, flipped off his blades, and stormed into the house.

"Coldhern," he said, rubbing his jaw, blood now pooling lightly at the corner of his mouth. "Lee Coldhern."

Raine skated up to Jameson and whispered something near his ear. Illumination registered on his face.

"So, you're the man who started this whole treasure fiasco."

Lee opened his mouth to say something, but Jameson's words had apparently taken him by surprise.

"I'm sorry?"

"You heard me. And, what's this about you trying to buy Nolan Place?"

"I assure you, sir, that my intentions—"

"Your intentions were anything, but honorable. Mr. Coldhern, I don't think you *might* speak with Miss Nolan today or any other day."

"Is that so?" Lee looked at Grace, his eyes soft and pleading. "Grace. Darling."

Gullible and of poor status. The words from the letter echoed in her mind.

"Darling?" Grace took a step forward, but nearly lost her footing. The last thing she wanted to do was to crawl across the ice to face Lee.

Tag swooped in next to her and took her by the hand.

Her confidence returned.

"Darling? After everything you've done, how dare you come here and call me, darling?"

Jameson skated back a few paces to give her room.

When Tag attempted to let go of her hand, she squeezed it tighter. He stayed.

"You hurt me, Lee," she whispered his name. "And after you'd promised me the world, you got engaged to that woman. All because she had money. Well, the joke's on you. Now, *I* have money. And I don't want *you*." It felt good to confront him. She took a deep breath, no longer wanting to look at him. "Go away, Lee. And never come back."

"I was trying to be civil here, Grace, but you've forced my hand. For twenty-five years your grandfather's property had been delinquent on its taxes. I'm afraid there's no turning back now, not even your little treasure can change that. Soon, I will be the owner of the little Nolan farmhouse in the middle of Nowhere, Kansas. Everything on that land will belong to me."

"Wrong." Ethan reemerged from the house, calm and collected. "You're too late." He stepped onto the ice next to Grace without his skates and took her hand from Tag. "I think it's time for you to go."

"What do you mean I'm too late?" Lee asked, his voice cracking slightly.

Ethan handed him an envelope.

It didn't take long before the Redbournes all clustered together around Grace. She saw the trepidation in Lee's eyes as he measured the men before him. Grace imagined that the sight of one of the Redbourne brothers alone—or their father—would be intimidating for anyone, but here, with all of them standing together with their arms folded over their chests, towering over Lee in both height and stature, they were a sight to be reckoned with.

Lee glowered at Grace as he opened the envelope. After quickly scanning the document inside, he shook his head. "This isn't the end of it."

"Oh, I think it is. Now, Mr. Coldhern," Ethan said firmly, wrapping his arm around Grace's waist and pulling her tightly against him, "it is time for you to say goodbye."

"But—"

"Now," Ethan growled, leaning forward. "Before I have my brother, the deputy here, arrest you."

Raine pushed his coat aside to show off his shiny badge.

Lee didn't say another word, he simply turned on his tail and headed back for the little carriage he'd come in.

"Thank you all." What else could she say? With several pats on her shoulder and arm, the clan dispersed and continued to skate.

She turned to Ethan, who looked at her with a raised brow. "Is it true? What he said about buying my house for unpaid taxes?"

"Nope."

Grace searched his eyes. "You realize he came all the way out here from New York?"

"Yep."

"How can you be sure?" She loved the playful smirk that brought out the small dimple just above the corner of his mouth.

"Because the taxes, love…have already been paid."

"Do you sing?" Grace asked Ethan as Leah directed everyone into the family room to sing carols.

"Not very well. I leave that to my brothers."

"Will," his mother said his brother, "go sit at the piano, will you?"

Grace followed them into the family room. Will moved to the piano against the wall. He sat down and started to tinker on the keys. Jameson reached behind the couch and pulled out a violin and started to tune the instrument.

"Excuse me," Ethan said. "I'll be right back." He disappeared down the hallway toward the back of the house.

Grace loved music. The Coldhern Estates had always been filled with one orchestra or another playing at their grand Christmas parties, and on occasion, a single musician would entertain their family through dinner. She'd always hidden in one of the rooms above the parlor and had put her ear to the vent, listening to their beautiful selections.

Ethan walked back into the room, heaving an enormous black case. To Grace's delight, he pulled out a cello and sat in the chair next to the piano. After a few moments of tuning, Grace recognized the tune Will's fingers produced on the piano. The stringed instruments joined in and Cole started the verse, *O Holy Night*.

Part way through the song, Raine joined in, then Tag until all of them were singing.

Grace couldn't help herself. She closed her eyes. "*O night…o ho-o-lee-ee ni-ight, o night divine.*"

When she opened her eyes, everyone was staring at her.

"Sorry." Maybe she had intruded on a Redbourne family tradition.

"That was brilliant," Will said, turning around on the piano bench.

"Where did you learn to sing like that?" Hannah asked.

Grace glanced over at Ethan. He winked at her and smiled. Will turned back to the keys.

Grace moved over next to Ethan. After singing a few more hymns, Jameson pulled out the bible and opened to the book of Luke, from where he recounted the story of the first

Christmas.

Ethan excused himself for a moment and he returned with a large basket. He cleared his throat and turned to her. "Grace, I have one more gift for you."

"But you've given me so much already."

He held it out to her. She opened the latch and pulled back the flaps. Bob jumped out of the basket and onto her chest, purring and rubbing against her cheek. She giggled.

"Is he ready for me to take home?" Grace asked with excitement. She lifted him up, so his face was close to hers, and she saw it, hanging on the red ribbon tied around his neck. A beautifully cut emerald ring. The setting was of an exquisite gold design and the stone was perfect.

Her eyes shot to Ethan. *Breathe*, she reminded herself.

He picked up the kitten, removed the ribbon and held the ring in his hand.

"Grace." He smiled when he said her name. "I have not experienced a dull moment since you've come into my life."

Everyone laughed, including Grace. Her heart raced and she fought to keep her breathing even. His beautiful sage green eyes had seen into her soul and now, more than ever, she knew she loved him.

"Somewhere along the way I'd lost my hope for ever finding happiness." Ethan looked down at the ground. "But, you...you brought hope back into my life." He reached down and took her hands in his. "You were the most perfect Christmas present I could have ever hoped for. And I want to share the rest of my Christmases, and every other day of my life, with you." He slid the ring onto her finger. "Marry me, Grace. I love you."

She bit her lip—her heart so full it took a moment before she trusted herself to speak.

Ethan groaned, shaking his head.

"Yes, Ethan," she said with a smile, "there's no place else I'd rather be than with you."

He lowered his head, his mouth merging with hers in a kiss that promised forever.

Three Weeks Later

Today had been the happiest day of Ethan's life. He glanced over at his bride, sitting in the window seat, staring out at the moonlit winter's night—his favorite denim quilt pulled up around her shoulders, and her hair tumbling in waves down her back.

He loved her. Trusted her. But something inside of him still feared her reaction to his scars.

He stepped toward her and wrapped his arms around the fullness of her blanketed form. "Come to bed, my love?"

She turned around to meet his gaze, fire alight in her eyes. She allowed the quilt to drop to the floor at her feet, exposing a gown of the softest fine white linen cascading down the length of her.

He rested his hand at the curve of her hip, longing to drink in the sweetness of her mouth.

Grace's fingers traced the lines of his shirt, but when they settled on the top button, he sucked in a breath. He fought the urge to turn away from her, to stay her hand. Within moments, his shirt gaped open, still tucked at the waist.

His jaw clenched.

Her hands felt wonderful against the bare flesh of his torso.

Ethan lifted a hand to her face, caressing her full lips with his thumb. He longed to pull her against him, to taste the sweetness of her kiss.

Grace's fingers glided over his chest, up to his shoulder, and down his arms.

He held his breath.

She smiled as she slid the shirt from his shoulders. It fell backward, draping his waist. Grace tilted her head as she looked at his scars. She traced over the mottled texture with her fingertips, and when her lips touched his dappled skin, he knew she loved him—no matter the scars he carried.

Ethan cradled her head in his palms and pulled her face up to meet his kiss, knowing that this beautiful woman would be his bride...forever.

THE END

WATCH FOR

REDBOURNE SERIES, BOOK FOUR
LEVI'S STORY

ABOUT THE AUTHOR

KELLI ANN MORGAN recognized a passion for writing at a very young age. Since that time, she has devoted herself to creativity of all sorts—moonlighting as a cover designer, photographer, jewelry designer, motivational speaker, and more.

Kelli Ann is a long-time member of the Romance Writers of America and was president of her local chapter in 2009. Her love of and talent for writing have opened many doors for her and she continues to look for new and exciting opportunities and calls to adventure. She feels very blessed to have a talented husband and son who inspire her on a consistent basis.

Her novels are on the sensual side of PG—without graphic love scenes. Great romance novels are those that make you feel the spectrum of emotion, that leave you wanting more, and it is her hope that every time you crack open one of her romance stories, that you walk away inspired, uplifted, and with a love of romance.

www.kelliannmorgan.com